MIRANDA MILLER was born in London in 1950, and was educated at London day schools and, for a brief period, at King's College, London where she studied history. After leaving university she moved to Rome where she combined writing with a variety of jobs: working as an au pair, a secretary, a teacher of English and a translator. She later lived in Libya and Saudia Arabia, and continued to teach English until the birth of her daughter in 1981. Her first novel, *Under the Rainbow*, was published in 1978, followed by *Family* (1979) and *Before Natasha* (1985). Miranda Miller now lives in London with her husband and daughter and is currently working on a collection of short stories about expatriate life in Saudi Arabia.

MIRANDA MILLER

SMILES AND THE MILLENNIUM

VIRAGO

Published by Virago Press Limited 1987
41 William IV Street, London WC2N 4DB

British Library Cataloguing in Publication Data

Miller, Miranda
  Smiles and the millennium.
  I. Title
  823'.914 [F]   PR6058.Y62

ISBN 0-86068-915-8
ISBN 0-86068-916-6 Pbk

Typeset by Goodfellow & Egan of Cambridge
Printed in Great Britain by Anchor Brendon Ltd. of Tiptree, Essex

For Tim and Judith Hyman

CHAPTER 1

✵✵✵✵✵✵✵✵✵✵✵✵✵✵✵✵✵✵✵✵✵✵✵✵

I'm bleeding, Simon thought. Worms of misery have colonized my intestines and they're building empires inside me. Soon they'll come sliming out through my pores and the children will love their disgustingness. The dwarf lavatories with broken locks were the only possible refuge from the loneliness Simon had woken up with and he realized how quickly he would rot if he didn't come to Smiles each day. He wanted the image of his life as something useful and energetic: a man on a bike crossing the river in the grey early morning. Simon remembered the wood he had carried with him, scrounged from one of the building jobs that were still being done to the houses near him on the other side of the river.

The ancient black iron stove dominated the downstairs room. Christy and he had dragged it there because they were afraid it would crash through the floor upstairs. Its rusting complex of doors, drawers, knobs and warming plates was an altar to times when people knew how to be poor. On a full belly of wood and rubbish the stove kept them warm all day; heated the children's milk, cooked their food and became for them a monster, castle or volcano. Simon thought it was beautiful and tended it with respect, sweeping and laying it each afternoon and reblacking it every few months. He felt the stove was the real building, strong and dignified within the flimsy, leaking shell of the other. The stove made the torn books and broken toys more pitiful.

Even when the orange tongues flickered on the other side of the glass door Simon wasn't comforted. He wished Christy would come, preferably at her bossiest, and clatter around. If he knelt there looking forlorn perhaps she would hug him. If someone didn't touch him soon, he thought, he would disintegrate. But of course she never hugged anyone over eleven and it was hard to imagine her having much physical contact with that boyfriend of hers. Simon thought that, like most heroic people, she lacked the ability to be private. Struggling with dirt, chaos, cold, hunger, children's tears and adults' apathy, Christy was defended by a wall of busyness. Yet she always looked as if she could leap over the wall into his undeserving little garden of weeds and worms.

Her sneakers came flapping down the concrete corridor and he heard her key in the only unbroken lock in the building. In her husky voice, which had a disappointed edge to it, she said, 'Simon? Oh good. They've delivered the supplies down by the road, we'd better go and get them before they're nicked.'

'Did you manage to find a place for the new kids to sleep in last night?'

'What? Oh yes, they're in the garage under Edith Cavell.'

'Is it safe?'

'Is any of it? One of the window frames over the slide is bulging outwards. I noticed it yesterday.'

'I'll go up and have a look at it later.'

The mud was up to the ankles of his rubber boots, reminding him of worms again. Christy's feet must be perpetually wet. I wonder why she doesn't get herself some proper boots. I suppose her volunteer's coupons aren't even enough to buy clothes. I couldn't manage on them if I didn't have the flat, and Bernard to pay my bills for me. I daresay I'm a convenient tax write-off for him. Christy marched ahead, almost military in her self-discipline. Simon noticed how thin she was under her lumpy sweater and how blotchy and tired she looked. He supposed she lived in one of those caravans, sinking into its individual patch of mud. She had been there for too long still to be in a tent, and the corrugated iron shacks were only for families. There were buckets and bowls everywhere to catch the rain that had been falling for weeks that spring. Around the washhouse, where parents sometimes tried to organize lessons for the older children, string upon string of bedraggled washing sadly danced. A few people were around, mainly those who were hurrying to catch the rush hour crowds. Sarah, who was six but rarely had time to come to the playgroup, pushed her legless grandfather over the rubble in a

2

home-made pushcart. They were on their way up to Sloane Square, where she would dance to his accordion music until the police moved them on. Mick the clown and Donald the knife swallower set off in dirty finery to walk to their regular pitch in Covent Garden. Half a dozen cardboard scavengers pushed wheelbarrows noisily towards Wandsworth Bridge, looking for boxes which they would sell that night to new arrivals on the streets of the city.

Ted drove up in his battered lorry to set up, in the back of it, the only shop at Smiles. Cash was illegal but the government turned a blind eye to small transactions. Because Ted accepted cash and barter, most of the people at Smiles were forced to accept his bruised apples, squashed tomatoes and potatoes sprouting with roots. His dented cans had long ago outlived their selling dates and he had an unappetizing selection of underwear and T-shirts that had been damaged in floods or had fallen off the backs of even less salubrious lorries. Ted knew he was hated by the people of Smiles and he refused to live there, out of a mixture of contempt and self-preservation. He slept in the lorry, on a pile of grubby bedclothes beside a stove where he made chips, tea and coffee, in a dusty glade deep in the forest of boxes and crates. He was a small, pale, weaselly man with sandy hair and eyelashes, quite young but ageing rapidly from sleepless nights when he lay in his padlocked lorry guarding his stock and cash savings, waiting for his enemies to break in. It was his ambition to save enough money to buy property and qualify for a Britcard, even a green one, so that he would no longer be a victim of the black cash economy he exploited. He had tried to ingratiate himself with the True Brit Information Agency on the other side of Wandsworth Bridge by accepting large consignments of Neuropepsi which he sold for a few pence less than other drinks. At Christy's playgroup most of the children arrived either with empty bellies, or sluggish and gassy after a can of Neuropepsi. Many of the mothers believed it helped kids to get to sleep, and helped them again in the morning, to calm them down.

Most people in the camp were clinging to the momentarily uncold and unwet darkness inside the tents and shacks. Simon paused outside one of the tents and tried to imagine what it

3

was like to huddle there each night with only a sheet of plastic between you and the frozen mud. He would never understand the discomfort unless he experienced it and he would never experience it unless he had to. Who would? The people who lived at Smiles weren't martyrs; they would think he was mad if he gave up his central heating and duvet to join them. Still he knew that every day he spent there was, amongst other things, an atonement for thousands of warm, dry, well-fed nights. Simon was glad, in a way, that they had taken away his Britcard when he gave up his professional job and refused to look for another, because his unpinability made him feel less cut off from the people at Smiles.

Christy was standing on the brow of mud that slithered down to the main road, where the UN lorry had dumped flour, rice, powdered eggs, powdered milk and orange juice. On the other side of the swirling traffic, on a roundabout, a dozen figures sat huddled in a cave of newspapers, cardboard boxes and plastic bags.

'Never mind observing the natives. Those pigs on the island have pinched another crate of orange juice – I told the driver not to deliver it so early.'

'I suppose, if they took it, they needed it.'

'We all bloody need it. Look, they're drinking it now. Sickly orange bottles instead of Neuropepsi cans –'

'You can't possibly see from here.'

'I've got eagle eyes. In the back of my head and the pit of my stomach, I can see food a mile off, specially before breakfast – Look!'

Christy laughed as an empty bottle hit a moving lorry. Simon watched one of her rare moments of triumph, as her eyes shone green with the fun of being right and of her enmity with the island people. Most of them were zonkies, or Neuropepsi addicts. When taken in vast quantities, the government panacea turned people into mindless, drooling idiots, subject to fits of arbitrary violence (although the True Brit Medical Research Institution denied this, insisting that it was possible to prove, statistically, that more happiness could only be better). In their passive moods, the zonkies sat for days in shelters made of garbage. There they were preyed on by the more aggressive junkies, alcoholics and the embittered ex-mental patients who were still waiting for the community to care. In their rare bursts of brutal euphoria, the zonkies had fights or looted shops. A few weeks before, a gang of thirty of them had descended on Smiles, where they had destroyed several tents and stolen ten valuable cans of UN soup dust. Poor Christy, Simon thought, she won't allow herself to dislike the people at Smiles and she can't take out her feelings on politicians because they're so remote. It amused Simon that Christy's contempt for the island people was identical to what the worst volunteers – the ones who disappeared after a few hours – said about Smiles: layabouts, zonkies, thieves.

Christy turned back to the difficult job of dragging the crates and sacks over the mud to the playgroup before the children arrived. Simon helped, and although he seemed vaguer than ever that morning they worked together in silent harmony. He was so polite and insubstantial looking, yet so reliable. He had no sense of informality; when he had flu in January and didn't turn up for a week he had sent a woman over with a note. Apologizing because after two years he had behaved like a normal volunteer. The woman was from his real world, surprised made-up eyes behind tinted glasses and little green leather pumps being sucked into the mud. It was funny to think he could wake up with that and choose to come to this. In a way, Christy wanted him to stop coming because that would place him as what Sean had always said he was: a middle-class prig waiting for a good job. Unplaced, Simon was disconcerting. But indispensable, Christy thought as she watched him prepare the children's breakfast of yesterday's bread mashed in lumpy milk.

Once the children arrived she and Simon hardly spoke to each other. They had been working together for so long that the daily jobs were divided scrupulously between them and the children picked up the qualities they needed, sharing the two of them out like sweets. Dimelza came in half asleep, stumbled over to Simon, wrapped herself around him and fell asleep again. He went on crumbling the stale bread into empty yoghurt cartons, moving only his forearms so as not to disturb her. Manic people of all ages were attracted to his calm, which he hoped they mistook for strength.

5

The Irish twins came in and started trying to sell Christy a pen she had lost the week before.

'Where did you get it?'

'Bought it in a shop.'

'Rubbish. You pinched it from my bag, didn't you?'

'Don't smack our bums.'

'I wouldn't go near your bums, you smelly little brats. Give it back!'

They made her chase them, throwing it to each other, and finally collapsed with her in giggles and hugs. All day long the twins whipped up each other's vitality until it reached fever pitch in mid-afternoon and they had to be shouted at. Christy admired them because they were unsquashable, whereas so many of the children were already crushed. The white ones were far too white and the black ones had skin disorders from lack of sunshine and vitamins. The first hour was spent feeding, warming and encouraging them to the point where they dared play. Organized activities were almost impossible because they ranged from six months to eleven.

Originally, when people still lived in the flats, the playgroup had been set up for children between two and five. Then, when the buildings became uninhabitable and people moved out into shacks and tents, children from Smiles were often refused free places in schools because they were disruptive or unsuitably dressed. Those who didn't come to the playgroup worked like Sarah or played down by the river at low tide. A few conscientious parents had tried to organize classes in the washhouse. Christy couldn't lose interest in kids she had known since they were babies just because they were five, and she let the children come as long as they wanted to. Most of them left abruptly at about puberty, which hit the children of Smiles ferociously; suddenly they saw beyond their childhood to the rest of the city which excluded them. When they realized they would never conform to the values that ruled around them they hated all values with a terrible, lucid intensity. Then they left and went to live in teeny camps – there were hardly any adolescents at Smiles, only children and rapidly aging adults.

That day more came than usual because of the rain. They couldn't play in the yard at the back so they swarmed into the

6

two rooms, which had seemed so cavernous to Simon in the early morning. He thought there was something nautical about Christy's place that morning, with all the water outside and inside all the children pitching and tossing, sealed in a fug of body warmth, noise, smells and salty shrieks. Only Simon wasn't a captain, more like a mast passively allowing insect people to slide up and down it, hang things on it, push it over and sit on it. He managed to stop the twins, who were holding the two smallest babies upside down. Dimelza had woken up and was demanding stories which he bellowed while a little girl put handcuffs on him and a two-year-old pulled his hair. 'Beauty and the Beast', or 'Beauty and the Monster' as she called it, was Dimelza's favourite. He had told her Beauty was black but she saw the book depicted her as a pink and golden Rhinemaiden.

'See. I told you, dinneye, princesses isn't never black.'

'Why do you believe the book instead of me?'

'You dunno. You're just making it up to keep us quiet.'

'Well I'm not doing very well, am I? I've never heard so much noise in my life.'

'In Africa there's black princesses,' Lily said.

She was a huge six-year-old with plaits that stuck out like short ropes and sad eyes bulging with visions of a fantasy Africa. She lived in a tent with an aunt and waited for her mother to send for her. Lily was too big and mournful to play but she loved stories and Dimelza's fierce, crazy agility and grace. Someone had brought in a radio which screeched tinny music in the background. Dimelza started to dance, whirling and flinging her arms and legs around as if she wanted to get out of her body, flashing smiles. Dumbly Lily stood opposite her, shaking her stiff arms. She would be happy for hours because she had danced with Dimelza. Simon felt he had more in common with Lily; in fact, watching them, he was reminded uncomfortably of his enslavement to Jessica when she was very young. Some of us are just born inhibited, he thought, then spun round as one shriek rose above all the others.

Hamid, who needed crutches to walk, had fallen downstairs. It looked as if he might have been pushed by Martha, one of the older girls, who sat at the top of the stairs glaring

7

down. But then she always looked shifty and bad tempered, she might not have . . . Unable to handle a confrontation, Simon took the sobbing boy in his arms.

Christy thought he was far too soft on them. Her regime upstairs was more orderly and subdued, which might have been why children were streaming down to the pandemonium. With a team of helpers chosen for their clean hands she was kneading the dough for their lunchtime bread. Neither she nor Simon were any good at baking bread (hers had lumps of salt in it and his never rose successfully), but they persevered.

'I saw that,' she said to Martha.

'Saw what?'

'He could have broken his back, falling like that.'

'He's all broken anyway.'

Christy had to plant her hands in the sticky mixture to keep them off the girl.

'Get out! Just sod off into the rain if you can't be nice to little kids. You haven't been to see us for weeks, you're only here now because you're hungry. If you're too old to play you're old enough to be useful so get up off your backside!' All the time she was shouting Christy was staring at Martha's face, dull but familiar, a face she had wiped and kissed and fed. 'You didn't used to be a bully.'

''seasy when you're little, being sweet.'

'You wait until you're my age. You get so sour nobody wants you even if you come free with a sack of sugar. Now go and change Jack, he's stinking.'

The other children were muted, waiting to see what shape her anger would take. If they were lucky it would cut off there, a short jagged tear in the morning. Otherwise it would spread into a gaping hole with threadbare edges, and being at Christy's would be as miserable as staying at home. She struggled, but all the reasons for anger bounced up and hit her between the eyes, where she already had a pain: Martha's spite, Simon's absurd niceness, the rain, the lumpy dough, the blocked drain and Sean's addiction to meetings. One day, Christy thought, the black pus of my anger will come shooting up out of my throat and nostrils and ears and I'll die of it, which will be a relief.

8

At lunchtime they distributed bread and orange juice and little plastic tubs of cheese made from solidified milk.

''sall watery.'

'It looks like sick.'

'My bread's soggy.'

'I don't like potatoes.'

''tisn't potatoes, stupid.'

But they ate hungrily, pushing and squeezing to get near the stove. Christy and Simon sat at the top of the stairs from where, like umpires, they could watch disasters with some aloofness. Dimelza kept turning round to make sure Simon was there.

'How's your kid? The one with the funny name.'

'All right. I think. I'm seeing him tonight.'

'I bet he's all polite and clean. Not like this lot.'

'No.'

'You don't live with him, do you? Do you miss him?'

'Every waking moment.' And because he wanted to save that pain for this evening, and inflict a little of it on Christy who seemed invulnerable, he asked, 'What about you? Haven't you ever wanted children?'

She looked at him incredulously. '*More* children?'

We've known each other too long, he thought, to suddenly start asking questions about our private lives.

'What did you do to Martha?'

'Only yelled. I nearly hit her though. Deep down I suspect I'm a murderer.'

'We all are.' Again, that awkward personal note he didn't want.

'No we're not. You aren't for a start, I can't imagine you hitting anyone even if you were provoked. Suicide would be more your thing.'

'I don't want to talk –'

'Well you ought to. It'd do you good.'

She got up lightly and went down to the window. In profile her face has a piggy look, he thought, with that thick nose sticking out at a snouty angle and the wide, flat cheeks. The nice thing about it is that it's all upward tilting, she never looks droopy though she's obviously exhausted most of the time. That frizzy black hair makes her look like a pharaoh with a perm.

9

'It's stopped!' Christy yelled.

The children scampered over to the door while she unbarricaded it and let them out into the playground. Before running to join the children Christy turned to give Simon one last look. She had large, greenish brown eyes, muddy when she was calm, but whenever she was angry or moved – most of the time – they brightened and opened unnaturally wide.

All the fences that had divided the old gardens had been removed so that it was one big space, once grassy but now a muddy swamp, surrounded on all sides by the looming vertical ruins of the old flats. Bricks and window frames had fallen into the playground, although no one had yet been hit. One morning years ago Christy had found a woman's body draped over the slide. She had probably jumped from the roof of one of the old tower blocks, but the police hadn't investigated her death as she was an unregistered person. Christy and Simon carried out amateurish repair jobs to prevent the most obvious dangers, propping up the shuddering cliffs. One day, Simon thought, they'll finally collapse, inwards on to the playground and outwards on to the shacks and tents. They had been shoddily built to begin with, not meant for this world at all but for the purer one of scale models, where crisp trees sprouted pea-green parsley and meticulous people thronged pedestrian precincts which, presumably, were never rained on or vandalized. The towers might totter suddenly and crush lots of people like that block at World's End, Simon thought, or stagger on for years shedding fragments. If I knew more about building we could dismantle them gradually and use the materials to rebuild our shanty town, as the Romans did with their imperial leftovers. Staring up at the scarred red towers, he looked for the dangerous window Christy had mentioned and found it on the ninth floor of Baden Powell House, the most doddery of the four tower blocks, built in the sixties. Samuel Smiles House, where the playgroup was, had been built and abandoned last.

Simon fetched his tools and loosened the boards on a ground floor window of Betting Poll, as the children called it. Betting Poll, Smelly, Eden Call and Liver Stone were the four points that had to be touched in their chasing games. Inside, damp bloomed on the breezeblock walls and puddles of urine, rain and beer lapped at the concrete floors. People still sheltered in the building despite the danger signs plastered all over the boarded-up doors and windows.

Simon pushed open the cracked glass doors and climbed the spiral concrete stairs. The graffiti on the walls were a thick mural of obscenities, calf love and assignations. Up past eight landings life was simplified to meetings between wankers and lovers. Then more shattered glass doors led to a windy balcony and two gaping entrances where front doors had been wrenched off. The flat still had orange and brown whorl patterned carpet decomposing in the sitting room where a black plastic sofa burst its foamy guts out. He stood at the bulging window and looked down at the children playing in their muddy valley, sheltered from everything except the avalanches of the mountains themselves. The aluminium window frame had pulled out from the concrete on three sides. Simon chipped away at the fourth until he was able to remove the frame. Then, as if he had opened the door on to the deck of a ship, freezing air billowed into the flat. The wind was exhilarating, it pushed out the smells of rotten domesticity and shook the remaining doors and windows. All the way up to the fourteenth floor the wind pressed its nose against the shuddering walls, waiting to reclaim its territory.

When Simon reached the ground again he was so chilled that he had to go in and sit by the stove. Lily was there with Hamid and the three babies, asleep in cardboard boxes. Lily was gazing at the red glow behind the glass doors, eyes huge with the contemplation of mysteries, relaxed now that she didn't have to pretend to be a child any more. Hamid was also enjoying doing nothing, he sat composed on his chair with his feet dangling a foot from the ground, his crutches beside him. His thin face flickered into watchfulness whenever the children's shrieks came near, in case he had to defend himself. When Simon came in he was disappointed and waited for him to suggest some pointless activity. Simon remembered how he and Rose, when they were about the same age, used to escape from the games they were expected to play into silences which for some reason had to be kept secret.

'Tell me a story,' Simon said to Lily.

Her heart thumped. It was the only thing she knew she

11

could do, if only she could speak. She closed her eyes and squeezed her voice out. 'Once in Africa where me mum lives there was a big fire. Like this one only much much bigger, big as this house, and it happened every day under a mountain. When they wanted to be warm all the lions and elephants and snakes and the people too, they opened a door in the mountain and went and sat there. And they cooked their food over it, their bread and bananas, and on Sundays it was chicken. But the fire had magic smells in it –'

'Spells,' Hamid corrected her.

'No, smells. You could smell all the things you wanted, like how it smelt in bed wiv your mum when you was little and 'spensive perfumes and chips. And you could see all the things you wanted too, in the flames. Lovely houses and toys and parties wiv people dancing in beautiful gardens and chocolate bars and big round moons.'

'Then what happened?' Hamid asked.

'Nuffing. They was happy so they stayed there.'

Simon said, 'Now Hamid.'

Lily longed for him to praise her story but he didn't because he thought it would embarrass her. She thought he hadn't liked it.

'I can't.'

'Of course you can, anyone can, there are millions of stories,' Lily said contemptuously.

'No I can't, I'm not good like you.'

'Lily's very good at it,' Simon said and her eyes filled with tears.

'Oh all right. Once upon a time there was this boy called John who's good at running and swimming and football. Then one day he goes to the swimming pool on his own and he falls in and drowns. And his mum was very sad. That was a stupid story, intit?'

'Short,' Simon said.

'You shouldn't tell it so fast,' Lily advised him.

Hamid appealed to Simon. ''ave we got to talk?'

So they sat in a shared silence, a luxury none of them had expected. The door was closed against the noise and the wind, the heat from the stove sat heavily on the air and wound around their faces like a scarf. The babies slept on and Hamid

12

soaked up the heat, the last time that day he would be really warm. Later there would only be damp blankets and the paraffin stove, which burnt your nose and hands and knees and left the rest of you in a draught. He couldn't complain about it because his father would say he was weak, and he was already weak about so many things. When he told his mother he was always cold and hungry except at Christy's she sobbed that they should go back to Karachi where it was hot enough to fry fish on the pavement. But she had never been there either; she only knew about it from her parents who owned a big food shop in Clapham where Hamid's mother had grown fat eating dates when she was small. The government had taken the shop away and put them in Smiles where the people, his mother said, were rubbish.

Lily sat with her eyes closed and her arms tightly folded as if her ribs were aching. She was going into the fire, walking through the scarlet and golden specks to play with Dimelza in the park. Lily-in-the-fire was small and agile with lovely arms like matchsticks and could make people laugh. Lily-the-balloon floated off above the glittering red trees.

When Christy came in with the others she caught sight of them for a moment, three lizards. She had never seen Simon's face so naked, full of broken dreams. She turned away, deliberately shouted and laughed and woke the babies. It was nearly time to go home; most of the children didn't want to leave. Christy looked forward to the time they had all gone but not to the rest of the evening, with or without Sean, in her caravan.

Rita, the twins' mother, came clopping downstairs in her pink suede mules. 'And how have they been today, the little bastards? Any bones broken or necks wrung?' The twins, who had just her frenetic and cheerful manner, ran over to her. 'Oh Jesus, look who's here! Have you been buying up the shop again, Beatrice?'

Dimelza stared up as her mother swayed downstairs, the siren of Smiles. At the bottom the children came to feel the silk of her orange blouse and inhale her wonderful perfume while Rita and Beatrice acted out their daily comedy.

'Off to work are you?'

'Thought I'd just give the kids their tea first.'

13

'Don't dirty your blouse. I've not seen that one before, is it new?'

'You should get yourself some new things, Rita. Jumble sales is no fit beauty parlour for a woman.'

'And where'd I get the money?'

'I told you before, there's plenty of money to be got in Brixton.'

'I'm an honest woman, Beatrice.'

'Maybe you're making a big mistake.'

'Maybe I've got my pride.'

'Pride is for when you're old and ugly. You still got pretty hair, Rita. I may be getting myself a flat pretty soon.'

'Where, Mamma?' Feverishly Dimelza smiled up at her and squeezed her elegant fingers.

'You washed those hands today?'

'Where is it?' Rita asked, choking.

'Up near Railton Road. Come on, Dimelza.'

Everyone watched her climb the stairs, because watching Beatrice was a pleasure. She was beautiful, with tiny bones under purplish black skin and hair plaited and beaded like a garden of reptiles. Her style was a combination of elegance, fearlessness and an indifference she was adored for. Every evening she left Dimelza with her baby sister and her older brother, Douane, to disappear until four or five in the morning. In return they cooked for her and vied with each other for the privilege of laying out her clothes. Often her lovers turned up at Smiles with presents and nervous eyes. She had dumped them after an hour or two but they came trailing over the mud after her, offering their hearts when she only wanted their money.

Having watched Beatrice with amusement, Christy sighed when she was gone. Beatrice made her feel earnest and heavy. Beatrice was to feminism what Hitler was to liberalism. And it was no use telling her she was exploited because it was visibly untrue: Beatrice did all the exploiting in her life, and flourished on it. Christy saw Simon looking at her with so much sympathy that she smiled back.

CHAPTER 2

✿✿✿✿✿✿✿✿✿✿✿✿✿✿✿✿✿✿✿✿✿✿✿✿✿✿✿✿✿

The long day and the bike ride across London had calmed
Simon. He was still in his working clothes but had washed as a
tribute to his mother's birthday and had even bought her a
present, a book about porcelain collections in French
châteaux. He turned off St John's Wood High Street, pedall-
ing into claustrophobia and unreality. The hedges were just as
neat, the detached brick houses just as perfidiously Georgian,
the cars just as new. Apart from a few armed guards and
roof-top heliports it hadn't changed since he was a child.
Outside his parents' house the number of cars in the drive and
the lights within warned him that there was a party. Freeman
Castle, Rose and he always used to call it, and now it lived up
to their ancient joke. Simon was seized by psychosomatic
pains – he prided himself on knowing his own neuroses – and
had to force his legs up to the front door. It was opened by a
man in a white coat. Either his grandmother had lost her few
remaining marbles or Madge had got away with the extravagance she had always dreamt of. Yes, the signs were everywhere: new carpets since his last visit, champagne bottles and
plates of salmon being carried by more white coated strangers
into the drawing room.

His father, Bernard Freeman, approached, emanating bon-
homie and aftershave. His face seemed only to get more
polished with time, browner and more knotted like well-
seasoned wood. Every time he saw Simon he looked thinner,
greyer; soon he would fade away into a dim mass of perpendi-
cular lines. The boy didn't eat properly, dress properly, needed
looking after. And yet he used to be good looking, so fair and
straight.

'My dear boy! So glad you could come. On your bike?

Marvellous exercise. All right for money?' He added in a loud stage whisper.

'Fine.'

Laying two fingers on Simon's frayed sleeve, Bernard guided him into the gold and blue drawing room. Business associates who hadn't known Bernard for long thought someone had come to mend a fuse.

'How's Merlin?'

'Splendid. Delightful little chap, be down soon.'

'Darling!' Her kiss was full of lipstick. 'Plenty of hot water if you want a bath,' she whispered.

'Do I smell?'

His mother and father exchanged crinkly smiles. My God I'm getting on a bit for a rebellious son, Simon thought. Be charming, be poised, be thirty-two. But somehow the same phrases always came out when he was there, everything about them was an implied criticism of his way of life and he was never old enough to take it. He smiled at his mother and handed over the present.

'How sweet of you to remember! Oh, all those gorgeous places on the Loire – thank you, darling.'

'You'll be buying one soon.'

'Yes, it's going pretty well.' Bernard glowed with the undeniable success that had come to him at last.

'Have you told him, darling?'

'What's that? Oh yes.' He leaned forward with his confidential stage whisper. 'Something very exciting. Get you in on the ground floor. We'll have a little talk when they've all gone.'

'What about?'

But Madge and Bernard had pranced off in opposite directions like the gilded figures in baroque clocks who come out and bow when their hour strikes.

'You're the architect, aren't you!' A woman with cropped black hair and a very red face stood before him, grinning.

'No. I used to be,' he added more approachably as he saw how desperate her grin was.

'I'm Thora Wainwright, I'm at the Ministry of Leisure, you know. We're so thrilled about the work your father's doing for the jobless.'

16

'Is he?'

'Oh yes. Such an imaginative idea, giving all those people a chance to relax and at the same time educating them.'

'Why don't you just find jobs for them?'

'If only it was that simple. What do you do now you're not an architect?'

'I'm jobless too. I'm a volunteer at a playgroup in Wandsworth, on one of the council estates that collapsed when the councils did.'

'How brave! I don't know how this city would run without people like you.'

'It doesn't run. Because there's no proper administration and no money, people like me just paper over the cracks.'

'It must be terribly squalid.'

'Yes.' He swallowed, wanting to tell her what Smiles was like but reluctant to expose Christy and the others to her blandly inquisitive eyes.

'Still, with your qualifications,' she gave him a conspiratorial wink over her glass, 'I should have thought your father could find you something a bit better.'

'I don't want anything better,' Simon said and backed away from her to a little scarlet and gold chair where he found he was churning with anger.

From his corner he would be able to wait for Rose and Merlin, the only two people in the house he really wanted to see. He found he was annoyed with his mother for having this ghastly party; if he had known he would have come another night. Annoyed with her too for always avoiding intimacy with him. Why couldn't they just for once talk about real things alone together? Poor woman. He watched her. Nothing poor about Madge, even when she had been she had made strenuous efforts to camouflage it, and now she was at last the hostess she had dreamt of being thirty-five years before when she married Bernard. It was a generous fantasy, and having practised it for so long, having read all those biographies of Lady Cunard and Lady Londonderry, Madge lived it out quite well. She circled and hugged and kept glasses full, she laughed a lot and looked genuinely pleased to see people and swept around in her sapphire sequins looking matronly but not lugubrious. Under the make-up that hardened her face was an

17

expression of joy, mummified innocence. His father too; all the bagginess and stooping of his years of failed video and cable television companies had vanished and left him firmer, taller, with a more resonant voice. My parents are expanding, Simon thought, easing into moulds they cast long ago. He overheard enough snippets of conversation to be convinced these were the people Madge and Bernard had always wanted to associate with.

'Unions in their place at last.'

'In the gutter.' (Laughter.)

'Getting the economy back on its feet.'

'Show those dagos a thing or two.'

'Terrible about Portugal.'

'What's that?'

'Found more oil. Beat us again with their GNP last year.'

'You don't trust their statistics, do you? We went to a Portuguese restaurant last week, greasy stuff, can't even cook.'

'Indian's the only foreign food I risk. Superb cooks the Indians, though they are getting a bit above themselves. Preaching disarmament. We gave them the only civilization they ever had.'

'Curry? Well, I like it when it's all prepared in a scrupulously clean Swiss kitchen and I can see the ingredients. But when it's cooked by our dear friends the Indians, I simply don't trust it.'

'Did you get some of those shares?'

'Just a few thousand, sold them the following week and did awfully well.'

'Oh, good.'

These are the voices of confidence, Simon thought. Madge and Bernard sing with them in perfect unison. Trilling their patriotism as an extension of their self-love, improvising whole arias in praise of profit. They're up there taking bouquet after bouquet, dividend after dividend, while I – crouch down in the cobwebs under the stage, shrivelling up, thin and critical and full of doubts.

As if in harmony with his thoughts Rose appeared in the doorway, noticeably thin and critical, but cool and chic to make up for it. He shouted her name and she came straight over to him.

18

'I thought you'd never come!'

'Is it horrible?'

'An orgy of old corruption and genteel new fascism.'

'Well, they've made it at last.'

'Made what?'

'Whatever it was they were always so anxious about not having made. They both exude contentment these days. Madge never phones any more, not even on their wedding anniversary to remind me what I'm missing.'

'Bernard has plans for me.' He mimicked his father's voice, 'Get you in on the ground floor.'

'I should think you could do with a bit of nepotism.'

'What do you mean by that?' His pride was wounded at one of the few points where it was vulnerable.

'Are you still doing that voluntary work?'

'Yes.'

'But it's such a depressing place.'

'Not to me. That job has really kept me going, you know, since Jessica died. This party depresses me far more.'

Rose accepted this because she knew her brother was basically truthful, however odd some of his truths were. She looked around the room with an air of calculation, not moralizing as he had done but weighing and labelling.

'I thought I might find Sir Maverick Pearson here. I've been chasing him for weeks, trying to do a piece on him. But it seems they're not moving in those circles. Yet.'

'Do you know what Bernard's up to?'

'Oh yes. He's going to make millions out of Bread and Circuses. He's turning the old football stadiums into holographic fun palaces. You stuff yourself with junk food and Neuropepsi (crafty, that, no vandalism you see). Then you personally win the Battle of Trafalgar or some other selectively glorious moment of our history. The unemployed will get in for free.'

'But where will the money come from?'

'Government grants. Sir Maverick's one of his keenest supporters, that's why I thought he'd be here.'

'Cunning old bugger.'

'Yes, I must admit we underestimated him.'

Simon looked at his father with the detachment he'd always

19

felt. He couldn't remember that there'd ever been any emotion stronger than affection or contempt on either side. 'They have changed, haven't they?'

'Power and money. You'll never understand what aphrodisiacs they are.' Rose, officially his younger sister, smiled at him as an old pander might smile at a virgin. But he knew she was on his side.

Madge was juggling with two conversations at once while keeping her most sensitive antennae directed towards her children. She was so annoyed that in a minute it would show. She didn't have to hear them; for years she had overheard their arrogant, superior, clever talk, all through their interminable adolescence. Not that they had got better, they had only gone away. If she let them upset her like this they would spoil her beautiful party, demolish the happy monument she had worked so hard to build. In the evening of her days. How she ached with pushing and pulling them all, Bernard most of all, but at least he had finally done something worthwhile. She turned to look at them again, huddled in their secret corner, blind to the stiffening backs all around them.

Rose had made a profession of her tactlessness and rudeness; it seemed she was paid to write nasty things about people. Paid well enough to buy those spiky, unfeminine clothes and live in a flat like an interstellar igloo where they had once been invited to an inedible meal. A career woman. Well, at least she had a job. Simon, once her favourite, had touched much rawer nerves in Madge. His way of letting her down had been more ingenious, designed to break her heart. Such a brilliant, handsome boy, full of life and wanting to do nothing but put up marvellous buildings, from Lego onwards. The first sign of trouble came when he fell for that silly girl, fell not in a normal, healthy way but head over heels, body and soul. Simon always got far too involved in things. Even architecture, though at least there was money in that. Every Christmas and birthday he wanted books about it, when they went on holiday he did nothing but look at old churches and he spent all his spare time on those models. That was all right, the real Simon. Brilliant people were always obsessive.

But Jessica hadn't been the right sort of girl for him. Extremely pretty and charming when she wanted to be but

20

scatty and in fact quite mad. Anyone who did that must be. She couldn't cope with the child: once when he was two Madge had dropped in at their dreary flat to find Merlin running round the garden stark naked, covered with mud and screaming with laughter. And Jessica had turned Simon against her. Poisoned his mind, neglected her child and did herself in. Thoroughly irresponsible. Terrible for the child and for Simon but these things happen, you just have to pull yourself together.

Simon had fallen apart: it wasn't obvious at first because he went so quiet. Then one day she had called round with a ham and some custard and had found him lying in the dark bedroom, with the child, at three o'clock in the afternoon. He had left his job and hadn't sent Merlin to school for weeks. So she had had to take the child over; she didn't mind as he was a nice little boy though he looked like Jessica and had her vagueness, not brilliant at all. She had told Simon he could come as well but he had chosen to cut himself off from them completely. They hardly saw him except when he came to see the child and he never told them what he was doing. Nothing, she suspected, except that so-called job in a gypsy camp.

By now Madge had stopped pretending to respond to the conversation around her. Although there were far more important people there, something drew her towards her children. Blood. They looked up at her approach as if she was wielding a hatchet. Close up, they were even more unsatisfactory – Rose so shiny and aggressive in her boots and suede trousers, Simon's face far too delicate for a man's. He must go scavenging in dustbins for those clothes.

'Darlings. Huddled together in a corner like conspirators. Wouldn't you like to meet a few people?' Then to Simon, casually, 'Aren't you going to say hello to Merlin?'

He was sitting in the opposite corner, very still on a tapestry covered stool. He wasn't looking at anything, his hands were piously folded on his long grey trousers and he waited as if it was his permanent condition, not as if he was anticipating pleasure. When adults lurched up to smile at him or spill drinks over him he glanced up at them without curiosity. To Simon's horror, when he finally attracted Merlin's attention,

21

the child gave him the same veiled look. Before he had time to think Simon raised and opened his arms as he used to when Merlin was two and ran towards him, shouting 'me!' Now it was Simon who needed to confirm himself, stumbling through the well-padded, scented bodies to crouch beside his son. At eye level Merlin's face was exquisite in its curves and hollows, chilling in its impassivity. Simon couldn't see it as anything but Jessica's face, framed by the same light brown waves, carved by overworking the same piece of alabaster and drained of vitality. The two of them didn't even know what to call each other.

'I didn't see you. When did you come down?'

'I don't remember.' He had a little Prep school voice now, to go with his fresh white shirt and red tie.

'I've got a present for you.' Simon handed him a laser torch which projected kaleidoscopic patterns on the air. The twins went crazy with desire for it every time they passed it in the window of a shop in Wandsworth. Merlin shook it and stared briefly at the rainbow shapes obscuring his father's face before placing the toy on the ormolu table beside him.

'Thank you for the present.'

'Is it all right? You haven't already got one, have you?'

'I've got the one with the story of Treasure Island, and you can hear their voices too.'

'Oh. Do you like your school?'

'It's all right.'

'Would you like to go to your old one again?'

'I don't mind. It's a long way to go, I might get tired.'

'I used to go to that school you go to.'

'I know.'

'Do they still have turquoise blazers?'

'Yes. And you have to have six pairs of shoes. Shall I tell you what they're for? One for outdoors, one for indoors, one for football, one for cricket, one for tennis and one for gym.'

'I didn't like wearing a uniform.'

'I do. I think it's lovely. Grandma bought it all new, all in the same shop at the same time. We had so many parcels we couldn't carry them all and they had to be sent.'

Madge was never more impressive than when she was striding through a department store charging things up to her account. Simon remembered such scenes from his childhood, always followed by his father's outrage at the bills. Now that she had a platinum Britcard Madge was quite regal in her extravagance.

'Do you remember when we used to go to jumble sales?'

'I hate jumble sales. All the things are dirty and smelly and you never know where they've been. Did you get those trousers at a jumble sale?'

'Yes I did. As a matter of fact.'

'Have you got a job yet?'

Simon looked at him incredulously. Give me a child for the first seven years, those bumbling Jesuits had said. Madge had turned his from a grubby little anarchist to an impeccable conformist in just two years. Knocked the stuffing out of him. But the stuffing had been so lovable and it was because it must still be around somewhere, waiting to be put back in, that Simon answered mildly, 'I've always had a job. I think you mean, have I got a salary?'

'Have you?'

'No. Just a volunteer's allowance. That wouldn't be enough to pay for a school and a uniform if you came to live with me.'

Merlin's face grew rigid with concentration, as if he had just heard a sound he had been listening for. But Simon couldn't tell whether he had been listening in dread or in hope.

'Would you like to come and live with me again?'

'Do you want me to?'

'Yes. I miss you, Merlin, I wish I hadn't let you go although I know Grandma and Grandpa have been very nice to you. But if you come you'll have to get used to going to an ordinary school again and not having new things –'

Simon was whispering now, because he could see Madge coming towards them and he knew he was bribing his son. 'You can have as many animals as you like and we'll go on camping holidays and cook sausages over the fire in the garden.'

'Can I have a tropical fish?' Merlin whispered back.

'Yes.'

'Cocoa time?' Madge said with the chime that was always in her voice when she spoke to children. She was looking flushed

23

and shiny, an earring had come off and an inch of blue sequins had come unzipped to reveal red flesh and pink nylon. 'Kiss Daddy goodnight.'

Merlin turned his face passively. Simon realized that he hadn't seen him smile all evening, couldn't remember the last time he had. He hugged the boy closely, burying his mouth in the soft hair and kissing his forehead, squeezing him to make it like the bear hugs they used to have when Merlin was small. But the thin body was sharp and resistant. So Simon stood up.

'We're going to the zoo on Sunday week, I'll come and pick him up at lunchtime.'

'Lovely! Won't that be fun, Merlin?'

But he had left the room, evading his grandmother's goodnight kiss.

Vol-au-vents, stuffed vine leaves and strawberries and cream were brought in for those who had stayed, and the party moved towards the centre of the room. Bernard was talking to his old friend Sammy, an accountant he had known since his theatrical days when he had backed not-very-successful West End plays. Sammy's favourite combination was solid money and a touch of Showbiz glamour; he loved actresses and casinos and was terrified of being thought dull. As he listened to Bernard's loudly whispered estimates of the amount of money he was expecting in the first year, Sammy winked at Simon and at Rose, whom he had fancied since she was twelve, to show them he wasn't just a dry old money man.

Madge was sitting on the gold velvet couch with Joan, Sammy's wife. Like Bernard, Sammy had married a very goy woman to secularize himself completely. Madge and Joan had both been flowery blondes and even now gave an impression of pink and orange ripeness. Madge was complaining about her mother-in-law.

'She won't look at me. Of course she's senile anyway, but at least she smiles occasionally at Bernard and the child. When I go up there she crouches in the corner and sneers, she's really malevolent. And she won't change those awful black clothes. My dear, the smell!'

'Very difficult. You know mine died last summer?'

'Really? Oh well it's the best thing for them at that age.'

'Have you tried getting her into a home?'

24

'Bernard won't have it. Then you see this *is* her house, she's never made it over to us though of course she ought to have done, years ago. And as Bernard says, one hears such awful things about homes nowadays, even the private ones.'

'I think it's the best solution. They get so little out of life over eighty. After all it *is* mercy selection not just bumping them off.'

'Is that what you –?'

'Well you know, the home arranges it all.'

'Oh.'

'You get tax relief.'

'Oh really?'

Two male civil servants were also on the couch, wishing they had gone home before the party became more intimate. They were stranded on either side of the two women, unable to talk around them or to avoid overhearing their conversation. They ate their strawberries slowly and stole glances at each other. They thought they might have been at the same school.

On the opposite couch a computer tycoon and the managing director of a hotel chain were trying to decide whether the catering contract should go to Chichi Kebab or Scrummy-burger.

Madge washed down her strawberries with a glass of Kirsch and reflected on the strange rightness of things. You married the wrong man, lavished your affection on ungrateful children and worked hard for nothing, it seemed, until suddenly the ugly grey lumps of your disappointment fitted together into a dazzling mosaic. And there you were enthroned at the centre of it, your splendour visible at last. Like the Emperor's New Clothes only the other way round. Simon and Rose looked up nervously as Madge tottered to her feet.

'You haven't seen my little man. Let me show you all my little man. Bernard gave him to me for a Happy New Century present.'

She left the room for a few seconds. Simon looked at Rose. 'Do you think she's bought herself a miniature residential lover, and Bernard's been too distracted to notice?' he whispered.

There was a whirring sound that reminded Simon of the

25

mechanical monkey band he had been given as a child. A humanoid entered the room: it was about five feet tall with long folding arms, a rectangular body and a walk that was too stiff to make it altogether good company. But it was a presence, like a waiter with a nervous tic, Simon thought. They all watched as it piled the dirty plates on to the trolley, emptied the ashtrays and offered cigarettes and chocolates.

Madge stood behind it, screaming with laughter. 'Isn't he gorgeous! He draws the curtains in the morning and runs my bath and gets the milk and the papers in. He's called Hero Ten, terribly Greek and romantic. You can get much smaller models that look like elephants' trunks but I think it's so sweet having a real little man – and he cleans everything. Do let him have a go at your shoes, Simon.'

In silence he submitted to having both his feet gripped by a metal pincer which applied polish and rubbed vigorously. He waited for his shoes, which hadn't been new to begin with, to fall apart under the strain.

'He does absolutely everything. Changes plugs, hoovers, polishes – Mrs Thompson only comes one morning a week now. He is a little insensitive in the garden, he tends to crush the plants. And I can't quite trust him with my crystal.'

'Marvellous,' Sammy murmured in the general chorus of admiration.

'You know, people knock modern technology, but think of all the boring little jobs we don't have to do any more.'

'He was a bit expensive. But wonderful value.'

Madge smiled at the computer tycoon, who smiled back. Simon looked down at his gleaming shoes while Hero Ten brought the coats.

CHAPTER 3

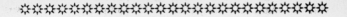

When the others had left, Madge tottered up to bed and Bernard indicated to Simon by loud whispers and furtive beckonings that their little talk was to begin. They went into his study, a room that had seen many changes. For years it had been shabby, full of unread yellowing scripts and curling posters advertising plays his father had backed, with titles like 'Once More Unto the Breeches' and 'Popping the Question'. Then, in the mid-eighties, Bernard had employed a secretary who had introduced him to gadgets, and he who had always prided himself on his impracticality had discovered he could master not only a pocket calculator, but also videos and computers. Now the room had been painted a cool blue and resembled a war controls bunker, with charts of potential sites for theme parks which lit up, a working model of a holographic game and numerous relations of Hero Ten. Beamishly, his father showed him to a chair and sat opposite with his hands clasped under his chin in a kind of monetarist prayer. Simon genuinely wished he was susceptible to his father's charm; everyone else was, and being left out made him feel uneasy. It was so familiar, this feeling, a suspicion that went back to early childhood that his father was living in a shoddily made propaganda film and was trying to drag him into it. Simon's resistance was no longer conscious but it was probably the deepest force in him.

'It's all looking pretty good, isn't it? As my old friend Joe Schneer used to say, there's no reason why you can't win on the swings and the roundabouts. And talking of the entertainment world, how's your knowledge of theatre and cinema architecture?'

'Why?'

'Well, I'll tell you since you ask.' Bernard laughed. His son's abruptness always made him nervous. 'Sammy's a bit of an old theatre buff as you know, and he's come up with the idea that we should set each battle in a building of the period. Sense of history and all that, you know how I loved History when I was at school. So, you walk through this Art Deco foyer, for instance, and there's Dunkirk. I think he's got something. Of course, we couldn't go mad on the idea or it'd cost the earth but I thought we could stick on a few plastic columns and things. Well?' Bernard's voice was slightly exasperated, as if he was waiting for a very slow mind to catch up with him. Simon as usual took refuge in dimness.

'Yes, that sounds like a good idea.'

'But don't you *see*? It's right up your street. All you have to do is design a few of these things, just big hangars really. One of the sites is just round the corner from you, the old Chelsea football ground. You could work from home if you like. You'd have a free hand, plenty of money and publicity – only a fool would turn it down.'

'No thanks, Bernard. Sorry.'

'Why not? Not highbrow enough for you?'

'I'm not an architect any more.'

'You've got the bloody qualifications, haven't you? We spent enough money sending you to that college.'

Simon realized how much his lack of ambition hurt Bernard and detracted from his own triumph. His father's eyes were bloodshot with anger and helplessness; he wasn't offering Simon a sinecure but begging him to accept a favour.

'No, I really don't want to.'

'Your mother's very worried about you.'

'She always has been.'

'She thinks you've lost your nerve. You've got to believe in yourself, Simon, if you don't nobody else will. Take it from me. Six years I've been plugging away at this theme park number. Trying to convince my bank manager, convince the mandarins, selling the idea, selling myself – if you just sit around moping you'll never get anywhere.'

'I'm not trying to get anywhere.'

'I just don't understand you.'

28

'I know. Never mind. I understand you,' he added, meaning to cheer him up rather than condescend. 'I'm really pleased you're going to make all that money.'

'It's not the money, Simon. It's the vision, the little piece of Jerusalem in the here and now I'm helping to create. I want to bring joy into people's lives – I might be surrounded by computers but I'm quite old fashioned really. A bit of a poet. That's where you get it from. No, I don't think you understand me at all.'

They faced each other obstinately, proud of being misunderstood.

'All I really want to say is, go ahead and make lots of, um, visions and don't bother about me. I'm all right.'

'But you're my son. It's my responsibility to worry about you.'

'Well, we can't all be successes like Rose.'

'She's a girl, it's not the same. Anyway she's not my idea of a success. I like a female to have some charm. Rose is too clever by half, and she drinks too much. No wonder she can't get a husband.'

'She doesn't want one.'

'I always said you two should do a sex change.'

Simon stood up. 'Maybe you'll pay for our operations when you've finished building Jerusalem.'

'Now don't go rushing off. Let me finish what I was saying. It's all very well being so superior but who pays the price? It doesn't help Merlin, does it? I mean how is he going to feel when he realizes he's got a father with no pinability? What if you had an accident? Won't you at least let me get a green card for you?'

'No. As a matter of fact I feel very bad about Merlin. I shouldn't have left him here for so long. I'm really trying to sort it out.'

'What do you mean by that? For God's sake don't push the child backwards and forwards, just when he's beginning to get a bit of security and order in his life. No, I'm not complaining. I'm just pointing out that there is such a thing as a sense of responsibility. Either you have it or you don't. Now personally I've always been very strong on that. My wife, my children, it's all been for you. Of course you're too sensitive and

29

intellectual for that. I sometimes wonder if you've noticed you've got a son.'

'I certainly hope that when he grows up he and I have more respect for each than you and I have now.'

'You won't have, don't worry, you won't.'

With a terrible confusion of guilt and fury he left the room. Rose met him in the hall and they went into the bright yellow kitchen. Now the moonlight pouring in stripes through the venetian blinds modified the strident colour. They sat at the table without turning on the strip lighting they both disliked, and enjoyed feeling like burglars in their parents' house. They couldn't see each other's faces except in zebra patches of light and dark, but each knew the other's face by heart anyway. Rose was holding a brandy balloon which shimmered and sparkled with her porcupine jewellery in the strange light.

'You look shattered. Have a drink.'

'I'll make myself some cocoa in a minute.'

'Always so abstemious.'

'I need comfort, not stimulation. I've had enough of that.'

'Was he spiteful?'

'Yes, although it was loaded with smiles of course. He wanted me to design kitsch cinemas for his ghastly games. Two thousand years of True Brit fantasies.'

'I saw that coming months ago.'

'Why don't you tell me these things?'

'I see what's going on because I've got a nasty calculating mind. You haven't, so you wouldn't believe me anyway – I hope you told him where he could put his games?'

'I wasn't really rude until he came up with the sex change crack.'

'About us? Pathetic. He's been making that joke for a quarter of a century.'

Rose had been named on the understanding that she would, like her mother, be pink and blonde and dewy. This alter-Rose had bloomed half-heartedly in a vase in her head when she was very young. It had restrained her excesses of intelligence and had made friends, for and through her, with a succession of dull, obedient children. Then, in early adolescence, she had turned on the flower like a summer gale, had blasted and shattered and shrivelled it, giving it one last shake

30

to make sure it was dead. Her parents' sardonic remarks about her had begun, and hers about them. She passed exams, joined women's groups, got drunk and abusive when she was supposed to be coyly delightful at her parents' parties, and finally left home with a poet in his fifties, who Madge still referred to as 'that filthy old man'. Rose's battles had been harder than Simon's, and fought more openly. She hadn't started with the dubious advantage of being the favourite, the boy who had everything and would accumulate more for his family's reflected glory. It had been clear to their parents that, whereas Simon was brilliant, Rose was just clever and difficult.

Despite being played off against each other the two of them had always been close. Before Rose was eight and her brother ten they had understood that Madge's cosmos, where boys who were tough and good at football opened doors for giggly, pretty little girls, had nothing to do with them. Rose's suspicion that her mother didn't really know anything was confirmed when she started to menstruate, and Madge put her to bed and told her she had flu; she told her brother about this mysterious virus which had no effect on her nose but produced a bloody flood in what Madge called her botty. Together they laboured over the *Encyclopaedia Britannica* to work out what was going on in her body. They concluded that it happened every month and meant she could have a baby, although Rose hadn't wanted a baby, then or at any other time. They helped each other through puberty and when boys and girls were segregated into different schools, to mix only at parties and self-consciously, they continued to feel they were the same race. Rose's feminism had been tempered by the idea that men, as long as they didn't assert their manhood too much, were friends and allies. Simon generally preferred women's company to men's, although the least hint of Madgeism – an exaggerated interest in food or clothes or a tendency to gush – could drive him into silence.

Nowadays, their best meetings were always here at their parents' house, once or twice a year, when shared wounds could be uncovered, licked and reminisced over. There was nobody else with whom they could discuss their childhood and adolescence. Outside they met stiffly but in this house they feasted joyfully on the past, picking out raisins and rich chunks that could only be digested late at night.

'Do you remember the first time you brought Jessica back here for dinner? They'd been inviting her for months and you kept making excuses, then you gave in. As soon as she left the room to go to the loo, and you followed her, Madge started on her. How she was scatty and not serious enough for you, and Bernard frowned anxiously and said he'd try to arrange something with Rowena.'

'What happened to Rowena?'

'She married Sammy's solicitor's son.'

'Perfect. No, I don't remember that evening well.'

'You both disappeared for half an hour and Madge was frantic, in case the food got cold, or that was what she said. What she thought was probably far more scurrilous.'

'God, yes, it must have been that evening. I knelt at the bathroom door until she let me in and allowed me to stroke her legs. Nothing ever seems really erotic now, not like it was then. Everything was bathed in sex.'

'Not for me. I never liked beautiful young men enough to sleep with them and men I did enjoy talking to were usually so fat and hideous I thought it was kinder not to notice their bodies. Like George.'

'I never understood that.'

'I didn't want anything young and tender like you and Jessica, I thought that was schmaltzy. I wanted someone who would fight Bernard on his own ground, and George did that rather well.'

'They hated each other. Do you know George swindled him out of quite a lot of money? He made up this story about a musical a friend of his had written, about King Arthur coming back to life and leading the British people to their former glory. 'Ring-a-Ding King' it was supposed to be called – I remember him singing songs from it, and Bernard tapping his feet. He actually handed over a cheque. But you weren't supposed to know, in case you married him.'

'Oh, I knew all about it, I helped him write the songs. I loved that side of George, I didn't mind at all about his being unscrupulous until he started on me. I saw him the other day.'

'In a pub?'

32

'No, coming out of one of those freaky sects. The Sacred Tabernacle of the Millennium, Ravenscourt Park, it was called. In an old church. And there was George in a long green robe, surrounded by young girls. He's some kind of high priest – I suppose it gives him a chance to monologue without being interrupted. He's given up practically everything, so he claims: drink, tobacco, sex, trying to get published. He bought me a coffee and then lectured me on how bad it was for me. We had a good talk. I offered to do an article on them but he seemed rather nervous.'

'You do have an acerbic pen.'

'Word processor. I think they're hilarious, these sects. And I'm not sure how seriously George takes it all, really. He kept making puns about being raptured and ruptured. He says we all have to be pure in body and mind to be worthy of the next thousand years. I asked how many people there were who qualified and he said eighteen. All the rest of us are predestined to be destroyed by war and plague – which seems only too likely, really – there'll just be this little Garden of Eden in Ravenscourt Park, George and his girls. What's the matter?'

'Just sour grapes. I was thinking how wonderful it would be to meet your first love like that, to talk and be friendly and casually go away again.'

'But if Jessica was – here – you'd be living with her, so you couldn't do that, anyway.'

'I don't know.'

'But it was such a grand passion, all consuming and non-stop romance. Not like me and George, we were like Pyramus and Thisbe. Do you mind talking about Jessica?'

'Not to you. When she died, you know, I had to make a sort of saint out of her. It was the only way I could cope. But recently I've been remembering all our quarrels, and how impatient she was with Merlin – I'm not at all sure we would have stayed together. What hurts most of all is the thought I can't talk to her ever again. It's left this gaping hole in my idea of myself, twelve years that seemed solid are ambiguous and full of questions I can't ask anybody. There was a lot of nonsense in that grand passion stuff and it was over, really, long before she died. But nothing else has ever mattered quite as much.'

33

'What's going to happen to Merlin?'

'Yes. Yes, that is the question, isn't it? I think he'll come and live with me.'

'Oh good. Shall we kidnap him tonight?'

'Don't be so melodramatic.'

'I saw it as more of a farce, really. He's such a nice little boy, though, I hate to see him being messed about. You can't lumber a child with a name like that and then just forget about him.'

'I've never forgotten about him, not for a moment,' Simon lied. 'But for the last couple of years I've been so uncertain of myself, I've really thought Madge might make a better job of him.'

'Simon! Look what she did to us.'

'I know, but she did it with such confidence.'

'That's the worst sort of interference. You can never escape from it altogether – I never have. I hear this running commentary of Madge's values, telling me that the way to a man's heart is through his stomach and men don't like clever women, and Bernard saying it's in the blood –'

'You don't seem to let those voices hold you back.'

'It's a constant struggle though, a sort of mad internal civil war. No, Madge is a wrecker. You should have sent him to me for a while.'

'What a disgraceful suggestion. Exposing him to all your alcoholic gay friends and your slovenly housekeeping.'

'You see! The same voices, you hear them too.'

They ended up, as usual, smiling at each other. The differences between them rarely made them quarrel; it was such a relief to be able to talk about old lovers and cast-off selves.

On the landing outside his room Merlin listened to them. He couldn't hear their words but found the long, surging phrases, punctuated by short light bursts, comforting like a game of tennis. He trusted Simon and Rose although he didn't think of them as his father and aunt. His mother was the only person whose relationship to himself he had entirely believed in, and when she died he had decided to be an orphan. It made him feel brave and romantic. There was something obvious about having two parents or even one, and although

34

Simon was more honest than most grown-ups he wasn't really distinguished enough to be his father.

Merlin felt squashed between style and character. He knew his grandparents weren't to be counted on but he was deeply impressed by their money and space and optimism. He felt much more important in this house, which had so many rooms that they weren't all used, than in the cramped and shabby flat where he had lived until he was seven. Here, he felt he lived in a castle, a prince surrounded by feasts and new-smelling clothes and delightful fuss about his education. The fuss went on all the time, about what he had for breakfast and what he wore each day and how he was taken to school and what he wanted for his tea. It made him feel hugely interesting and he absorbed it through all his pores, thirstily, like a famous beauty soaking in expensive lotions. He loved his big room overlooking the garden, with its pale walls and furniture, and the way his toys and books were always neatly arranged when he came back from school, no matter how much chaos he had left them in. The old witch upstairs was a confirmation that some kind of magic had entered his life; often in the night he heard her muttering in the room above his, and last summer when he had a temperature he had seen her in the corridor in her long black dress with a gun she was going to shoot his grandmother with. Things like that could happen in a castle.

Simon's air that none of this really mattered put either his father or himself in the wrong. To live at Simon's again would be to turn his back on a dazzling view he had just discovered and pretend it wasn't there. No, thank you, I won't have anything comfortable or beautiful today, I'll just live in my dark little hole and wear awful clothes and eat brown rice. Simon seemed to be saying that all the time and Merlin was bewildered. Simon always pretended that bicycles were nicer than big fast cars and burnt home-made biscuits tasted better than gooey bought cakes and cheap toys, like the one he had just given him, were superior to the magnificent gadgets his grandmother bought him. Yet you couldn't accuse Simon of lying. He hurled the truth around like a flame thrower, distorting and destroying. This castle wouldn't be nearly so exciting if Simon wasn't there to disapprove of it.

Merlin knew he had made a pact now, to go back to the

dark flat, and he was pleased and surprised to be asked. But he wasn't sure that he would go. Last thing at night when he lay in bed it was to Simon he narrated the events of the day; his grandparents had to be given a censored version because they were only waxworks really, though very realistic.

He heard Rose and Simon moving around downstairs, and got up to dash into his room before they opened the kitchen door and saw him at the top of the stairs. Then he heard the other door, the witch's door, and stood paralyzed with fear. She wasn't an evil witch but she was ugly and smelly and followed him round all the time. He thought she snooped in his room when he wasn't there: sometimes he could smell her old age and cologne when he came back from school. He couldn't complain to his grandparents because they were deaf, dumb and blind to what went on in the castle and, anyway, Madge hated the old woman, and Merlin didn't want to get her into trouble. Trapped between two sets of late night noises, he knew someone was bound to catch him. The stairs above him creaked, he closed his eyes in the dark and didn't dare turn round. He could smell her now, long before she reached out her tree root hand and spoke in that hoarse, croaky voice.

'Darling? Little one? Would you get your old ancestor a drink before I die of boredom? I can't sleep.'

'What sort of drink?'

'Brandy and soda.'

'Rose and Simon are down there.'

'So invite them up. We'll have a party in my room, have my wake a few months early.'

'How can you wake up if you can't sleep?'

'Go, get me the drink and don't ask questions.'

She was sitting on the stairs above him breathing heavily, her breath dry and crackly like scrumpled newspaper waiting for fire. Her voice was funny, nasal, with a trace of the cockney accent Madge said he had picked up at his old school. Now, she said, he had a nice little voice.

Reluctantly, clinging to the wall, Merlin slipped down to the drawing room and felt his way over to the table where the drinks were. He had to switch on a standard lamp to illumine the rancid array of flashy bottles. There wasn't one called just brandy, only a pretty red one, cherry brandy. The tumblers were in that silk lined cabinet with the sticky door. Hating what he was doing, thinking how stupid he would look if he was caught, Merlin coaxed the door of the cabinet open, got the glass, half filled it with the cough mixturey liquid and added a squirt from the soda syphon. He could hear Simon and Rose on the other side of the hall. He left the lamp on to guide him back to the door although Bernard would notice in the morning. He still complained about bills.

On the landing Connie grabbed the tumbler and spluttered, 'What is this muck?'

'What you said. Cherry brandy.'

'My God! Even the child is trying to poison me.'

'Isn't it right?'

But she was moving away from him down the corridor, her jewellery and the shiny black dress she always wore clicking and swishing.

CHAPTER 4

�֎✾֎✾֎✾֎✾֎✾֎✾֎✾֎✾֎✾֎✾֎✾֎✾֎✾֎✾

While they were having their party Connie played her old
records, which was what had made her so restless. On the
cover of one of them was her photograph, the one that had
caught her at her loveliest and most vivacious, an image of
perfection that had flickered and died as soon as the camera
finished blinking. For hours she had swayed in her chair to
tangos, black bottoms, congos, rumbas and cha-cha-chas.
her career had started to go downhill with the cha-cha-cha;
she had been too enigmatic for those short, bouncy syllables.
Her eyes so long and green and beautifully made up, every lash
like a feather, her voice husky yet sweet. In the ENSA songs it
swelled to mother all those boys with cups of tea and white
cliffs and chins up. Her other hits were tantalizing, seductive;
although she was born in Hove she had an instinctive
understanding of mystery. That was why the fifties, with all
that girl-next-door nonsense, had been a bad time for her.
Connie had often considered cultivating a foreign accent but
Bernard's father had been against it. Dietrich overdid it
terribly really, with those legs.

Seeing the face again had made her nostalgic, it caught at
her heart like the memory of love. It was her love, none of her
men had moved her half as much. Tiny bones, a creamy white
bird, the heart-shaped face broken by high cheekbones and
framed by the deep red waves of her marvellous hair. A raving
beauty, everybody had said so, never just pretty or attractive.
Eyebrows plucked fastidiously, apostrophes above her extraordinary eyes. Not the great bushes women went around with
now, over noses so shiny you'd think they polished them. It
was ridiculous to go on about being natural; beauty had to be
slaved for, created, lived up to and then worshipped. For years

as a young girl she had done exercises to form that long curved throat sloping to white shoulders. There had been no hint of a double chin until she was well over fifty. And clothes. It had pained her when Bernard had married a woman who wore crimplene and carried plastic handbags. During the war the textures and perfumes of Connie's wardrobe had been intensely sensuous. She used to stroke the silks and satins and cold hard spangles, trying on half a dozen outfits before deciding what to wear for the evening. At one point she had had fifty stage dresses, all cut to the same basic pattern that flattered her so perfectly: sleeveless, the neckline low, and the skirt long, skilfully slit by that little woman near Leicester Square. The same dress, in silk and lace and satin and sequins, in purple and green and black.

The woman in the photograph was holding a Turkish cigarette in a long ivory holder and a brandy and soda. It had been a real one too; she had got on rather well with that photographer. What she missed most of all was being surrounded by people who looked after her – dressmakers, hairdressers, photographers, head waiters who made a favourite of her. Bernard's father Maurice had looked after her very well, really, until they were married, when his demands became unreasonable. That was the beginning of the end.

In the silence between records she could hear the party downstairs which, she knew through several walls, was excruciatingly dull. All of them invited for business reasons, not a single one because he or she was fun or beautiful or talented. Madge trying to copy the style of the parties she used to give when Bernard was a boy, parties where Madge was usually the drabbest figure in the room. Awful droopy dresses she used to wear, with plastic slides in her limp yellow hair and visible agony in her face whenever Bernard talked to another woman. The original girl-next-door, only in fact she came from Epping. Connie found it so hard to talk to her that she used to pretend to be fascinated by the forest, asking her endless questions about the trees, the reputed wild animals, the flowers. She didn't mean to embarrass the girl, she only wanted to improve her by a touch of romance, the wood-cutter's daughter instead of the mayor's niece.

The house then, before most of the real antiques were sold

off to pay the children's school fees and help Bernard through the long periods when his luck and judgement failed. Connie remembered her fury when she had gone downstairs one day to find her Louis Quinze chairs and inlaid Florentine chest missing. The crude way Madge and Bernard had pretended not to notice. As if the tacky matchbox reproductions they bought were really substitutes, as if Connie had spent twenty years making a dazzling setting for herself only to forget what she had put in it. They had never understood that she had stayed for the house and the children, not for them. As soon as Maurice died – his death as low profile as his life – the house had become too big for her. But there was no question of her moving or of Bernard going to live in the flimsy suburban house that was all he would have been able to afford. He was too incompetent to take over Maurice's string of betting shops, so he and his mother had just shared the income, less and less over the years. Connie had given them money as well as space in her life, with their noisy children, their money-grubbing friends who never had enough money to do quite what they wanted and the kingdom of plastic they brought with them: gadgets for the kitchen, toys, sweaty floral garden furniture, bathroom fittings, suitcases, trays, coat-hangers, cutlery and crockery. Madge must have gone shopping for it all over London; whenever she wanted something that would properly have been made of wood or metal or leather she must have demanded plastic instead. In hot weather the house stank of it, a sickly, headachy smell that rose above polish and honeysuckle. It was unbreakable, Madge explained, as if all the other objects in the house lay shattered around her.

The children had in fact been very destructive when they were small. They didn't belong to the same species as neat, nannified Bernard but she had liked them far more. For a few years she enjoyed them more than anyone, more than her surviving friends who had grown thoughtlessly old and ugly. She had gladly let her household revolve around their bright, voracious little faces and had loved them uncritically, to her own surprise, when they were dirty and ill and bad tempered and spiteful. She had thought Madge too strict and possessive and said so, which caused a lot of trouble. It seemed incredible that such enchanting creatures had been produced by such a puddingy marriage. When she was Grandma, Connie had believed in herself for the first time since the devasting impact of the cha-cha-cha.

Now nobody called her Grandma. Simon and Rose hardly came to see her although she always knew when they were in the house. That quaint little thing downstairs was afraid of her. It was her tongue, she said the wrong thing although she was on the ball, too many balls perhaps, rolling around her head like a billiards table.

They had stolen the house from her while she was being Grandma. Squeezed her out of this room and that, always for the children, when really it was for themselves and their tedious friends. They started to give more parties; at first they invited her but only until she used the opportunity to tell their friends what was going on. How Madge kept her out of the kitchen and said she was dirty and banished her photographs from the drawing room.

The brandy and soda had been just to hold, to face the mirror with. They stopped her drinking years ago because of that thing in her throat, cancer, but they had a new name for it now. The darkness seethed with the aroma of Courvoisier, cigars, pickled walnuts, the ghosts of pleasures past. The sickly goo Merlin had given her would have been a joke a few years ago, she would have laughed and sympathized with the child's mistake. But now the unexpected enraged her. A new brand of lavatory paper or a strange car outside the door were reminders that she no longer had to be consulted.

The side lights in her room were small and discreet, pointed under dark red, semi-circular shades fringed with bobbles. With the gestures of a very young actress about to make an entrance Connie checked her make-up, ran her fingers through her brittle hair and touched the plain where her flesh met the black spangled neck of her dress. Then she carried the glass over to her audience, the long swinging Edwardian mirror.

The parody of her photograph was complete. Only her colour scheme, the red and white and black, raised a banner to the lost cause of her beauty. But the red was the clowning orange of too many henna rinses on white hairs, the white had

41

the yellow tinge of dough and the black was coated with fungussy green; she was staring at a rectangle of ditch-water with tributaries of shrivelled paper overhung by dusty autumn weeds. The fragile bones were just waiting to become a skeleton now, draped with a worn out tarpaulin of flesh. Her eyes had got much worse over the last few years but they weren't short sighted enough to dim the shock. The little phrases that had comforted her for so long, fine figure of a woman, doesn't look her age, shouldn't have retired so early, sounded flat and insincere. She would never be able to believe them again. She edged away from the mirror, not wanting to sit up all night with that grotesque image. When Simon was three his favourite insult had been, disgusting old banana skin. Connie muttered the words aloud, an incantation against the malevolent old witch. People didn't understand that you lived years behind your flesh. While it rotted away your soul went on blushing and trembling.

No party noises now, no sound at all, she was reeling through the night alone again. The blackness outside the window was as peopled with monsters as it had been when she was a child. Her pretty lights didn't penetrate the shadows of disappointments, losses and betrayals she had carried off before her flesh betrayed her. Someone else was awake, Simon her last love, thumping in the room below. For a moment Connie hoped he might be making love down there. It was terrible the way he became desexed when that fickle girl (whom Connie had rather liked) died. But it wasn't a rhythmic thump, only the bump and shuffle of furniture being moved around. Another fidgeter in the night. Connie couldn't remember the last time she had been really comfortable.

CHAPTER 5

The past was thick in the house that night, coating the newly decorated walls with the fuzz of time lived through but not absorbed. Simon, unwisely sleeping in his childhood room for the first time in years, realized as soon as he opened the door that he hadn't a chance; the ravening beast of his unfinished business was there, drooling. A prehistoric beast, pre-Jessica, pre-Smiles, whose fangs were under the embroidered cloth, a kind of altar cloth, which his mother had thrown over the model on the big table in front of his bed. He hadn't been able to bear to look at it closely since he had last worked on it, when he was eighteen.

Its foundations had been a big hardboard partition which Madge had had cut and had then decided not to use, when Simon was ten. Already a hoarder, he had dragged it up to his room and used it as a base for his plasticine figures. Snakes, elephants, trees, a witch, dinosaurs, giants, soldiers, a mermaid and a clown, all of them mottled with dirty colours from when he had squidged them together into a ball each night. Planted firmly on the board, relationships sprang up between them – the mermaid inclined her head towards one of the soldiers and trees grew up around the witch to screen the others from her. The settlement became more ambitious when Simon began to build on the shiny brown plain that stretched between his creatures. In the centre he built a cathedral/ mosque like the one they had seen in Cordoba, with spires of gold and silver paper and a dome of marbles. In order to support the weight of its roof, the base had to be some building blocks Rose had discarded. He had cut out paper insets for the doors and windows, painted with onyx pillars and golden altars to suggest the real interior. Around the piazza circled thick dark versions of every kind of building that had ever intrigued him; there were flat roofed rectangles with stairs on the outside and courtyards in the middle, where he imagined his father's Jewish ancestors living in their striped robes, thatched cottages grouped around a village green, a squat French château topped with cone shaped disposable cups, a medieval castle with a moat and a vaulted cave with a hermit.

As soon as he began to people the city, Rose became interested. She decided that plasticine was too soft, you left fingerprints all over people when you moved them, so they made clay inhabitants. There were peasants with scythes, a chatelaine, Muppets, nuns, goblins, Joan of Arc, Elton John and Julius Caesar. There were no extras; all the people had names and characters and moved with complicated purposes through the droopy streets. Narrow lanes like ditches wound where plasticine foundations had been pressed to the board. The whole city was perpetually on the verge of falling, wobbling, melting like candle wax, and this had given Simon a delicious sense of impermanence. It seemed to him now that he had felt more confident moving the brittle figures around than at any time since. Rose had written stories and plays about the feud between the big-nosed aristocrats in the château and the boy and girl in one of the cottages. They were always trying to free the serfs and help Joan of Arc to escape from the stake. Rose and Simon were quite happy to delegate their adventures. Their own childhood was urban, sedentary and greedy.

The city took up most of their spare time and pocket money, just as that other City took up so much of their father, who was always sighing over pink pages covered in arithmetic. For three years they had an outlet and even their quarrels were vicarious, wild fights between the boy and girl who lived in the cottage. Over their heads Simon and Rose glared at each other. During the school holidays their saga was only broken into by demands for them to consume milkshakes, tongue and coleslaw sandwiches and Grandma's Christmas Cake. Simon wondered if Rose had kept all those stories, and decided she wouldn't have bothered. After their talk finished at two in the morning she had summoned a taxi to take her back to the present. Rose was better at disengaging herself than he was.

She could hardly be worse. Whenever Simon thought he had some hard, undeniable truth to hang on to – unhappy childhood, tragic death of wife – it twisted and spun, sucked into the vortex of his fair-mindedness. The first city was now just a few dull plasticine smears on the edge of the board, but he could remember it in every detail, and how he had felt: absolutely secure in his talent and unbreakable promise, just practising on the city for all the fine buildings he would raise outside it. Even then Madge was more to be dreaded than anyone. There were always her rages to fear, her disappointments to be avoided. The whole household seemed to revolve around that. But then there was her food to be eaten and her admiration to wallow in. He had projected most of the unhappiness later, when his parents had humiliated Jessica, and again when he felt he would explode with his effort to reconcile life at Smiles with life in St John's Wood. He could only keep his foothold in both by blaming his parents for their smugness, their attitude that anyone who wasn't doing as well as them had only themselves to blame and anyone who was doing better was cheating. He had moulded and crafted that unhappy childhood of his but now he thought, painfully, that it had been far safer and easier than his son's.

He had demolished the plasticine city one day after looking through a book of scale models of ancient Rome. Years of inner life scraped and squashed into a grubby football and thrown away.

Rose had wept furiously when she saw what he had done.

'It was my city too.'

'It was in my room.'

'I made all the people and the stories – what have you done with the people?'

'I put them in a shoebox for you. Joan of Arc got a bit chipped, sorry.'

'You could have put it in my room if you didn't want it. It was horrible what you did. Like dropping a bomb. You could have told me.'

'It was terribly childish Rose, clumsy and messy. I'm going to make a much better one. Look at this, isn't it beautiful? You can see all the doors and windows, all the details are perfect. You can help me. We'll put the same buildings in if

45

you like, only properly made in wood and plastic and all done to scale.'

'It's boring. It looks like something in a museum. And it's empty, what's the point of a city without any people?'

'You can buy little figures to put in it, and lovely feathery trees. I'll take you to a model shop on Saturday.'

'I don't want bloody damned feathers. I want my city back, and I don't want titchy little houses like that, I want something my people can move around in.'

She had clasped the shoebox and he remembered with surprise her passionate misery. Rose had been very small for her age, with a pale yellowy face always strained forward to understand. Her child hair was dull too, short beige curls, and the only splash of colour in her face was the green flecks in her brown eyes which had looked at him then so bitterly, her tears making the edge of the shoebox soggy. She had so often been angry. She sat out her childhood with brooding malevolence, waiting for it to finish so that she could get her own back.

Now to avenge her the second city looked just like a minor exhibit in a provincial museum. Neat, resolutely modern, no anachronisms and no surprises; the vision of the man who was later to give the world an underground car park in Kuwait and a public lavatory in Aberdeen. The two cities brutally illustrated the point that always struck Simon when he went to see children's art exhibitions. The younger age groups produced work full of vitality and courage, cheerfully breaking all the laws of perspective and shouting with bright reds and greens and yellows. Then at about twelve the children who were 'good at art' discovered the tyranny of realism, and tried conscientiously to reproduce what they saw around them. Walls of repressed, muted, accurate paintings of wine bottles and bananas, nature very dead indeed, killed by the longing to imitate adults. That made him a very ordinary child, with an imagination just big enough to fill a hardboard partition. Yet at his most confident – not this evening – Simon still felt he had spires and piazzas and eclectic twenty-first-century boulevards swirling in his head. He replaced the cloth, moved the table further away from him, over to the window, switched off the light and felt his way to the bed.

His body still remembered the layout of the room. His feet

avoided the chair and his hand reached out to put the glass of water he had carried upstairs on the bedside table. He had a bruised, heavy head from his twenty-hour day and from the alcohol he had consumed. He would let himself oversleep. The sheets were cool and fresh as his own never were. He lay back and floated on comfort.

Simon dreamt he and Christy were making love. On a bare impersonal floor they staggered together, kissed, touched, licked, sucked, stroked, hugged, fucked, fingered, melted the entrails of each other. It was so intense that he couldn't remember later whether the light was on or whether they were clothed or naked. He didn't have to see her to know she was Christy, Christy and he deliriously happy together on the floor of a dream cube.

He woke up as shocked to find the sheets soaked with sperm and sweat as he would have been twenty years earlier. There must be some mistake, one part of his mind tried to reprimand the other, Christy and I keep our distance. He had even been proud of their working friendship. Since Jessica's death he hadn't really been sexual at all and that had been a source of pride too: how clean life would be if he could only be celibate and devote himself to Smiles and Merlin. A secular, paternal priest. Now he lay in a puddle of cold desire and burning curiosity. Instead of shrivelling away his sex force had ripened inside him and had picked this unlikely setting to burst into fruit. It was such an old habit to lie in this bed and feel guilty about sex. But he didn't, only surprised and grateful.

The dream hovered over him as he bathed in the hedonistic bathroom and devoured the vast Freeman breakfast. Delighted to see him at that hour, Madge plied him with mushrooms and scrambled eggs and toasted buns, while her little man whirred around the table. Christy was the dream and the dream was Christy. The smell of her dream skin clung to his and her amused eyes watched his decadent morning. They were displaced by the wistful stare of Merlin, who said nothing but sat in frozen expectation.

'Coming upstairs to see Grandma?' Simon asked with forced joviality.

'No. I don't like her room, it smells.'

Madge smiled approvingly.

'We'll all smell when we're her age. Come up for a few minutes and then we'll go to the park.'

'I'll come if you stay to lunch.'

Connie could hardly believe that they were the end of her vigil. They stood in her doorway looking so fair and English, she was glad her descendants looked more like Nazi officers than their victims; you never knew when things would start up again. She remembered her mother getting a letter just before the war and moaning, 'All of them they have taken to the camps.' One of the few actions of Bernard's of which she had thoroughly approved had been his changing of their name from Friedstein to Freeman. She had looked it up once in a book of Old English surnames: 'Derived from Free Man. A common name in Anglo-Saxon villages'.

'My little British princes,' she said, and clutched their pink hands in her dry yellow ones.

Merlin's eyes began to swivel, as they did when he was so embarrassed by adults that he couldn't bear to look at them. But he liked being there beside his father, in front of her, because it was as if they were brothers, their age gap closed before someone so ancient. The smell of old clothes, stale make-up and shrivelling flesh was terrible. Simon had to give him a push before he would kiss her.

'I've been thinking, you should find yourself another girl-friend,' she said to Simon. She wanted to get in everything important because she would probably never see him again.

'I've been thinking much the same thing.' He smiled but he could hear in his voice the jollity he would use to foil the excessive frankness of a lunatic or a drunk.

'Your mother is trying to get rid of me.'

'Oh. I'm sure you're wrong about that.'

'Yes. Put me down like a dog, they do that now.'

'I really don't think – '

'Yes. Don't argue, there's no time. But I want you to have it, not her. I want her out of the house with all her plastic and her fat greedy face. Take me to a solicitor.'

'What now? It's Saturday.'

'Bernard's cousin used to be very good. Spencer his name was. Is he still alive?'

Simon felt the power of her will to die right, rising above all

48

the smells in the room. That was all a will was, and why shouldn't she have her way? He didn't want the house but he was just as deserving, or undeserving, as his parents. Perhaps he could use it to help Merlin.

'All right. Are you sure you can manage, Grandma, if we go out? How long is it since you left this room?'

'I'll wear my mink and my Fascination Tango dress, I won't disgrace you. You're a good boy. But they won't let me out.'

'Oh come on, they don't keep you locked up, do they?'

'Like that woman in Jane Eyre.' Merlin shone with excitement.

Suddenly she was exhausted and had to sit down. 'They sold the keys. I haven't slept for five years, nobody realizes.'

They were still standing over her but she could see them flicker, retreat, she didn't know whether it was their bodies or their sympathy. 'Jack Buchanan said I should have made films.' She wasn't sure whether they were still there. Her eyes kept closing, the nerves at the corners twitching, and she really had no idea what her tongue was up to.

'I'll make an appointment anyway, Grandma, and we'll go along if you're not too tired.'

'He ought to have married that nurse.'

Her head was like a toy being moved around on a stick. It lolled at improbable angles as her mind careered from sleep to waking confusion. Merlin thought it was spiteful to be so ugly, and he tugged at Simon's arm to take him downstairs where people at least knew how to keep their heads on their necks.

'Goodbye Grandma. See you soon.' He kissed her, to Merlin's disgust.

She didn't hear them go. She was on the roof of the Gargoyle during the Blitz, Hitler's fireworks everywhere, twirling to Bunny Haskins and his band, pausing only to powder her nose in her mother-of-pearl compact.

Merlin kept his grip on his father's arm all the way downstairs so that Simon felt he was in the custody of a very small policeman. And upstairs the sequinned spider queen spun webs to catch them all in: if the house was his he would somehow be pinned down. So he had handcuffs on now, a fine insidious mesh of family feeling bound his torso and Christy's dream hands reached out to caress his heart and balls.

49

As Madge called them for lunch and stood at the bottom of the stairs, a big over ripe mango bird, Simon caught himself enjoying life. Pleasure and love, to which he had been immune for so long, were suddenly accessible again. They flooded the staircase with seductive colours and their sap rose up from the four corners of his being, making him laugh with surprise.

CHAPTER 6

✵✵✵✵✵✵✵✵✵✵✵✵✵✵✵✵✵✵✵✵✵✵✵✵

Thirty people were sitting in the old portakabin that was Smiles' communal room. There were more women than men and they were all wearing coats – fur coats, army coats, heavy tweed coats that looked as if they had once stridden over Scottish grouse moors. One small black woman with a shaven head was wearing a blanket with three holes cut in it, and clutched a supermarket trolley full of elaborately tied tangles of rags.

The April night was so cold that the speakers' voices could be seen on the air. Hot air, Christy thought sadly, exhausted fumes. She had already given her report, nervous and apologetic for her own pessimism; no, the children weren't learning anything, they were just being kept out of danger for a few hours a day, and they weren't getting a balanced diet, just enough to stop most of them from getting rickets. Now the woman from the Squattery at the old County Hall was speaking in the detached, level way they all tried to adopt. Her voice shook as she told them a child had drowned last week as he played on the mud at low tide. The police had said they ought to look after their children properly.

'There are three thousand people there now, maybe more, I don't know. If there's a room we give it to a family. What else can you do? More than half of them are children and the schools won't take them, so of course they play by the river. There's no play space in the gardens now because of the tents. I teach as many as I can but a lot of them won't come to lessons. Then as soon as they're eleven or twelve they're off to a teeny camp, my daughter was saying last week she can't see the point in staying.'

'They had a fire in one of those kids' camps last night, over in North Kensington,' someone butted in.

51

'Order, don't interrupt,' said Sean as the woman sat down in tears.

'Order's a funny name for what we've got.'

'Law 'n order, that's what we were promised.'

'We won't get that or anything else with all this middle-class chit chat. We should be out there on the barricades fighting, tearing up paving stones.'

'We are fighting,' Christy said. 'Only not with violence.'

The man who liked paving stones sniggered.

Sean had the quiet authority of someone who spent more time in meetings than on his own. 'I say order, not because there's any out there but because if we don't have some in here we'll starve. Who's next?'

A big, elderly bruiser of a man stood up. Christy, who hadn't seen him before, was surprised by the eloquence that flowed from his squashed plum of a mouth.

'Jim Stearne, from what used to be St John's Hospital near Clapham Junction. And in case you're wondering, I'm not a doctor but a down-and-out same as the rest of you, only there's some of us with voices and some without. Now before I give you my report I want to say something else: this is the first time I've been here and I don't mind telling you I had my doubts about coming. Talking's all very well, and I do more than my fair share of it, but in my opinion talking shops are not what's needed at the present time. I used to be in the Old Seamen's Union before that was outlawed and in the Printing Union before that was outlawed too, and if I had a sausage roll for every meeting I've attended I'd be fatter than what I am. Be that as it may, I've not come here tonight to knock you, and seeing as how I've got the opportunity I'd like to say how much I appreciate what you're doing. It isn't easy and it isn't thankful but it's a service to us all to have a place we can come to and meet others what have been ground down like ourselves, due to policies beyond our control and beyond theirs too if you ask me. It's given me heart, brothers and sisters, to hear you tonight, and heart is not a commodity I come by very often in these dark times.'

His listeners had been wriggling with impatience. They were all tired and cold and wanted to get home; going on and on was the worst possible crime at these meetings. But his

52

fluently booming voice reassured them; it was like a pianist who you know won't hit the wrong note.

'Things was bad to start with where I come from and it's rapidly gone from worse to worse. At the beginning – a couple of years ago now – it was all barbed wire and guard dogs. The concentration camp, they used to call it locally. Now it didn't take long for them as had no home to see there was a perfectly good one crying out for tenants behind all that barbed wire. So we cut the wire and administered arsenic to the dogs – judicious, not cruel. But I'm buggered if I can see why dogs should live in luxury when there's people sleeping out in the rain and snow. Once we was in we stayed in. It's been my experience that once you break the law, more often'n not, the law doesn't bother you. What's the law want wiv a bloody great empty hospital anyway? So there we stayed and very pleasant it was too, wards full of beds and clean linen fresh as it was the day the National Health got the last nail in its coffin. There was kitchens like cathedrals and bathrooms fit for Royals to shit in, if you'll pardon the expression.

'I say the law didn't bother us but that was before we started on the gas and electricity. If you've got a couple of hundred people and God knows how many kids in a place, it's no good having it all unplumbed and disconnected. So we done it ourselves, done a good job and kept quiet. Up until that moment the lights went on and the hot and cold water flowed you'd think we didn't exist. Then all of a sudden it was swarming wiv blokes in overalls turning it all off and talking about prosecution. All right then, we says, we'll pay same as everyone else. You're a bunch of scroungers and meths drinkers, they says, how are you going to pay? That's our business, we says, you provide the services and the bills is up to us.

'Anyway the upshot was we stayed in the buildings but they cut all the comforts out of them and over these two years it's degenerated something terrible. Smells, damp, leaking roofs everywhere, broken windows, old geezers popping off in the middle of the night on account of the cold. We got the zonkies moving in now, downstairs, can't stop them. Fights every night. I wouldn't know how to start cleaning up now and as for repairs, you'd have to rebuild the place. My missis

53

died in March, only sixty-four she was. She'd always had bronchitis but it'd never of killed her if we'd've been somewhere dry and warm. All the time I was nursing her I thought, couldn't help it, them bastards at Westminster are murdering her sure as if they come after her wiv an axe.

'So it's not the Hilton where we are. It's a pigsty but there is a roof and as all of you here tonight will appreciate, on a freezing, bloody, muddy night that's a very considerable difference. When I was employed in the printing trade I walked past Charing Cross Bridge every morning for close on fifteen years. I'd watch those poor sods wiv their cardboard boxes and the despair in their eyes, there wasn't as many of them then as what there is now but there was never less than a coupla hundred. And I'd think to myself, must be bleeding horrible sleeping out like that. I wonder why they don't get themselves a job, young blokes too some of them, anything'd be better than what they've got. Terrible what booze and drugs does to people.'

'I'm afraid I'll have to stop you there,' said Sean.

'Let him go on,' Christy said sharply.

Jim looked round the group and saw most eyes fixed on him with sympathy. 'I wish now I'd of got a closer look at them. I wish I'd of studied them, worked out how you stay human never mind decent when you're living in a cardboard box on bread and tea. And I'll tell you why, because I'll be joining them. We had a visit Monday morning from a flash looking fellow tells us our presence is no longer required, not that it ever was. Gives us a document all signed and sealed informing us as how Freedom Enterprises – beautiful name isn't it – is taking over our site and the bulldozers'll be in next week. So me and a coupla hundred more'll be investing in cardboard boxes. Some of us drinks when we can get it and some of us doesn't, speaking for myself I don't take drugs and I don't hold wiv 'em. But talk to me in a year and I might have neuropeps and meths coming out of my earholes. I'm not a despairing man and I'm not one of your revolutionaries either. But it's my opinion that the majority of people in this country is getting its rights nicked one by one by the minority. And if the majority, that's us, doesn't sit up and take notice, we'll all be sleeping out.

'It's not just comforts, though discomfort does terrible things to the brain. Take me, seven years back I had a cheap flat down the Fulham Palace Road wiv a good job and coming up for retirement, so I thought. Then they go and do away wiv controlled tenancies and the next thing we know we're living wiv our son and daughter-in-law, looking for something else. Well, there isn't anything else unless you buy it, and who's going to give me a bloody great mortgage at fifty-nine? All of a sudden I'm old and poor and my wife's sick. But she can't get into a hospital because we've got no Britcard, we paid our stamps for thirty years but that don't count. So she gets worse and Dave and Annie gets fed up wiv us, I'm not blaming them. It gets harder and harder to get up in the morning or go home at night but I carry on at work because that's all there is, and there's only a year to go before I collect the pension. Then along comes that story about the KGB infiltrating the printing unions, they got us on some new law and we're out on our arses negotiating for twenty quid a week. Negotiating, mind you, because as Commie agitators we don't get no redundancy and forfeit our rights to the pension fund. Forfeit your human rights is what it boils down to, if you've no property and no job. Two years. That's how long it takes to get from running a car and going out for meals to scrounging round the dustbins. Right. I've introduced myself and I daresay I overdid it. I'll sit down now but I'll be back, and I'm gratified for your attention.'

Christy felt the misery in the long silence after Jim stopped talking. You met once a month and talked, enjoyed it in a way, yet you knew that at the next meeting nothing would have changed except that there would be more of you. People started to go home. It was after tea and raining; most of them had a long walk home and nowhere dry or warm to sleep at the end of it.

Christy and Sean were left alone together in the hut, facing each other across the empty circle of metal and canvas chairs. She watched him add to the minutes and knew he would keep his eyes on the page, away from hers, for as long as possible. Now it was more a matter of disguising than exchanging thoughts between them. She wished he wasn't so skinny and withered inside his sweater and jeans. With his small soft-skinned face crinkled with anxiety and his greying wing of hair he looked like an old woman. We'll still be here when we're both old women, she thought angrily.

Christy yawned. 'Will you write it up for the *Prodigal Bum* or shall I?'

'I'll do it.' Sean always volunteered to do extra jobs and then acted as if he had been martyred. 'There's not much to say really. Did you see that cartoon in the latest issue?'

'The one about Neuropepsi?'

'Yeah. Do you think it's true?'

'Probably. I never touch the stuff, I won't have it in the playgroup. But the kids are given it at home all the time. God, I'm so tired. But there's no point in dashing back now through the rain. If I get wet now I'll stay wet all night. The rain's coming in under my door again.'

'Coming through my window too. Wettest May since 1837.'

'Oh, well as long as it's historically significant.'

'Pity that bloke dominated the meeting.'

'Jim Stearne? I thought he was wonderful, I hope he comes again. I wish people did that more often, just stood up and talked about their own experiences and feelings instead of pretending we're bureaucrats representing something.'

'But we are, we're delegates.'

'Delegating what from who? It's a mockery of the old system: it's pathetic the way we cling to motions and agendas and minutes.'

'Now don't start on my poor old minute-book again.'

It was true, she resented the battered exercise book as if it was a mandarin in an immaculate suit strangling them with red tape. She came and sat next to Sean so that she could read what he was writing in his small, not unmandarin-like handwriting.

'This is exactly what I mean. You've reduced that man's life to one sentence: "The delegate from St John's Hospital in Clapham introduced himself interminably".'

'Well he did go on.'

'And for ten minutes I forgot I was here.'

'We don't come here for escapist entertainment, Christy.'

'Why not, for God's sake? It's the only chance of entertainment I get.'

56

Sean looked up at her and smiled. 'Bet's having a party tonight, in the washhouse. She says she's leaving again, going to live with her sister in Sunderland, I suppose she might. Would that cheer you up?'

Home-made booze, dancing in the mud, couples fumbling against corrugated iron walls, Bet's face toothless and sagged at forty. Sean and Christy obliged to jollify and prevent fights . . .

'No, I'm going home. I'm thinking of going to see my mother soon. Will you look after the children for a week or two while I'm away?'

'If I must, though I shouldn't really leave the stores and admin for so long. Can't Simon handle it on his own?'

'It's too much for one person, and he is a volunteer.'

Christy turned off the paraffin lamps and stoves and slipped out into the freezing rain before Sean could think of something mean to say about Simon.

They padlocked the door, although the hut was broken into and slept in almost every night, and armed their bodies against the cold; hoods up, heads down, hands in their pockets as they squelched their leaden feet in and out of the ankle-deep mud. After another few weeks of rain, Christy thought, the mud will be deep enough to drown in like at Passchendaele, then we'll all be tentbound and shackbound. Sounds rose above the clatter of the rain and the mud gulping at their footsteps. A child howled, a woman screamed and a man yelled a fluent incantation of obscenities.

When they reached their caravans, which were linked by a canvas porch, they touched cold hands in the dark before turning away to their separate, leaky shells. It was rarely now that they went to each other in the night, they had so little left to talk about and it was lonelier, though warmer, to lie together in silence.

Christy lit her paraffin stove, took off her wet things, laid them on a chair beside the evil-smelling, flickering blue flames and hurried into the huge sweater and thick socks she slept in. She knew it was dangerous to sleep with the stove on in the confined space; every week there were fires at Smiles. The fumes would give her a headache – but she had to wake up to dry shoes, even if they only stayed dry for a few minutes. She

57

cleaned her teeth with some of the water she had left in the kettle and got into bed.

It was narrow as a coffin. Her feet inside her sleeping bag poked out over the end and above her the rain slashed at the roof while the caravan rocked in the sea of mud. Slowly her body warmed and relaxed, she shut her eyes and was thankful the day was over. Christy experienced a sense of well-being, the absence of discomfort, and the certainty she had the night to herself. She lay on her back with her arms at her sides, effigy-like, the rough wool of the sweater and socks as itchy as sackcloth. Falling backwards into sleep now, Christy jerked convulsively and then plummeted another few thousand feet. She saw herself as a corpse, not of marble but of knotted veins and muscles and battered skin, being lowered into a soggy grave. She lay on a wooden tray made of scraps of wood nailed together, murky brown against the wet sludge landscape. Nobody watched as ropes lowered the rickety coffin into the mud. The ropes swayed in the wind, a plank of wood swung loose and catapulted the body into the cold slime. Slithery bog filth packed her eyes and ears and nostrils . . . Christy didn't trust sleep after that.

She got up, though she could have touched most objects in the caravan from her bed, and made herself a cup of coffee from the UN dust that had no smell or flavour; coffee dust, milk dust, oxtail soup dust. Observing how her hand shook as she poured the water from the kettle, she wondered why the image had shocked her. She and Sean had often ridiculed pompous wedding and funeral rites. Because there had been no man, woman or child there to watch. Christy knelt beside the stove with her face on the bed, and sobbed with loneliness. Not too loud, because then Sean might hear and come, and that really was the last thing she wanted.

Her face still puffed and sullen, she looked down at the patch of flesh between the sweater and the socks. Two thin, hard lines, mauve in the wobbly paraffin light. They might as well be table legs for all the connection she felt with them. She had no mirror in the caravan and hadn't seen her own reflection for months. Christy touched her black pubic hair, still sprouting hopefully though you'd think it might give up and drop out, and felt the numb rubber of her clitoris. She

58

hadn't felt any pleasure in her body since she had joined the queue at the Vasectomobile the previous September.

She hadn't gone, like most of the others, for the free food hamper (baked beans, a tin of biscuits, a jar of marmalade and a Lymeswold cheese). She had wanted to make sure she wouldn't produce yet another unwanted, unloved and damned near unlovable child. As a professional carer – Sean's phrase, not hers – she felt entitled to choose who she cared for. And the possibility that one of their half-hearted bouts of lovemaking might result in a shivering, undernourished Smiles baby was unbearable.

The queue was long and jocular. The men wisecracked about castration, impotence and savings on Durex, while the women complained about their pregnancies and children and relished the thought it was over. Beatrice was there; she flounced out at the other end looking radiant and went straight off to work. Dimelza saw her mother's hips were swaying with even more confidence than usual and she wondered, together with the other children, what was going on in the big caravan where they gave grown-ups presents.

'No more fucking kids,' her mother had snarled when she asked. Then the children thought they were going to be sent away with the ghostly white-coated food givers, and fled across the mud.

Christy was glad when the children left because children Dimelza's age were her weakness, as she saw it then. She wasn't ashamed of loving them but she felt it was wasteful to love your particular child when there were so many others who needed you. She was the only woman in her section of the queue who hadn't already had at least one child, and grew edgy listening to their stories of miscarriages and abortions and sleeping out on winter nights with tiny babies. Memories she wouldn't have, grim ones perhaps, but Christy felt her experience narrowing to the white, opaque door. She hadn't told Sean she was going to be 'done', a word she remembered her mother using years before when they took their female cat to the vet. Sterilization was an ugly concept that required euphemisms and evasions – anyway Sean and she had agreed they didn't want children. Just before her turn came the woman in front of her abruptly walked off. Christy remem-

·bered bitter jokes at delegates' meetings about gas chambers, and experienced a moment of panic before she opened the door.

Behind it, of course, was a bland white smiling place, irreproachably clean and painless. Done. Tore the life out of her with sympathetic faces and handed her a leaflet, 'Toeing the Line', boasting that the government had met its population target three years in a row. 'Our island cake is big enough for everybody just so long as there aren't too many of us,' it began. Christy scrumpled it up, threw it in the mud, and stumbled weeping over the ruts, garbage and rubble that iced her slice of the cake. She had given the children a morning off because she couldn't face them, so she went straight to her caravan and stared desolately at the food hamper.

'I hope it didn't hurt?' Sean asked when he found her there.

'Not physically.'

He sat beside her on the celibate bed, holding her hand apologetically. 'I think you were absolutely right.'

'Why didn't you do it, then?'

'Too busy this morning. I'll go next time they come round.'

She glared at him, furious to think he could father children until he was senile. In some better place and time with – 'Oh, they'll be back. Can't have dregs like us breeding.'

'You're far too valuable to disappear into a morass of babies.'

'They would have been your babies, Sean.'

'Yes, but look how they drain women. Look at Ellen. Until that child was born she was as active as any of us, driving supply lorries and mending roofs and co-ordinating all the South London camps – a really practical woman. Now she just sits around with that screaming child and she can't even mend the leaks in her own tent.'

'He's always ill, that's why he screams, he's always cold and hungry and so is she, I suppose.'

'Anyway, you don't want to be like that, do you?'

'No. That's why I did it.'

Sean never doubted that a point proved rationally was a point proved. Christy, as he had admiringly observed, was capable of rational argument. But she often privately despised it. So it was with her lost fertility; she approved of it, saw its loss as both inevitable and sensible, but every night for eight

60

months she had mourned it. She had lost touch with her body and with some inner garden where a bucket of weedkiller, smilingly thrown, had annihilated thirty years of growth. She worked hard, shrivelled and dreaded her nights alone.

This one was particularly long. The thick blue atmosphere pressed like oily fingers behind her eyes and nostrils. She turned the stove off, crawled back into bed under a heap of blankets and waited for the cold to hit her. If she didn't fall asleep now she would feel the chill of the April night seep right through her flimsy walls, hear the rain plop dolefully into the bucket in the sink, the blurred anger of the traffic on the motorway and the shrieks and yells of people returning from a night out. But if she didn't sleep she wouldn't be able to work tomorrow, or not without uncontrollable bad temper. It was a relief, sometimes, to let her spleen overwhelm her but the price she would pay was too heavy; her own guilt, the children's disappointment, Simon's awful tolerance. Well he and Sean could tolerate each other for a few weeks and see how they liked it.

I'm in a bad way, she told herself, and tried to make a mental list:

Can't sleep
Can't concentrate
Can't relax
Can't enjoy myself
Can't love the children or anyone else
Can't get rid of my headache

I need –

I'm not really sure but my mother will help. She always does.

CHAPTER 7

Rachel poured goat's milk over her porridge and ate it beside the fire she had just made. Her morning rituals filled at least the first two hours of her day. She liked to feel that her time was slow and stately, it was the only way she could ennoble her solitude. Rachel knew she had a talent for justifying her lifestyle, whatever it was, for she had been just as happy living here when the house was a fish farm co-operative and, long before that, when Martin and Christy were still around. Her most characteristic trait was an obstinate refusal to complain or become bitter, and she understood why it put people off.

Rachel collected the hens' six eggs, picked some sage, parsley, carrots and potatoes for her lunchtime soup and walked beside the stagnating trout pond. The last trout had died years ago, rising to the surface bloated with some horrible fishy disease. They had fed them too much or too little or the wrong stuff, none of them really understood what went wrong and, as the co-operative had gone sour some months before the fish died, people started to drift away towards the coast. They were all younger than her, couples; she had watched their security in each other's bodies as they lived and worked together. In a way it was easier, not to have to watch them any more, or hear their children playing where Christy used to play. Rachel wished she had made more friends, now it was too late, now she had no transport or money and it tired her to walk more than a few miles. People could come to her, but they didn't.

The atmosphere around the isolated, shabby building wasn't gloomy but benign. Christy picked it up as soon as she came within sight of the house, crouched on its hillock waiting for the Dartmoor weather to punish it.

Rachel had heard the lorry rumbling over the track; in the silence she had even heard the engine stop and the door slam. She had assumed it was taking supplies to some remote farm. When she saw her daughter marching towards her, camouflaged by a hood and bulky clothes but unmistakably recognizable as Christy by her angular stride and snouty nose, her mother gave a shout of pleasure and ran towards her. Both moved as fast as they could over the ruts and holes that, a month before, had been plugged with snow. They met, hugged, and stared at each other in amazement. For Christy the surprise was that her mother never changed, for Rachel it was that her daughter could have been so many people. Now she looked tired and sallow.

'Did you write to say you were coming? They often don't deliver the post now.'

'No. I only decided to come the night before last. I set off yesterday afternoon – quite a smooth journey really.'

'You hitched all the way?'

'Oh Rachel! You used to hitch yourself. It's only because you're my mother you feel you have to disapprove.'

'Hypocrisy's part of having children, you'll find out.'

'I won't. It's so clean up here, even the mud isn't dirty like our mud.'

'Pure and empty. You'll help to fill it up. Are you on your way somewhere?'

'I just wanted to see you. Can you stand me for a couple of weeks?'

'I think so. If you can stand a diet of eggs and carrots.'

Their words were light and quick in the early sunshine, their arms wrapped tightly around each other as they moved forward, warm and energetic, both feeling how much easier it was to be purposeful together. Two tall, strong women, one with frizzy dark hair and the other with a grey bun that dragged back all her features.

They went in through the back door into the kitchen, hungry for talk. As Rachel made tea and toast she kept glancing around to make sure Christy was still there, and her daughter's greenish brown eyes followed all her mother's competent gestures. The woodburning stove had been lit for an hour and had warmed the small, low ceilinged room. The

63

only furniture was the wooden table where they sat, a big dresser and a sagging couch, scratched and slobbered on by long dead cats and dogs. Heavy blankets hung over the door and window to keep out draughts, so that even in the morning the air in the room was muffled and nocturnal. Christy took off her shoes and socks and laid them on the stove.

'I sometimes think there's a conspiracy to keep my feet wet.'

'I remember at Greenham nothing ever dried properly. Rubber boots with thick socks are the only answer, I'll buy you some. And now you're living in a tent too.'

'Caravan. Why don't you ever come to see me?'

'I can't take London any more. All that decay and poverty – it breaks my heart and then I feel guilty because I'm not doing anything about it. Besides, how could I get there? My pension's hardly enough to pay the rates and buy wood.'

'Hitch, like me. Then I can worry about you.'

Rachel decided to scratch the surface of the crisis she sensed in her daughter's life. 'Are you going to stay at Smiles?'

'I suppose so. I've nowhere else to go and anyway I don't see how I could leave. It's not like an ordinary job, it's more as if I'd adopted a few dozen children.'

'*Do* they pay you?'

'I get free accommodation (a leaky caravan) and food and clothes vouchers. I save some of them. I don't know what for. You got me into the habit of saving. I suppose Sean and I are the richest people there.'

'How is he?'

Christy had turned up with him once, three years before, and Rachel remembered a dry, puritanical man, smaller in every way than her daughter.

'He's all right. Harassed, I expect. He and Simon are looking after the playgroup while I'm away.'

'Who's Simon?'

'Oh, he's an amazing bloke. You'd like him. He's been a volunteer for two years now, he helps me with the children – I couldn't run the place without him. He's very sad and mysterious about his life. I think he's married but he never talks about his wife, and he's got a son who doesn't live with him, and he used to be an architect. That's about all I know about him, really. The wonderful thing is that he always turns

64

up, and never gets impatient. Not like me. Sean can't stand him.'

Her eyes were as green and shiny as two oval pieces of glass washed by the sea, Rachel noticed, and her cheeks were vivid with warmth and interest.

Christy kept having to remind herself that there was time and space all around. She felt like a mangy animal who had just been let out of a dark cage into a sunlit forest. After lunch they went for a walk, straight up on to the moor where they saw only sandy ponies, sheep and wild flowers. To Christy's urban eyes it wasn't so much the beauty of the countryside that was spectacular, as the absence of people, dirt and noise. She had spent the years between ten and eighteen here, most of the time wanting to live in a less inconvenient place. But now she could see her mother's grandeur, swooping like a great bird over all this green airiness.

When they went back to the house Christy sat at her bedroom window and stared out, while her mother read downstairs. Hours without looking at a clock or feeling that anxious contraction in her heart because she ought to be doing something else. When it was dark they would talk again, and then there would be milk and honey in a capacious bed, the exquisite pleasure of unbroken sleep and waking up to silence. I want to be like her when I'm old, Christy thought, but that still leaves thirty years of confusion and ugliness. Fear clutched her at the reminder that when she was old her mother would be dead. And who would love her then?

After supper they sank into the crevices and broken springs of the sofa.

'Such a comfortable room,' Christy muttered, drowsy from the weight of the home-made bread and peach brandy.

'In winter I live in here all the time. I've only just moved back into my bedroom. The snow cut me off from January until a few weeks ago – I was burning chairs at Easter.'

'Didn't you see anyone all that time?'

'Nobody could have got here without a snow plough, and anyway there was nobody to come.'

'I ought to have known.'

'I wasn't unhappy. I bought dozens of books in a jumble sale at Christmas and I had my tapes and the radio. I wrote a lot of

65

poems – it was like being an adolescent again, that kind of indulgent, luxurious solitude. I had enough food and I fed on memories too, I must have relived every important incident in my life. Oh, and I wrote you lots of letters. I didn't send them because of course I couldn't get to the post, and when I read them after the thaw they seemed too – heavy.'

'I'd love to see them now. Can I?'

'If you like.'

Rachel pulled some envelopes out of a drawer in the dresser. 'And here's your Birthday Special from Martin.'

'To show he cares.'

'He does, in his way.'

'Where is he now?'

'The last letter I got came from India. Terribly mystical. I think he's married again but he didn't have the nerve to say so.'

'Toying with oriental religion, I suppose. How predictable. I always feel older than him.'

'He's genuinely ageless, I quite admire him for that. He loved us both for quite a long time, you know. I think he still loves you.'

'It's bloody easy to love someone when you're thousands of miles away and you never see her.'

'Don't hate him, don't cast me as the martyr. It's an insulting role for me and anyway I often think I drove him away.'

'How?'

'By not needing him enough. Read my letters, there's quite a lot about me and Martin.'

'Well I needed him.'

Sitting there with her mother, Christy remembered the evenings after Martin left, when she was twelve. He banged out of the house one windy autumn night after she had lain upstairs listening to their angers, Rachel's quiet and contemptuous and Martin's noisily dramatic. Every time a door or window shook she was afraid they were throwing things as they sometimes did. Christy wasn't on either side, she only wanted to hear both sets of footsteps come upstairs so that she knew they were both there, keeping the house safe for her. She heard his: running, slamming doors, bumping downstairs

66

again with something heavy. The next morning her mother said, 'Martin and I have decided we can't live together any more. But we still love you.' Every night until she had left home six years later, Christy had looked out of the kitchen window, expecting his knobbly black and white and scarlet face. As if his absurd travels were just a fantasy and he was really still waiting on the other side of the door he had walked out of.

'Read me *The Snow Queen*,' Christy said, curled up beside her mother, her eyes puffy and red with the strain of her twelve-year-old feelings. She was so relieved she wasn't really twelve any more.

Rachel brought the book, which had tissue paper between thick creamy pages and shiny, sentimental illustrations of stained glass window people. They were all beautiful, Gerda had hair like golden chain-mail and a pointed, elfin face, Kay was a marble page boy and the Snow Queen in her pagan furs was fantastically elegant. Often in the long silent evenings when they were snowed up Christy had hoped the Snow Queen would come for her, because a magic castle in the Northern Wastes would be far more fun than her squat, nowhere house. And the Snow Queen was glamorous, whereas at that judgemental age Christy found her mother dowdy and fat in her muddy clothes. She had been Kay, seduced by ice and fire, and then, rather as an afterthought, she had been Gerda as well because she was a girl and you were supposed to like the goodies. But privately Christy thought she was doglike and pathetic, following Kay around like that when he obviously didn't want to know and dragging him away from that fascinating Garboesque witch. Now the story had other resonances for her; she knew splinters of ice got into your eyes and heart when there weren't any witches around, and even improved your vision.

Rachel watched her melancholy face over the top of the book. She still knew the story by heart and still found Kay despicable. It was a long time since she had last sat in this room with her daughter with so little strain. Christy no longer wanted to escape, and Rachel was glad, as she had never meant to be a gaoler and in fact had virtually thrown her out at eighteen, just to stop her complaining about the house. For

67

ten years after that Christy had returned home with a constraint that implied her wings were being clipped and she longed to beat them again, far away. Rachel knew there was no duty in this visit, Christy really wanted to be with her and would be reluctant to leave. Rachel was triumphant but she feared for her daughter's life outside.

That night in bed, Christy held the letters. She wouldn't read them yet, she would save them, and when she returned to Smiles they would go in the box with Sean's early notes to her, Martin's nineteen birthday cards, poems her mother had written for her when she was a child and drawings the children had given her. Her personal life fitted into a rather small wooden box. She told herself it was because she had no room to hoard possessions. Warm, dry, floating on the sensuous imagery of the Snow Queen, Christy fell asleep.

But she woke to find the room still dark. The idea of Martin, or perhaps some dream of him, had torn her out of sleep and her brain fizzed. She sat up, switched on the bedside light and opened his envelope. A card with flowers and teddy bears; he found them all over the world and would presumably go on sending them until she was fifty. Because she was always twelve to him, just as he was always young and vigorous to her. She imagined him trailing round Asia with his backpack full of saccharine cards.

> My Dear Christina,
>   You don't write. Is that because you hate me or because you don't know my address? In fact I shall be quite stable in Delhi for a few years. Perhaps you will come? Rachel tells me you're a social worker so I suppose you have even lamer ducks than me to put up with.
>   In March I shall be in London, making a film for Indian Television. I'll be at the St James' Towers from about the seventh to the twelfth, and I would love to see you. But only if you would like to. I don't expect raptures after all this time. I've always loved you though God knows who you are.
>   Your affectionate and inadequate father,
>   Martin

He had come and gone six weeks ago. And what was he doing

at a hotel like that, was he rich? The possibility that her irresponsible father might have done well, according to the values her parents had taught her to ridicule, made Christy angry. Anger at the sight of one of those cards was almost a reflex reaction, anyway. Then, because of the conversation with her mother, she questioned the anger. What ought he to have been, then? A stream of adjectives gushed out: protective, interested, encouraging . . . . then, because they were so gushing, she cut them off. Well he should have been there, at least. Yet so many other fathers she knew of were none of these things, and she couldn't really blame Rachel and him for separating if they couldn't bear to live together any more.

Quite suddenly she identified with them instead of with herself. How deadly to be stuck in this remote house with someone you loved as little as she loved Sean and a child who was beginning to be obnoxious, as she was at twelve. You couldn't spend years at Smiles and imagine that united families were the norm. They were freaks of human nature, nearly always temporary, and for the first twelve years of her life she had had the good fortune to shelter in one. She wished she had gone to see Martin in London. Instead of the self-pitying confrontation she had always looked forward to she could hear a friendly conversation.

Mentally, Christy drafted the letter she would write if he really had an address:

> Dear Martin,
>   I didn't receive your letter until yesterday. If I had read it in time, I would have come to see you. I don't hate you any more, I can't say I love you either but you're a big part of my childhood. I suppose I see you as a romantic figure, someone who strode off into the night. Perhaps that's how you'd like to be seen. I don't find Rachel romantic but then I know her. Social worker's a bit grandiose for what I do: I live and work in a shanty town in Wandsworth, looking after children. I daresay you've seen that kind of poverty in India. People used to think it would stay there.
>   I've just hitched here to see Rachel so it's not very

likely I'll be able to fly to Delhi to see you. Perhaps you'd like to send me a ticket? Or perhaps you'll come to London again?

Rachel sends – I'm not sure what. I would really like to be friends with you if you gave me the chance.

She was pleased with this and jotted it down in case it still looked good in the morning. It seemed guarded and acerbic without being ungenerous. Christy didn't see why she should make too much fuss of her long lost father. He had wanted to get lost and she had been the real loser, she hadn't trusted a man since. For the first time Christy admitted to herself a deeper fear, that Martin's disappearance had given her a taste for men who were elusive, which was why Simon intrigued her so much more than Sean. It was easier to be honest about her parents than about her own muddled emotional life.

Christy turned to her mother's letters.

CHAPTER 8

✿✿✿✿✿✿✿✿✿✿✿✿✿✿✿✿✿✿✿✿✿✿✿✿✿

There were a dozen letters, written on sheets of lined paper torn off a cheap notepad and folded in brown envelopes. Rachel's round loopy handwriting covered every inch of both sides so as not to waste paper. Before she even read them, the letters touched Christy because they looked like the secret diary of a very young girl. She imagined her mother, alone for all that time, sitting downstairs beside an inadequate fire, trying to be honest with her daughter. A lot of what she had written was conversational, remarks they might have exchanged if they'd been in a room together; how cold it was, what she was reading, how it was both cosy and desolate to be cut off like that by the snow, and how bored she was with lentils and potatoes. Her mother had written a long letter each week, with daily entries. She had thought of Christy as a sympathetic companion all through that long winter, when Christy had hardly thought of her at all.

The general tone of the letters was cheerful, but in some passages Rachel admitted to weaknesses she couldn't have spoken of. Although her mother had handed her the letters Christy felt she was snooping. She had to force herself to accept this new intimacy.

'. . . I often read these letters aloud, or say poems, or sing just to relieve the silence. It's a deliberate noise, less dotty than talking to myself. Really of course I could scream and yell and bang dustbin lids twenty-four hours a day, nobody would know or care. But I am incurably sane, I've never been able to let go. I couldn't at parties, even when I was young and had had a few drinks. I admired your father because he was so good at being funny and silly and light. I don't think he knew I

71

admired him, I never told him and in fact stared at him disapprovingly whenever he got drunk or giggly. Then, very occasionally in our lovemaking, we were able to enter each other. I took on some of his blitheness and he became serious as I desperately wanted him to be. Then we were happy . . .'

'. . . I'll tell you something. I only stopped feeling guilty about not giving you a father (or not for long) when I saw you had problems with men too. Now I feel I can tell you what happened and you won't judge me too harshly, or him either.

It wasn't casual or sudden, our separation, though it must have seemed so to you. We lived together for seventeen years – five before you were born – and we thought we'd been through every kind of upheaval. Do you know who we were when we met? I wonder if you would have recognized us. I was a bit younger than you are now, I was a librarian at a University in Surrey that had just opened. It closed down years ago because it ran out of money. Martin was doing a Ph.D. on the role of women in Dostoevsky and we used to have great arguments in the bar. I accused him of making the women too passive. He'd been doing this thesis for years and he really had no intention of finishing it, he got by on a bit of money from his parents and a few hours of teaching.

I often think we'd have been perfectly happy if we'd been able to drift on like that, living near but not with one another, working but not too hard, no long term plans or responsibilities. Sorry, that's not very flattering to you. Martin looked a bit Dostoevskian himself at the time, all burning black eyes with curly black hair and a beard, and that very dramatic white skin with red lips. He had a funny nose that stuck out too far, come to think of it you've got it too. Even when he's ninety that nose will look as if it's escaped from a child's face. When he argued it was like an epileptic fit, he'd rage and thump and insist, and it was terribly exciting to shout back and stand up to him. That was before people became open about sex. It was still a secret we'd discovered against our parents' will. And I was attractive then, if you can imagine that. I'm not sure I can any more.

I was active in my Union, which was legal at the time, and we went on marches to protest about nuclear weapons and

Vietnam and apartheid. We despised marriage and I was never going to have any children because I had no right to bring them into a world where a nuclear holocaust could happen. My most vivid memories of the first three years we knew each other are of marching to Trafalgar Square with our arms around each other. Sitting in pubs later, talking and arguing. A feeling of warmth and pageantry.

Then they called his bluff, he had to finish his thesis which was very eccentric and Martin-like; full of references to Manichaeism and Marxism and Albigensian heretics – I think he dragged in almost every religious and political idea since Plato. The qualities that made him such a charming talker made him a flighty academic, though his lectures were always fun. Anyway he got a teaching job eventually – there were still plenty then – in a Polytechnic near Coventry. I got a job as a librarian in the same town and we finally, formally, moved in together. That was still considered quite scandalous by my family, who were Methodists from Yorkshire. They sneered at almost everything I did and I think they're the reason I'm writing to you like this: I want you to know all the things I didn't know about them.

We lived in a rather ugly new house and put on weight. There were lots of children in the street and I discovered I liked them. The holocaust didn't seem quite as imminent so we got married, rather furtively, and you were born. You were the great love of my life and Martin was very jealous of you. We both fussed over you, adored you, couldn't keep our eyes or hands off you. I think you must have been the most photographed and recorded baby in history. But there was this veiled resentment of Martin's, I always seemed to be defending you when he'd say you were spoilt or manipulative or selfish. He didn't see you as a tiny baby but as an equal and a rival. We never seemed to be able to turn into a family, perhaps it was because we spent so much time criticizing nuclear families before you were born. Then I stopped work, which made me restless. I used to stare in at the living room windows of the people who I imagined were Omo families and wonder how they did it. We all loved each other but somehow it wasn't synchronized . . .'

'. . . .You had a terrible temper as a child, you used to scream and shout and kick me. I used to hold your arms until you calmed down in case you hurt yourself. But Martin lost his temper with you, you used to have these horrible double tantrums. I'd tell him he wasn't grown up enough to be a father and he'd groan with fury, say how arrogant it was of women to assume they were the only adults in the universe.

Then he fell in love with one of his students. And I went off with someone too, a colleague of his, just out of spleen really. We were appallingly frank, we told each other everything and there was a period when we were so busy destroying each other that we hardly noticed you. You went to stay with my parents for a while. You must have been about three. Do you remember any of it?

Somehow we didn't destroy each other, or leave each other, we became closer if anything. Now it seems to me that we're always at the mercy of the spirit of the age: you absorb it from the air around you, if you're responsive it blows right through you and alters the contours of what you thought was your personality. I think that's what happened to us, when the hot winds of drugs and sex wafted towards Coventry in the late sixties. Suddenly there were late night films and all night parties in a place where the steak house had been the only night spot that stayed open until midnight. It was fun. The only trouble was that you were there, a perpetual reminder that we weren't young, also I've never been particularly good at having fun. I worked hard at it, wore mini-skirts and got drunk and tripped, but the more frivolous I tried to be, the more solemn I felt. I brooded and my brooding became feminism, a protest against Martin's attitude to me and the attitudes of most of the men I'd known to their wives and girlfriends. I became more aggressive, made my own friends and went back to work. Another bloody library. I think I deliberately turned you against Martin, which was wrong of me. I let myself slip into a relationship with him that was humiliating for both of us: I sulked when he came back at four in the morning but didn't ask questions. I hated him so much that I began to confide in you, I wanted him to come back to this set piece of you and me clinging to each other. The ogre returns to his lair. I often slept with you, then, instead of with him . . .'

74

'. . . He was drinking and swallowing pills like a nineteen-year-old and of course his body couldn't take it. He got fat and baggy, his skin went from ivory to the colour of old newspapers and he got an ulcer. He staggered in late to lectures and took a lot of time off work. Gradually, over several years, he became rather seedy and absurd, an easy target for contempt. I wanted to despise him.

I was much crueller to him than he was to me. I waved the threat of leaving him and taking you with me and he was excluded from our treats and adventures. Though there were still nights when we'd end up all in a heap in the same bed, hugging each other, terrified – at least Martin and I were. The tension, the sense that the fire had started but we couldn't smell the smoke or trace the crackling heat, was so unbearable that I was glad when he was sacked. It meant a move, a visible, clean-cut upheaval instead of all the painful changes we had pretended not to notice. Martin's reaction was so characteristic; having forced academia to reject him, he violently rejected it, jobs, mortgages, urban or suburban life. This sloppy romantic streak he'd always had in him broadened. As a matter of fact he became more attractive again and he and I were happier than we'd been for years. We discovered a taste for being shipwrecked together.

I admitted a lot of nasty truths I'd suppressed since you were born; to disliking our ugly, flimsy house, the town beyond it, my job, much of what Martin had become, the shops we went to and the parties we gave. It all felt wrong, forced and uneasy. But I would have continued with a sense of vague discontent, the quiet, miserable neurosis most of our friends managed to live with, if Martin hadn't jumped overboard. I was still, resentfully, following him.

I set about finding a desert island. You said you wanted to live in the country and ride horses. I was sick of the Midlands and had dismal memories of the North, where I'd grown up. But I did hanker after walks I'd had on the moors as a child, a sense of infinite space and possibility I wanted you to know. That summer we spent a month driving around Devon, the bleak inland bits nobody would want to retire to, and bought this place cheap in an auction. You must remember that holiday, it was euphoric. We really felt we were in control of

75

our lives again, escaping from a dirty world into a cleaner one we would make ourselves. Perhaps there is no more seductive fantasy.

The trouble is, its appeal rests on being watched. Very soon after we moved in here it was clear that nobody was watching us; a few friends threatened to come and stay the following summer but most just wrote facetious letters about the simple life. Very soon my list of correspondents dwindled. The first summer was fun, anyway. We camped out here while we planted things and almost rebuilt the house. I turned out to have an unexpected talent for carpentry and plumbing, I really enjoyed doing jobs that were immediately useful. You helped, and ran around and looked a lot healthier, though you must have been lonely. But poor Martin, having staked his future on being a son of toil, found it bored him stiff. He couldn't concentrate enough to do jobs properly, he hammered nails in crooked and fed the chickens with an overdose of vitamins that killed them and nearly cut off his thumb with an electric saw. We laughed, of course, but he was mortified. He always expected to be good at things. I kept saying there was plenty of time to learn but he didn't really want to learn, not in a sweaty uncomfortable way, he felt those tasks were a waste of his intelligence.

And there wasn't much time. In September it began to be cold at night and the roof was still leaking. I was working all day to get the house weatherproof for winter but I didn't really know what I was doing. We couldn't afford to pay anyone to help us. You were still happy, do your remember? You found a stables where they let you ride each morning in return for helping them and in the afternoons you helped me, you handed me my tools and you were good at growing things. Martin just used to hang around, so again you and I must have looked like a conspiracy. Then when your school started he drove you there and back, which filled up a lot of his day.

We decided not to sell the jeep although we needed the money. We'd never been really poor before and Martin had never been really cold. To me the winters here seem milder then the ones I remember as a child in Yorkshire. The snow seems warmer and gentler, the air less grim, even now when I'm alone in it. But Martin grew up in London, he thought winter was a time when you turned on the central heating, wore a few sweaters and spent more time in the pub.

The meaning of our glorious isolation only hit us with the first snows. I realized how we had needed all that padding of jobs, friends, being able to say to each other whenever we met, "I've got so much to do." Face to face, trapped for months in this house, there were no illusions and no trivia. That first winter we both expanded into the timeless space around us. Small foibles threw monstrous shadows on the walls and little differences of opinion became schisms. You felt it too, there were lots of days when the snow was too deep to get you to school and Martin taught you at home. He enjoyed that, he was good at it and it gave him something to do, but you felt the oppression in the house and became hysterical. I used to spend whole days locked in a room, reading and writing, resenting any sound outside the door. Martin was paralyzed. He couldn't go out or see anybody, and all those years teaching literature seemed to have put him off reading. We looked forward to spring, pathetically, as if the sight of grass and flowers would really restore our faith in each other. Half a dozen times that winter Martin nearly burst out of the house. We both knew if he left he wouldn't come back. I thought you knew too, you were such a sharp little girl, and that's why I was surprised you were so upset when he finally went. It wasn't something that happened suddenly one night, it had been inevitable for years, I think. But how do you explain that to a twelve-year-old?'

'. . . Now I wonder why it never occurred to me to be the one to leave. I would have taken you, we could have gone to my parents, who were still alive then and would have been delighted to see my marriage break up. My father was a great pessimist who only cheered up when things went wrong and proved him right. They never forgave me for moving to the South. I had other friends too, more than Martin, who made and broke friendships too easily. I think I'd already come to love this house, I knew I could be happy here with you. Martin was the obstacle and he came to behave like one: an obstinate, boorish, sulky presence at the kitchen table, getting sozzled on vinegary home-made wine.

Then the thaw did come and it was better. It was wonderful to watch the landscape come back to life. It was all new to you and Martin, you wandered around together gasping at the sight of lambs and snowdrops and rainbows, things you'd only read about. But I think Martin preferred them as literary symbols, he found the reality trite and obvious. We earned a bit of money letting the field to campers, made some friends in the town, began to feel acceptable again. But not to each other.

People came to stay. We drove to the sea and you looked after your horses again. We told the story of the terrible winter so many times, in the sunlight, that it almost became a harmless anecdote.

Then the second winter came and it was worse than the first, longer and colder with more opportunities for quarrels . . .'

'. . . Before that night Martin got so drunk he was indifferent to the cold, it had been a foregone conclusion for months that he would leave. We'd discussed it, made lists about it, told each other a hundred times we still loved bits of each other and would always be friends. It became like a train that just won't start though you've said your goodbyes and you want to go off on holiday. The holiday was from each other, all the hatred evaporated as soon as he was out of the house and I even missed him. I still do – in a comfortable way.'

'. . . It was only then, in my forties, that I discovered an intense pleasure in solitude. Not a negative, sterile feeling, though I suppose it might look like that from the outside.

The worst thing about those years was that I felt guilty about you, about giving you such an abnormal life in a place where your only chances of social life were with very conventional people. I'll say this for you, though you loved horses, you never wanted to be one of those awful hunting and gymkhana little girls. Your sympathies were with the horses, not their owners, and I liked that. I liked you altogether, I've always been more or less uncritical of you. It seems to me we've already talked about everything – except Martin, the most important thing of all. I've let him build up in your imagination as a sinister and mysterious force when really he was nothing of the sort, a far more open nature than mine in fact. So now, if you have any more questions, please ask them.'

'. . . One of the worst things about these winters is the sense that my consciousness is shrinking. There is myself, tenuously linked by frail branches of memory and feeling to you, Martin, certain books and pieces of music, a few friends I see once or twice a year. All the rest is snow, miserly fires and boring meals.

I think a lot about Greenham, the one time when I felt at the centre of things. I do miss that sense of involvement and companionship, the belief that I could have an effect on world affairs. It might have been an illusion but it was a magnificent one. The few friendships I still keep up, with Liza and Marie and Stephen, were all made during that year.

I keep asking myself why I went there, and why I left. Neither action seems to have any connection with the rest of my life. I think I went because of you. Having finally pushed you out of the house I missed you terribly and wished I'd had six children. I admired you for the way you went straight to the heart of things, I couldn't understand how you'd acquired such lucid vision. You left this house in the middle of nowhere, as you and Martin had both complained incessantly, and went straight to the middle of London to help people. You made me realize that only two things really mattered: that people were dying of hunger and cold (and that was already happening here in England though the authorities didn't like to admit it); and that most of our intelligence, money and resources were directed at destroying our universe, and we seemed about to do a good job of it. I'd never thought of it as being "our" universe before; it had been "theirs", owned and controlled by powers far beyond my control. I felt I'd done my bit by going on the odd march before you were born. But suddenly, because you were out there, lines of communication opened up between me and people shivering on the streets of London, and weapons of mass destruction primed to wipe out the whole country. Even me. I started to hitch into Bodmin twice a month to go to CND meetings. I volunteered to do things – I had more time and space than anyone else. But it wasn't enough; I felt pitiful, making jam for peace like my mother in the Women's Institute. So when someone suggested at a meeting that we should go to Greenham, I went for the weekend, and stayed there for a year.

It was the only time in my life I felt I was part of a great force. I think that was why the cold and discomfort were so easy to tolerate, at first. I'd been miserably cold and lonely, in various ways, for most of my life. Now I felt useful, courageous, surrounded by companions. We were righteous, I suppose, but then we were right. My ideas about feminism, which had been very vague, hardened as I saw how generously women there behaved. We did share everything and help each other and manage without leaders. Then the issues were polarized by the horrible examples of masculinity we saw: the jeering, sneering, brutalized soldiers on the other side of the fence, the oafish policemen dragging us by the hair through the mud, the petulant magistrates who couldn't see or hear us and doled out prison sentences like free samples. It was easy to despise them, and perhaps all great movements depend on the assumption your opponents are stupid or mad or both.

Certainly I became drunk on the strong wine of heroics, with its bitter sediment, the suspicion that nothing you can do will ever be enough. I began to need more and more encouragement. When they put me in that funny little prison in Kent – they tried to split us up so we wouldn't attract too many visitors and supporters – I realized how tired I was. I slept twelve hours a day in my cell, woke up and lay in a contented stupor, dry and warm under my blanket. After I taught my cellmate, a prostitute, some Greenham songs (she taught me some dirty limericks), they put me in a cell on my own. That was glorious. I managed to get hold of paper and pens and books, the place was very slack. Meals came every few hours and the heating was tropical. After a few days I realized I had recreated my life at home, and felt perfectly happy and healthy. For the first time that year I didn't have a cold and my joints had stopped creaking. Of course I felt bad about this sense of well-being, and perhaps you remember how when you came to visit me I was at my most evangelical and fist-banging.

Soon after that I left the camp and went home, with a

terrible sense of anti-climax. Some of us would have been pleased to be treated more harshly by the State we dissented from. Absolutes are comforting. Instead we were famous for ten minutes and then ignored, all but the strongest (not me) worn down by discomfort and bickering. It was as if the zeitgeist picked me up in its mouth like a huge, warm, many-headed monster, shook me, and dropped me again. I've never felt so alive and powerful since.

Not that I lost interest in disarmament. But my interests took small, partial forms again; going to meetings and organizing film shows and writing pamphlets. Half the profits of our fish farm were supposed to go to CND, only there weren't any.'

'. . . I've discovered a kind of pride in loneliness, in holding out for these long, silent winters. I couldn't do it unless you were there, and Liza coming to stay in May, and Martin in India, turning up some time with a new wife and kids I expect. It's a bit like being dead but keeping in tenuous contact with people from Beyond. As a matter of fact I've had enough, I'd dig myself out now if there was anywhere to go. If there was still a Greenham camp I'd go there. But there are only camps like yours and I don't think I'm patient enough or ascetic enough to be any use there.

Are there things going on secretly, do you hear anything? I heard rumours after they outlawed CND but nothing since. I often think of those stories we used to read about Russia, all those poor people who weren't allowed to form trade unions or strike, all those persecuted intellectuals. Well the truth is there are never very many intellectuals, and they either change tack or disappear quietly like James and Catherine, who are still in prison on sedition charges. The rest of us don't really know we're being oppressed, we just moulder and make a virtue of our isolation, tear up the things we write because nobody's ever going to read or publish them . . .

I day-dream a lot. All my life I've avoided trashy novels because there was so much stuff to read. But my day-dreams are utterly banal, Vicki Baum and Barbara Cartland, you won't remember them. Shall I tell you one of them? I look out of the window one morning and a van is coming up the track, loaded with cases and boxes. You're driving it, with a faceless man sitting beside you and small children crawling all over the boxes. You're happy with the man, whoever he is. You stop in front of the house, lift the children down and they come running to me. It's awful, isn't it? You'll wince when you read this. But I find the urge to have grandchildren is almost as strong as my desire to have you was. You confirmed me as an adult and now I need them to confirm me as an old woman. I babysit for the Parkers sometimes, he picks me up in his car and for a whole evening I touch and smell and talk to those children. I'm quite embarrassed to be so eager to do something that's supposed to be a chore. Bathing that baby and telling the older one her bedtime story are the high points of my month!

But I suppose the feelings I channelled into you are used up by your work. You must have to love fifty children instead of one, and the supply will be endless. I'm just a bourgeois relic (Martin's favourite insult), with my obsession with *my* daughter and *my* grandchildren. Still, they're very powerful, these feelings. I wonder if you have them at all? Now I must stop or you'll think I'm going soft, or interfering, which would be worse.'

CHAPTER 9

When Christy finished the last letter she looked up and blinked with surprise to see daylight in the room. She still had tears in the corners of her eyes because of the grandchildren she would never produce. It was a shock when that long monologue ceased, she wanted more, wanted to give back something of herself, to confide and ask questions. But she was alone again. The bare room, whitewashed years ago and greyish now, with dusty naked floorboards radiating from the bed, made her feel marooned. Her blankets were hidden by the blue and white leaves of paper; as she struggled out of bed they floated and danced in the early sun shimmering through the thin, white curtains. Christy put her shoes on and tiptoed deafeningly over the creaking floors to her mother's room.

'Is that you?'

'Can I come in?'

'Of course.'

Rachel, like her daughter, was wearing a sweater in bed. Her grey hair around her shoulders made her look older, haglike in her big bed under a patchwork quilt. Christy sat on the bed and edged under the quilt to shelter from the cold wind that swept through the house and on across Dartmoor.

'I read your letters. I've been sitting up all night over them.'

'I'm glad I didn't have to watch your face.'

'They're wonderful, I'm so glad you let me read them. I kept thinking, these are the kind of papers you usually find after someone's death, when it's too late to talk. I'm so glad you're here, and alive!'

'They weren't embarrassing?'

'It's good to be embarrassed sometimes. If you keep all your thoughts to yourself they get frozen up, blocked inside you. I'm so glad to know more about Martin.'

'That's as much as I can tell you. I realized while I was writing about him, it's not that we lie but the truth always gets away. I never knew very much about him, really. You'll have to ask him about me, one day.'

'Maybe. He wrote to ask me to meet him in London, last March.'

'Would you have gone?'

'Probably, out of curiosity. But I'd rather meet him after reading what you say about him and you.'

'I suppose I ought to have forwarded his letter. He wrote to me too, but I wrote back and said I didn't see why I should do all the travelling when he had cars and aeroplanes at his disposal.'

'Well, why should you?'

'He seems to have become very busy and grand. Or perhaps he just couldn't bear to meet in this house, wanted to meet on neutral ground. Anyway it's the closest we've all come to meeting for nearly twenty years.'

'You know what you said about grandchildren?'

'Ever since I gave you those letters I've been wishing I'd destroyed that one. It's none of my business.'

'It *is* your business. I'm tired of this awful privacy, I want to *be* someone's business for a change. I've only told Sean and he looked as if it was the most boring news he'd heard for months – well, last September I was sterilized. So there won't be any grandchildren.'

They were sitting up side by side in bed, almost touching, looking at each other with intense caution, in fear they would hit the wrong note and recoil into their old formality.

'Well, of course it's your body,' Rachel said carefully, astonished at the pain she felt.

'My body came out of yours.'

'That was a long time ago.'

'You're not angry with me?'

'Christy, what a thing to apologize for! Nobody could suffer for it but you.'

'That's what's been so hard. The feeling that I have no possible connection with anybody else. I think that's why I wanted to involve you.'

'I'm glad you told me but I can't judge. I hummed and haaed

a good deal about having you, and that was in a much more solid world. I think perhaps, in your situation, I would have done the same.'

'Oh, good.'

'You don't love Sean then?'

'Not now. Do you think I'd necessarily want to have a child with him, if I did?'

'I suppose not. Just another of my bourgeois relics. I don't understand very much about your life – do you live with him?'

'In adjoining caravans.'

'That's funny. Martin always used to say we could have lived together quite amicably, in adjoining flats.'

'Amicable is putting it a bit strong.'

'Then who *are* you close to?'

'To the children. To you, though we see so little of each other. And to Simon, who I work with – do you know, when I think of Smiles he's the only adult I really miss?'

Rachel waited.

'Have you ever felt close to someone you didn't really know at all?'

'Oh, yes. I fell half to three-quarters in love with Martin just watching him work at his desk in the library. He had such a flamboyant way of effacing himself, and he used to produce this stream of Mars bars and bananas from his bag. I'd come to hate the quiet of the place so I enjoyed his noise.'

'They're so silly, the things that attract you about people. Simon is very still and rather slow, not dim at all but you never feel he's entirely in the room with you. As if he lived in a Trappist monastery inside his head and was perpetually listening for the bell to release him from his vows. The only time he really comes to life is when he plays with the children – I suppose I do too – we catch each other at it, then stop and become self-conscious again.'

'He sounds very interesting. Perhaps you'll bring him here some time?'

'I never see him outside Smiles, hardly outside the doors of the playgroup. I don't know what he means to me. For the last few weeks there I felt so aware of him I could hardly breathe, yet I just carried on working. I didn't know what to do, so I didn't do anything.'

85

'Well, go back and do something now. There aren't so many people you're drawn to like that, blood to blood, I think it's a kind of blasphemy to throw it away. Renunciation is different, but why should you renounce him? It doesn't sound as if you owe Sean very much. Is he married?'

'Simon? I think so.'

'Find out. Why are you so disgusted by your own emotions? Do yourself some good, for a change.'

'I don't feel entitled to a complicated private life. Sean's all right because he's semi-public.'

Rachel laughed, putting her arms around her daughter as she had wanted to ever since she came into the room. Christy lowered her head against the rough wool on her mother's still jutting bosom and stayed there. It was the closest she had felt to another person for a long time, and she didn't have to see the irony in Rachel's eyes.

'I'm not laughing because you take your work seriously. I think you're right. But if you're valuable at Smiles it's because of your energy, and there's nothing like happy love for giving you more of that. You don't seem to have any energy at the moment. Don't let yourself shrivel up out of some sense of duty, I couldn't bear that.'

'Do you think we'll go on talking and writing to each other like this?'

'There's nothing to stop us. Except that neither of us lives in a place where the post is delivered reliably.'

'It's the first real talk I've had in months.'

'Me too.'

'Don't go away.'

'Let's go down and have some breakfast.'

Rachel made biscuits, with oatmeal and cinnamon and raisins, a deliberate attempt to recreate certain smells and tastes of Christy's childhood. In the warm fragrant kitchen Christy felt like an invalid anticipating recovery. She was tired but very relieved to feel she had a centre again. She thought, I can only stand the ugliness of Smiles if I know I have Rachel to escape to. And Sean can stick the sociological implications of that up his – but the thought of Sean's backside was a flat bassoon note in the flute duet of their morning.

86

'I'll go back soon. Next week.'

'Maybe I'll come to see you. Would you mind? It seems absurd to know so little about what you're doing.'

'You can if you like but I'd rather come back here.'

They ate the hot, crumbly biscuits.

'Do you still like cooking?'

'In my caravan I've got a flame like a bunsen burner. Perhaps you ought to come, just to have a look.'

They walked over the coarse, rolling ground where Christy had galloped in her horsy incarnation. Shrieking yellow clumps of gorse like the heads of jaundiced ogres protruded from the shaggy, dull green grass. Two ponies with coats the texture of the grass they nibbled looked at her, and she hugged them, inhaling their pungent, yeasty, friendly smell. When she used to ride alone here she had been terrified of the prisoners. Wild eyed, shaven-headed, bearded men wielding chain saws had played a major part in her fantasies, and whenever they received a warning that a man had escaped Christy used to go to bed with her grandfather's cosh under her bed. Now, she thought, I probably know some of the poor sods locked up over there. If I meet one I'll help him, hide him and take him back to Smiles with me.

'Does it all look different?'

'No, it hasn't changed, though I think I have. Shall we walk into Princetown?'

'It's a long way.'

'Good.'

The sky brimmed with rain, then gulped it back like a tearful child. The sun came out and blinked weakly. A few big drops fell, then ragged white clouds rushed to the coast to soak the early tourists there. Christy and Rachel walked fast over the landscape, which was alternately menacing and richly dappled.

'God how I remember this kind of weather. Waiting at the bus stop and willing it not to rain before the bus came.'

'You hated that journey, didn't you?'

'An hour and a half each way, enough to put anyone off school.'

'I kept thinking I'd be able to save enough from letting to campers in the summer to buy a van. But I never did.'

87

'I still hate buses. I never get one if I can help it.'

As they walked they helped each other over difficult ground and laughed when it finally rained. Rachel was happy, thinking of all the times she had walked alone up here and brooded over her bad relations with Martin and Christy. Now she no longer felt like a mad old woman, Queen Lear howling in the wind. She gripped Christy's arm as they dropped down into the pretty, prosperous, smug little town.

'Aren't we too bedraggled to go in there?' Christy asked timidly on the pavement outside the tea room.

'It's all right. They take cash.'

They braved the horse brasses and gingham tablecloths and went inside. 'It's all so rich,' Christy whispered hoarsely over her gingerbread. 'I'd forgotten how much money there still is outside London.'

'There is this little county ghetto in the centre. But as a matter of fact they're terrified of the people just outside, on the housing estates they built in the sixties. They've got 75 per cent unemployment and there's a tent settlement there. The farmer who owns the field they're in is always prosecuting them but he can't get rid of them.'

'Even here! Now why am I so pleased to hear that?'

'Because it's a sham, now, to live in your safe little area and ignore what's outside.'

'Part of me wants to sit at the window throwing cream slices at all those Range Rovers and jodhpurs. The rest of me wants to enjoy the Earl Grey tea and the Georgian houses opposite.'

'I expect they all give donations for starving children in Africa.'

'Starving English children are so distasteful, aren't they? We had another outbreak of rickets last winter.'

'Oh, look! There's Steven.'

He farmed hundreds of acres near her mother's house, a massive, handsome man in expensively practical clothes who waved and came over to their table. Sean would have hated him on principle but Christy couldn't help being charmed by him. He agreed to give her a lift to the motorway the following Tuesday.

On the morning she left, Christy came down to find her mother already making breakfast. She saw with admiration that the pile of books and notepads was ready on the table with the teapot; Rachel would get on with her own life as soon as she was gone. They were shy together, not knowing how to seal their old-new friendship. Christy followed her mother around, helping uselessly.

'For God's sake sit down.'

Before she did, Christy looked at her and Rachel stared back. A few inches away, Christy saw the lines and moles and crinkly grey hair that were coming to her, and the impatient humour that might, with luck, come too. Rachel saw herself just after her daughter was born, tough and serious and longing for a reassurance nobody gave her.

'You'll come back soon, won't you?'

'Very soon. And you'll post some of those letters?'

'All of them.'

CHAPTER 10

Like so many corners of London, the cemetery was alive to Simon with different periods of his life. And because he liked being haunted, he haunted it. He often cycled through it after work and at weekends he heightened his loneliness by solitary walks there; his mind half in the past, half in the present where gays picked each other up, zonkies and drunks of all ages sat on benches gazing ahead and people came crawling out of the catacombs, the best built and most macabre squat he had seen yet. He knew that on Friday nights his ability to care, as Rose sarcastically called it, switched off abruptly and he was able to ignore poverty and misery until Monday.

Simon turned off the central path, which was only partially overgrown, and made straight for the luscious tangle of the interior, where rose bushes, buttercups, dead leaves, waist-high grass and sticky trees rotted on a rich compost of broken graves. The smell of early summer and Victorian death went to his head. This was where he used to come with Jessica, twelve years before, when her flatmate monopolized the only bedroom each weekend with her boyfriend. Anyway they had both found love among the bones romantic. Then, the ceme-tery had been patrolled by gardeners and policemen. There had been flowers on some of the graves, rumours of foxes in the catacombs now so much prized by human beings, and a faded nineteenth-century formality to the place. Now that the decay was total it intoxicated Simon far more. It was the forest of thorns that had sprung up around the princess, only the beauty wasn't sleeping, she was dead. In fact Jessica wasn't buried here. They had baked her like a cake or a pot, put her ashes in a casket and her casket high up in a wall honey-combed with dead love. That other cemetery was meticulously kept, lawns and flowerbeds that stretched for miles in some southern suburb, Mortlake or Morden or Mortown. He hadn't been back there since her funeral and the place held no associations for him. He knew that Jessica's discriminating spirit would have scorned so flavourless a storage place and would have wafted straight back to their cemetery.

Simon was well aware that he used grief as a substitute for thought. For over two years it had worked rather well. The time was right, that desolate lumpy hour after Sunday lunch, and the heat fermented the vegetation to a soupy thickness that clogged his brain. Somewhere in there, he thought, our bodies made a hollow, my sperm left a trail the worms still slither along. She was wearing those white dungarees with a bright red T-shirt, she always wore clothes more garish than she was. And she shut her eyes when I kissed her, I did too, we both fell backwards into a blind, scratchy place that smelt of damp and hair and blackberries. Acutely uncomfortable, squashed between the graves. Kneeling there, his eyes shut again, Simon tried to repossess her as he had done on other summer afternoons. This was his sacrilegious shrine. But Jessica had gone; he could only think the words of his memory and see their two figures sprawled on the grass, not here beside him but far away and small and foolish.

Simon opened his eyes, shivered, got up and kicked the tangle of stone and leaves. Objects around him took on a callous solidity and the cemetery became ruthlessly itself, no longer a repository for his nostalgia. Down overgrown paths he saw the ruined, decapitated angels and lions, crosses lying in the grass, graffiti on all the little stone temples and pyramids that had been built for eternity and had turned so quickly into miniature slums. Simon set off down one of the green tunnels, stooping and reading the inscriptions that were as exotic as hieroglyphics from another civilization; 'Jo hua Whi Esq'; 'De ly be ved ife'; 'Sq re f Ke in on'; 'Ga f is li Ki & co ry'. Loud voices of people firmly placed, more confident even in their staccato, muffled state than he had ever been. But Jessica's voice, low, monotonous and a bit nasal, had faded.

Simon heard a rustling and threshing over to his right, near the wall, and thought it might be one of the rabbits or beavers which had returned to many of the London parks now they were so overgrown. Simon moved towards the noise, silently he hoped, though his heavy, urban feet broke leaves and twigs like a bulldozer. Through a screen of bushes he saw two white rumps of indeterminate sex, thumping away at each other amidst a pile of clothes that outsmelled the vegetation.

Simon backed away, shocked that the materialization of his memory was so harsh. He ran down the path that led to the opposite side of the cemetery, past a sweeping vista of ruined cloisters and a round, dome-topped building where several families lived. From behind a wall came the aggressive roar of construction, although it was Sunday. Freedom Enterprises, working overtime on his father's fantasies, more robust and lucrative than his own. He could see pagodas, minarets and crenellations above the wall, rising on the site of grandstands where crowds used to cheer and stomp and riot and kill. Presumably these future crowds were going to be more passive, though he couldn't see why, since they were the same people. He wondered if it was true that Neuropepsi, promoted so vigorously by the government, contained a tranquillizer that suppressed the urge to violence, and most other urges as well. Certainly those kids on the benches with the piles of red and black cans beside them looked as if they hadn't been lived in for years, grinning, silent, rapturous about nothing. He stared at them and then watched a crane lift a big dome into place.

A drill screeched a hole in the ground to plant his father's money trees. Dozens of voices ordered, whistled, grumbled, swore, gossiped, jeered, sang; hands sawed, hammered, nailed, dug, glued, painted, plastered, wired and raised mugs of tea. He could almost hear his parents on the other side of the city, complaining about the British Workman and His conspiracy to bankrupt them. The Grand Freeman Circus soared up a few yards away and he was torn between embarrassment, revulsion and family pride. He knew he would go to the opening day ceremony. In a hundred years from now Bernard's folly will be an architectural treasure like the Albert Hall. He often found comfort in meandering a century or two backwards or forwards. He wondered what Christy would think if she knew he was the son of a theme park tycoon. He wanted her to think he was a rebel, courageously breaking away from his family. Even my self-illusions are ten years out of date, he thought bitterly. More likely she'd think I was patronizing them, I'm sure that's what Sean tells her, or spying for my father to find out what the masses want . . . The less he saw of Christy the more he worried about what she thought of him.

When he had arrived at work one morning to find her gone he had stumbled around in a panic, which increased as he realized the importance of hiding it. Certainly Sean had seen it. He had fended off all Simon's questions with monosyllables and glares. The children had picked up the tension between them and even the cause, to judge by the five million times they asked where Christy was and when she was coming back. 'Home' and 'soon' were the only tightlipped answers Sean would give, and by Friday attendance had dropped by half. A disaster, Simon thought with real anguish. He felt like a criminal unmasked. All week he and Sean had silently duelled, wordlessly acted out a passion of jealousy. Despite all this repression things did come out into the open. Simon was sure now that Sean loved her, though this had never been clear from Christy's behaviour. And his own feelings, which Simon had often dismissed as being too nebulous to act on, bewildered him by their intensity. Smiles without Christy was so grim and dull that he was forced to admit he wouldn't have worked there for two years if she hadn't been there. He was still recovering from this blast to his vanity: for all that time he had believed he went to Smiles because he needed to help. Perhaps at the beginning it had been so.

On Friday when the playgroup closed he hung around until Sean locked the doors and, openly rude at last, handed Simon his bike. Over the last few days Simon had been reduced to feeling utterly pathetic, a caricature of Sean's worst opinion of him. He wanted to sit outside the locked door all weekend, drooling, 'Sorry, sorry, but please, please tell me where she is.' He didn't, of course. He found it so hard to behave badly.

Instead he looked straight at Sean, who looked away, and asked, 'Do you know if Christy'll be back on Monday?'

'I've no idea.'

'Have you heard from her?'

'No. Goodbye, I've got a meeting now.'

He left Simon on the muddy slope at the edge of the rows of

tents that descended to the road. Here, exactly a week before, he had said a ridiculously inadequate goodbye to her.

'Have a nice weekend, Simon.'

'Cheers.'

He squirmed now at the fatuous echo of the word. He'd always hated it, with its reverberations of cocktail parties and false jollity; why had he used it? What if that had been the last opportunity he would ever have to talk to her? This is love, he thought, suffering torture over the wrong choice of a word. This is love and very awkward it is too. I'm too old for this sort of thing.

Still Simon had leaned against his bike, unable to leave her stamping ground. Here there was at least the reverberation and promise of her strong, warm, honest personality. But if there wasn't the promise, if she'd had enough of drudgery and her sulky co-caravanist or whatever he was? As he realized his ignorance of all the details of her life, Simon's entrails dissolved into hot water and slurped up into his gullet. He had never asked, never bothered; for two years he had missed every single opportunity to know her better.

Standing there with his bike, it occurred to him that he was waiting for her, even though he knew she couldn't possibly come. His eyes were reassembling every figure that came into sight to construct a thin one with too much black curly hair and a bossy walk. He said to himself, I can't go home until I've seen her. Mad, he added, and repeated it to make sure. There must be other people who know where she is. Ellen. If I knew I could at least go there or write. I've been as cautious as a squirrel, hoarding my acorns of passion. I bet her friend never chased her anywhere.

Fortified, Simon padlocked his bike to a lamppost and set off over the mud. Moving among the tents, Simon realized that Smiles without Christy scared him. He had always gone straight to her and the children and straight home again. So while he complacently believed he was a necessary part of their community, most people in the camp didn't know him any better than he knew them. The first three people whom he asked about Ellen glared at him in silence. He walked down a rutted path about two feet wide that wound between uneven rows of tents, caravans and corrugated iron shacks. The top of the mud, where he tried to walk, was dry, but although it hadn't rained for a week the little valleys between the ruts squelched with slime. He knew from the smell this was a mixture of shit, urine and garbage. There were lavatories in the washhouse and in the abandoned tower blocks but most of them were blocked most of the time. Christy and he used to have to unblock the playgroup lavatories at least once a day. What a romantic courtship; Simon smiled and refused to be discouraged by the stench and the hostility. She had lived with it; it wouldn't hurt him to spend half an hour in it. He knew he would leave before dark. A lot of people were sitting outside in the warm afternoon sunshine but none of them looked at him until he had passed them, at least he thought so. He saw his back view with their eyes, the loosely hanging Chinese shirt and the new brown cotton trousers clinging to a bum that had only known clean, functioning lavatories. The St John's Wood one with its own wardrobe of little towelling covers, deodorizers and a musical paper roll with a union jack on it. His head pelican-like in the air, sniffing disdainfully. Yes, he would hate him too.

Lily's head appeared in one of the tent flaps. 'It's my teacher, Auntie.'

'Yeah? What you want? You want tea?'

The woman, the child and the boiling kettle seemed to fill the tent so Simon squatted outside, grateful that someone had recognized him.

'She been a bad girl at school? You beat her. Or send her to me. I beat her.'

'Lily's never naughty, she's a great help. She tells us stories and looks after the little ones. If she ever does go to Africa we'll miss her.'

'What's all this Africa crap? You been telling those Africa lies again?'

Afraid that he had got Lily into trouble, Simon dolloped more praise on her. In the dark tent the black pools of the child's eyes swirled with pleasure.

'You sure Lily she don't make trouble?' the aunt insisted. She was only about thirty but pitted and ravaged.

'No. Never. Thanks for the tea, see you on Monday, Lily.'

Simon realized that, wherever he went here, he was a figure

95

of authority. It made him feel a fraud. Still looking for Ellen, he wandered over as far as the main road near the zonkies' island. Below him a group of people surrounded Ted's van. He could hear shouting and the sound of glass being smashed, and recognized several of the mothers of children from the playgroup, including Beatrice and Rita. At first Simon thought they were protesting, as usual, about the length of the queue for Ted's stale, overpriced bread. Then he saw Beatrice and one of the other mothers jump up on to the lorry and start to hurl crates out of it. Ted's face appeared in profile, waving a stick like Mr Punch and shouting hysterically while the women laughed and jeered.

Simon turned and saw Ellen whom he recognized from the play group where she sometimes helped. She was standing just behind him, clutching her baby as she watched the scene. She was a small fair woman, prematurely aged like everyone in the camp. Her face was full of pouches and wrinkles and she clutched her six-month-old son, Jack, as if he was her only shield. She fought for him as ferociously as she had always fought for herself. Yet the baby was always ill; he had kept her up all night with a fever and a rash. Ellen grinned at Simon and he grinned back, thinking how attractively resilient she was. He tried to imagine the friendship between her and Christy.

'Hello, I've been looking for you. What's all this about?'

'Ted's had it coming to him for a long time. I'd join in if I had anywhere to leave Jack. They tried to get Ted to dump all his supplies of Neuropepsi in the river, and he wouldn't, so they're smashing them.'

'But why? I thought it was their favourite drink.'

'It was the cheapest drink he sold. And I admit some of the women used it to shut their kids up, Beatrice did herself for years. But lately there's been too many rumours, then there was that article in the *Prodigal Bum* –'

'What was that?'

'Said it retards kids, rots teeth and acts as a kind of tranquillizer by killing off millions of brain cells. Done tests on rats or something. I dunno, I never drink it and I'd never give it to Jack. The last few weeks most people have been refusing to drink it: Ted got worried so he reduced the price again and that made them even more suspicious. What are you doing here, anyway?'

'Looking for Christy.'

'She's gone to see her mum, hasn't she?'

'I don't know. I'm trying to find out.'

'Sean's the person to ask. He lives –'

'I know where he lives. He won't tell me where she is.'

'Oh.' She looked curious and amused. 'You Simon?'

'Yes. Why?'

'I just wondered. Anyway, I reckon she's at her mum's.'

'Have you got the address?'

'No. Devon or Cornwall, somewhere like that. I expect she'll be back on Monday. Don't worry.'

'Will you phone me if she turns up?' He handed her his phone number on a scrap of paper. She laughed.

'OK. I hope you know what you're asking, though. It's half a mile to a phone that works.'

Simon didn't care that she saw he was desperate. He liked her, and now that he had decided to be a lover he submerged himself, with some relief, in the role.

Later, as he cycled over Wandsworth Bridge, Simon heard the words of an argument about housing he had had with his parents months before:

Madge: I don't see why they have to live in these awful places, darling. Anyone with a bit of initiative can buy a nice house, around here for instance, or further out in the suburbs somewhere.

Simon: Initiative to do what? Rob a bank?

Bernard: They could damn well borrow the money. And work to pay it off. Too many people think the State owes them a living.

Madge: If people must live in these awful camps why don't they look after them properly? Even Rose was shocked by the state of that place where you work.

Simon: It's not a question of where people want to live, the point is there's not enough housing to go round. And none's being built.

Madge: Honestly darling, you do exaggerate. There's that lovely development going up on the Heath, where the

97

Dobsons are moving to, and the Finchley Road is full of building sites.

Simon: I'm talking about poor people for God's sake. People who haven't got jobs or investments or friendly bank managers or anything at all. Where the fuck are they supposed to sleep at night?

Madge: There's no need to speak like the scum of the earth just because you choose to spend so much time among them.

Bernard: As my dear old father used to say, the poor are always with us, all we can do is keep away from them. And he ought to know. Started out as a newspaper boy on ninepence a week, left school when he was ten. In those days, if you didn't work bloody hard you starved.

Simon: There are people starving now, you'll be glad to hear. Children dying of malnutrition and cold, just a few yards away from Harrods, in the park.

Madge: Rubbish, darling. You're so gullible. Those people get paid a fortune in stamps and vouchers and whatnot, I was reading about them the other day in the *Morning Glory*.

Simon remembered the conversation he had had with Rose that night, in their parents' kitchen. Yes, it was true, their voices were always in his head.

All Friday evening and all of Saturday Simon had waited for Ellen to ring. It was as if, having decided to let himself love Christy, he was unable to do anything else. Couldn't even read. That afternoon he had had to struggle out of his web of loneliness to get to the cemetery and, now he was here, Christy was hammering on his brain again. If he went back to the flat now, there would be seven hours before he went to bed, fifteen before he could possibly see her – Simon left the cemetery and hovered near the phone booths outside the gates, in the Fulham Road. Who could he phone? Rose. Chris, his only remaining schoolfriend. Daniel, his ex-colleague. They were the only three people who, he was sure, would be pleased to hear from him. He heard Madge again: The trouble with you is, you get far too involved. It was true, he loved too few people too much. Both the telephones had been ripped out of the wall, so his decision was made for him. He would go and see Daniel and Frankie, who lived within walking distance.

Their flat was in the conservation area near the Boltons, two big, sunny floors at the top of a white plaster mid-Victorian house. The gardens at the front and back were enormous and branches pushed against the windows at either end of their sitting room, throwing lacy shadows on the pale carpet. The flat was Daniel's and Frankie's lifework, they had converted it and decorated it and kept it up with infusions of money from their full-time jobs. They sat in it proudly, part of the carefully planned decor.

Daniel was tall and dark, with a big, beaky face framed by wavy hair, and Frankie looked remarkably like him. Simon had always thought this was a sign that they both felt comfortable with themselves. They borrowed each other's clothes and finished each other's sentences. They lived their life together with an intelligence and competence that made Simon feel utterly inadequate. Yet he loved to breathe the alien atmosphere in their house. Downstairs in the garden their children played, quietly and efficiently.

Daniel and Frankie sprawled together on a scarlet couch under the window, their heads illuminated by a halo of compatibility. Simon sat on the edge of an armchair opposite and on the low, marble topped table between them a bottle of white wine joined the books, newspapers and toys. Simon gulped his wine, preparing himself for the questions they always asked.

'George was asking me what you were up to, on Friday. I never know what to say.' Daniel smiled protectively.

'Neither do I.'

'I suppose you might go back to architecture some day?' asked Frankie, for whom the world outside professional life was a nauseating blur.

'No. I can't see the point of the kind of buildings I had to build, and the kind I believe in will never be built now.'

'Have you still got your models?' Daniel asked.

'Some of them. What about your work?' Simon didn't see why he should always be the one to be cross-examined.

Daniel was designing a hotel in Tokyo and Frankie was promoting a book on toy soldiers. She showed him an article about it in the *Sunday Hope* magazine. But they soon returned to Simon: he was unplaced and therefore public property.

'But what's happened to Merlin?' Frankie asked.

Then Simon realized he had forgotten about him all weekend. His guilt showed and his friends pounced.

'Um, he's still with my parents.'

'But how could you just dump him like that? I mean I could understand it at the beginning, just after Jessica – but that's ages ago. And it's not as if you're on good terms with your parents. Who knows what they've been telling him – I know if Daniel's ma got hold of Lisa and Toby there'd be a lot of little cats carefully let out of bags.'

Daniel wanted her to be quiet but Simon welcomed her brutality.

'I do want him to come and live with me again. But I keep putting it off until my affairs are sorted out and somehow they never are.'

'Nor ever will be. Meanwhile he's getting more aware, keeping score, blaming you – how can you *bear* it, Simon!'

'Because I don't see much of him. Up until now I honestly believed he was better off up at the Castle.'

'Don't you miss him?'

'Very much.'

'At least bring him to play with our kids sometimes?'

'I will. Next Sunday?'

'That's fine. And will you stay to supper?' She felt she might have probed too deep, but wanted to probe some more.

While Frankie was downstairs playing with her children, Daniel and Simon had a civilized, neutral conversation about Gaudi and Lutyens. Then Frankie came to sit with him while Daniel cooked, and opened fire immediately.

'I had a dream about Jessica the other night. She looked really spiteful and angry, and kept saying we'd betrayed her.'

Why is it, Simon wondered, that it's only with women that I'm able to talk about myself?

'Did you really have that dream or did you make it up?'

'Yes, I really did. I often dream of her, and always guiltily. It's strange, because when she was alive I felt she twisted us all around her little finger.'

'That's just her way of doing it from – wherever.'

'Simon! How cynical! And you the broken-hearted widower!'

'You can't go on being broken-hearted forever or you might as well be dead yourself.'

'I couldn't agree more. Oh, I am pleased. Let's have another drink.' Then, as she poured it, 'Do you know, for the last two years Daniel's had to restrain me from inviting you to supper to meet various women?'

'It wouldn't have worked. I could have done with the suppers, though.'

'Oh, it is nice to hear you being funny. I thought you were never going to smile again. Will you bring her to see us?'

'Frankie, don't be so obvious!' Daniel roared from the kitchen.

'I'm not, it's just natural curiosity. What's her name?'

'Christy. But there isn't really –'

'If you live with her will you grab Merlin back from your parents?'

'That's an impossible question.'

Daniel came in with a dish of pasta and a bowl of salad.

'You ask nothing but impossible questions, Frankie.' He wondered why they both looked so relaxed.

CHAPTER 11

Half drunk, well fed and warm with the confirmation of their friendship, Simon let himself into his flat late that night. The silence was less unyielding when you had just come from laughter. He walked down the linoleum corridor, dirty chess squares, and put Fauré's Requiem on the tape recorder. Then he switched on all the lights in the sitting room, drew the curtains (Jessica had a habit of transforming herself into a branch and scratching at the window) and lay down on the couch. He knew that before he could really get away from her he would have to move. This wasn't a flat so much as a museum of superstition and nostalgia. Jessica's clothes and books, Merlin's toys and his own models – all as unexciting as the one at his parents' house – filled the rooms. Every step he took there, every gesture he made, reverberated with actions from his past.

When he was twenty and Rose was eighteen, their father had bought them each a flat in this house with money their grandfather had left them in trust. They had all realized, Madge and Bernard tacitly, their children noisily, that they couldn't go on living together. Rose soon earned enough to buy herself another, more glamorous flat but Simon had stayed on, mouldering inside his increasingly shabby adolescent shell, too poor and, in a way, too faithful to uproot himself. Besides, he loved the room he was sitting in now. It was long, green, and sprouted like an underwater cave at the end of the grubby corridor. On the wall opposite the couch he was on, there was a door leading to stone steps that crumbled down to the weedy garden, a large bay window and a small church-shaped one. On his right was an open fireplace which he still blacked and polished and used. The room was always a refuge;

as soon as he entered it he breathed an air so familiar, stale and heavy that the doors of fear clanged shut behind him.

Lying on the couch he stretched his arms and legs and felt the length and power of his still young body. Desire might be a nuisance but it was also a conclusive proof of vitality. His hands slid down to his flies, drew out his hard prick and stared at it. It wasn't a familiar sight. But at the grasp of his hands sensation flooded his detachment, relief and delight as his nerves burst and dissolved. Oh, matter over mind, flesh to flesh, Simon to Christy! Panting, his eyes shut, his face expressing agony as his pleasure burst, he called her name again. And realized, in the cool and slimy deflation that followed, that he had just carried out a kind of exorcism and consummation.

Simon made a fire with the rags and newspapers he kept in a basket in the corner. Then, padding up and down the corridor in his socks, he carried Jessica's possessions from the bedroom and piled them on the carpet in front of the fire. The bedroom was a sad place, a more truthful monument to Simon and Jessica than the charming back room. There were the fitted cupboards he had half built before he lost interest, the long mirror in which Jessica had stared at herself with growing discontent, the dressing table that had disappeared beneath bottles of sleeping pills and tranquillizers.

Whenever Simon entered the room he saw Jessica sprawled on the bed that morning with her white nightdress around her thighs and her long brown hair stuck to her face with vomit. He had come back from his parents', where there was a party. He had phoned Jessica to tell her where he was but she hadn't believed him, she never believed him, she had an insatiable appetite for suffering – and now that image of her wiped out all the other erotic, tender, angry or happy memories he might have had of the room. She was dead on the bed forever and the squalid waste of her death had poisoned what he had loved her for when she was alive. In the ambulance he had been embarrassed because she wasn't wearing any pants.

Merlin had followed him into the bedroom. 'Is Mummy drunk?'

'She's got to go to hospital.'

'In an ambulance? Will it have the siren on? Can I come?'

'Yes, you can come.'

Simon had known she was dead but couldn't say it, even to himself. He said it for the first time to Merlin the next day, because he couldn't bear the standard euphemisms about going away. Madge was there; she had come round as soon as she heard the news.

'How can you be so brutal!' She sobbed, and clutched Merlin.

'Don't spit at me, Grandma.'

'My poor little boy! He doesn't even know how to cry!'

'Can I go to school now, Simon?'

'I'll take you, if you like.'

Simon thought of Merlin as he took her most beautiful clothes, the ones he loved to see her in and couldn't bear to give away, soaked them with lighter fuel and put them on the fire. He ought to have made a bonfire in the garden, but that would have been too public. The fumes gave him a headache and made his eyes stream; he opened the back door and sat at the top of the stone steps, looking out over the dark gardens.

Concentrate on Merlin. I haven't really thought about him since. Jessica's been a veil between us, as if I wanted it to be my tragedy, not his. That day I told him she was dead was the last time I really saw him, felt him. I sent him up to the Castle to avoid his eyes because he knew how mixed my feelings were. As if I had wished them both dead, wanted to smother his perceptions in the fat St John's Wood air. Nothing will be straight until he's back here. Phone him, then it would be so easy. Not at one in the morning.

Simon had left Merlin's room unchanged, the room in the middle, between their bedroom and the bathroom. Through its thin walls God knows what had penetrated. But they were cheerfully papered with Winnie the Pooh flying away on his balloon, and the small room was full of dusty boxes of Lego, a rocking horse, a table football game . . . Merlin hadn't needed to take many toys because Madge had given him so much. Not making him wait for birthday or Christmas but taking him out right away to conjure with a Britcard. No wonder Merlin's feelings about coming home were as complicated as Simon's about having him here.

Often over the last two years Simon had considered letting

the second bedroom, which would have trebled his income. But that would have been to admit Merlin wasn't coming back. Besides there was nobody else Simon could have lived with; it was months since he had even invited a friend back to the flat. It had been his private wart for so long, accreting his smells and ghosts and sprouting new, more leathery, layers of skin. To take a knife and cut it out would be crude, so much else would wither. He couldn't move; all he could do was to burn his past.

Tomorrow Christy might be back. Simon had been about to go to bed but the thought that in the morning he might see her, for the first time openly loving her, kept him crouched beside the fire. It was less smoky now, feeding calmly on the ashes of Jessica's books. He had kept her children's books for Merlin but had ruthlessly burnt the poetry and novels, the books on Astrology and Herbs and Cats and Great Buildings of the World. They were too much hers, so many of them presents from him, inscribed on the flyleaf. He could remember the slightly patronizing mood in which he had bought them, choosing good-looking books because Jessica didn't really read but looked at the pictures, wasn't capable of serious thought but somehow absorbed ideas. One of these had been almost blind respect for Art. She had loved him, to begin with, as an artist and had gazed adoringly at anybody she met in a pub or at a party who announced that he or she wrote or painted. She was convinced it was far more admirable to produce an unpublished poem than to organize a car hire firm (her job until Merlin was born). It had been her dream to be drawn or painted by a 'great artist', for she knew her face was memorable, a Pre-Raphaelite mouse Simon had once called her. He had disappointed her by his failure to immortalize her and she had posed, in various states of undress, for quite a few closing time geniuses. He had so often laughed at her art-worship: but perhaps it had sustained his ambition, which had disappeared almost as soon as she – how had she got back into the room?

In a way it was Jessica's uncritical acceptance of the so-called artistic that had killed her. They were on the verge of leaving each other and so she had chosen an operatic death. Only instead of swelling voices and beautiful effigies, there had been a cold, white corpse sprawled indecently, a nasty ambulance ride, a hospital where suicides were shovelled along like cars on conveyor belts.

It's the living that count. Merlin, oh, Merlin, fill the space she's expanded into so voraciously.

Slowly in the firelight the child materialized, cautious at first, the pale, thin, over-polite boy at Madge's party. Then Simon recalled his presence when he had been happy, before the messy tragedies of grown-ups paralyzed him. Merlin laughed, shouted, ran, played in the garden, splashed in the bath and dressed up in his room. His father thawed, smiled. And Christy could enter here too, soon when the silly barriers between them were down. Then the rooms would be warm and strong again; he would at last be armed against his past. It was so good to have a dream. In the fading glow Simon lay down under a rug on the couch to dream it.

CHAPTER 12

As Rose drove down the Somerset lanes on her way to Sir Maverick's she was nervous, though Gerry, sitting beside her, would never have known it. Rose knew she was going there as Bernard's daughter, an identity she loathed, and that if she displeased Sir Maverick she might make herself unemployable. He had influence with both the newspapers she worked for, and there was only one other. Rose's instinct to annoy powerful men was so strong, and so much beyond her control, that she stopped to light another cigarette because her hands were too shaky to do it as she drove.

'You don't want to stop on these bloody corkscrews. Combine harvesters'll mow you down soon as look at you – lost again?'

Rose was screwing up her eyes at the unhelpful tangle of Arthurian waffle on the Ordnance Survey map: Mount Guinevere, Knights' Bridge, Morganswood. Somewhere around here there must be a monument to poor little Merlin. 'You're supposed to be doing this, you're the passenger.'

'Sorry love. I've got no sense of direction when I'm sober. We passed a pub in that last village –'

'I can see turrets through the trees over there, let's have a look.'

Past a Georgian lodge full of unpicturesque armed guards, a park rose to a house that was unique and very famous, although it was only six months old. A small medieval castle with a moat was flanked on the right by an eighteenth-century neo-classical mansion and on the left by a Tudor manor house.

'Identity?' One of the guards asked, and scanned their Britcards.

'Made a lovely job of it. I'll get some shots inside the gates if you don't mind stopping.'

'If they let us in. I think it's horrendous, like a film set.

'But it's the real thing.'

'Turned into something completely ersatz.'

After a phone call the guard waved them on. Gerry jumped out with his camera, and knelt and crouched with the showmanship that earned him half his salary.

This wasn't really meant to be an interview but a Souvenir Colour pull-out on Sir Maverick's unconventional, controversial, tasteful, eccentric (the Morning Glory had already used all these adjectives ad nauseam, she would have to find some new ones: extravaganza. Tired of moving between five houses, he had decided to combine three of them, so he had dug up Jermyn House in Berkshire and Tyndall End in Suffolk and moved them to the grounds of Lancelot's Keep. Conservation societies had roared at him, questions had been asked in the House and smoothly answered by him, a television documentary had chronicled every stage of demolition and reconstruction and, Rose knew, millions of readers would drool over Gerry's pictures with their titillating captions: *Nash's North Wing safely in place now, at a cost of £3m.* Any less than adoring comments she slipped in would be edited out. The Morning Glory had no time for ambiguity; Sir Maverick was a leader of men, a director of newspaper and TV companies and a patron of the arts. Rose was allowed to hold up a mirror to him and watch it flash but not in any way to distort his magnificent reflection. She knew she would, as usual, write two articles, one in her head and one with her fingers. This kind of double-think was such a habit that it caused her very little discomfort.

> *Rolling over the verdant parkland I was struck by the guts and determination of this man who, not content to have one stately home, moved heaven, earth and the National Trust to get three. Larger than life in his brown monk's robes, a reminder of his recent conversion to the Catholic Church, Sir Maverick strode towards us over the twelfth-century drawbridge. The peacocks screamed . . .*

He leaned in at the window and kissed her.

108

'Rosie? I've just been talking to your dad. So glad you found us. You can leave your car in the cloisters.'

Gerry hopped around, like a sparrow pecking with his camera at Sir Maverick's human interest. Feeling like a vandal, Rose left her car on the grass in the Romanesque ruined cloisters and walked back to them. Sir Maverick had contrived to stand so that his elegant brown length was reflected in the moat. Rose could smell on her skin the fragrance, charm and cruelty that emanated from his. A hot, florid face that would quickly turn red with anger.

His wife Pandora sat on a window seat in a low-ceilinged, sunny room, wearing a green linen dress. She's so beautiful, Rose thought, that she puts down every other woman for miles.

'This is the one, I think, do you know I still get lost now we're facing south instead of west – here we are Pandy! This is Rose, Bernard's daughter.'

Rose was kissed again. Gerry, who earned four times as much as her, was treated as her sidekick. They hadn't met his parents.

> *Pandora Clough Whittyng gave up a successful modelling career to marry the man who was, in 1979, only the dashing young Tory candidate for West Throgmorton. Now she is a radiant chatelaine and political hostess, cheerful mother of five and an accomplished cook. We lunched on her game pie and raspberry fool, washed down by Samuel Beckford's favourite wine . . .*

Close up, Pandora's milky skin was taut with a much pummelled look. She had dark blonde wavy hair, a delicately moulded beak, high cheekbones, hooded eyes and a body like a greyhound. If upper-class beauties are ever cloned, Rose thought, she'll be their mould. She would have been happier as an Edwardian lady of the manor, then she could have been utterly useless, arranging flowers all day. The years of flirting with cameras and pushing for Maverick have strained her, coarsened her, as if a marvellous swan had to be trained to squawk limericks like a parrot. What about me, Rose thought angrily as her head rushed with alcohol, to most people I'd seem just as remote and spoilt as her. It's only because I went

to school with girls like Pandora that I can see her so clearly –
Rose concentrated on what Sir Maverick was saying over his
second glass of port.

'. . . given people back their sense of pride. It's the most
natural thing in the world to love your country, to feel better
than the rest of the world, it's nothing to be ashamed of. I was
at Oxford during what I call the trendy liberal age – didn't last
long, thank God, because they were too bloody liberal to
assert themselves, ha ha.'

Giggles from Pandora.

'I had a union jack waistcoat made for me, wore it everywhere. You wouldn't believe the abuse I had to put up with.
Fascist was the least of it. Now all that's changed. We said
we'd put the Great back into Britain and we have. Your dad's
idea for instance, great stuff, it'll give people a sense of their
roots and traditions again. A lot of these black kids don't
know where they come from, that's why we had all those race
riots. Well they're here now so we should welcome them, let
them share Blenheim and the Battle of Britain with us, get
them to write songs about that instead of all this alienation
and hate.'

'I do think hate is awful, don't you, Rose?' Pandora said
earnestly.

'You've often been accused of racism. Would you describe
yourself as a racist?'

'Certainly not. If my great grandfather hadn't married a
sugar heiress with a very dark complexion we wouldn't be
sitting here today. Probably be in Battersea or somewhere.
And I have nothing but admiration for the Jews, like your
family my dear, who came here a few generations ago, worked
hard, educated their children, and made it their business to
integrate.'

Sixty years ago you wouldn't have had me to lunch, Rose
thought, staring at him.

'But it all takes time, brains, and, frankly, money. This
country has been inundated with people of different races –
poor old Enoch had a point, you know – and not all of them
are well-endowed with the qualities I mentioned. So we've got
to help them, give them a sense of belonging to a great
civilization. A little campaign every few years to stir their

110

hearts in the right direction. The more you keep the enemy without, the cosier it is to be within – am I being indiscreet?'

'Yes,' said Pandora, suddenly unsmiling.

'Never mind. Who's your editor now, Rosie?'

'Johnny West.'

'What happened to Duncan? Someone was telling me –'

'He got sacked last week.'

'I'll phone, er, Johnny later. The *Morning Glory*'s all right.'

Gerry knelt in front of Pandora and caught her at her most fragile, willows and moat swirling behind her. She was smiling again; she liked to see men on their knees.

Maverick sat on his Queen Anne chair at the edge of the long, polished table, drumming on it, his grey channel eyes darting impatiently from idea to idea. All ego and energy, Rose thought, a force waiting to be unleashed. She sat very straight, not sober but in control of her thoughts and words.

'A lot of people have criticized the government's record on housing. It's been estimated that fifty thousand people sleep out in London every night.' Later, when she played the tape back, Rose was surprised at the anger in her voice.

'Really? Who by? It's true we've had to cut public expenditure. In my view this is a necessary part of developing again as a great people. Now in the nanny state, the average man never had to do anything for himself: born in a free hospital, he lived in a Council house, went to a free school. Then he either passed exams, got a job and joined a Trade Union which held the country to ransom and blackmailed and betrayed its members, or lazed around for the rest of his life receiving huge dollops of taxpayers' money. Now *is* that a life? I don't think so. That's not my idea of an Englishman. People now have to struggle a bit, they have to shift for themselves and they get out what they put in. In some cases, nothing. In other cases, the satisfaction of knowing that everything they have is the fruit of their own effort. People have got their pride back and they can't run to Nanny State any more because she's not there!' Maverick filled up Rose's glass, and his own, and toasted himself.

Rose didn't drink. She was remembering that morning when she had visited the camp where Simon worked. Urgently, she wanted to tell him about cold and hunger and

111

dirt, to turn his party political broadcast into a conversation.

'Have you visited any of the shanty towns the homeless have built? People living in tents without electricity or proper sanitation, knee-deep in mud most of the year?'

'I visited one before the last election as a matter of fact, on the outskirts of Birmingham. Yes, it was squalid. People find their own level. But by God, some of the faces I saw there! Splendid, real English faces, like something out of Hogarth.'

'Toothless and drunk, you mean?'

'I'm talking about spirit, Rosie, the will to fight and survive. One old chap came up to me and shook my hand and said, "It's a bitter medicine, Sir, but it's the right one and the country knows it."'

'Weren't you attacked?' Rose asked incredulously.

'We had a spot of trouble with a bunch of yobbos but the police sorted them out. No, by and large, people realize now we're the only alternative.'

Rose sighed. It was easy to imagine him striding blithely through a barrage of eggs, tomatoes, stones and mud. He would think they were offerings from admirers or some quaint old English custom that had been revived.

'Perhaps they're too stupefied by a diet of Neuropepsi and chips to rise against you. Yet. You know, a lot of people think Neuropepsi contains tranquillizers, and that the government keeps the price down deliberately. Why did you decide to distribute it free in the theme parks?'

'It's a very pleasant drink. Very popular with young people.'

'You don't drink it, do you, Sir Maverick?'

'No, personally I prefer a nice bottle of Château Lafitte.'

'And prefer to keep your wits intact?'

'That's a very serious allegation you're making. And a paranoid one. Particularly when you consider your own father is launching these theme parks. I hope you're not going to print any nonsense about Neuropepsi? Are you all right over there, Pandy?'

'Oh, yes, we're getting on frightfully well. I'll just show Gerry the rest of the house, darling, he wants some more shots.'

Pandora flashed her ubiquitous smile at them and swayed out, followed by Gerry who looked like a dog with a newspaper in his mouth. Rose, who knew how successful Gerry's combination of flattery and lust could be with women, wondered. But Maverick's eyes were still glittering with the light of future worlds and he showed no concern. In a way, Rose thought, he's above such things, above human relationships altogether. Or, to put it another way, deaf and blind but certainly not dumb.

> *Sir Maverick's lifestyle is not modern. Perhaps he would say he embodies many periods in our national heritage; he is a medieval monk contemplating in his cloister, a knight dedicating himself to his lady, a squire in a Peacock novel relishing good food and wine and talk. What about the future? Sir Maverick sees it as a flower sprouting from the sturdy roots of our collective past. He believes his beloved England will once more show the world what greatness is and what stuff we are made of: stern stuff, strong stuff, great stuff.*

Wearily, Rose turned on the tape recorder again. Maverick's words were definitely slurred now and she would gladly have fallen asleep on the floor. He staggered from his chair to a huge wooden chest, lay down on it and started to do press-ups.

'Power, Rosie, that's what it's all about. Not letting yourself get flabby and muddled and soft. Fifteen minutes of this and I'll be ready to drive to the House this evening. Now a so-called Socialist wouldn't be able to carry on like this.' His voice came between pants, in staccato bursts, but it didn't stop coming. 'Have you heard about the latest opposition party they've formed? The Anti-Poverty Front. APF. I ask you, who's going to vote for a mouthful like that? It's not as if the opposition hasn't had a chance. We had that coalition for a few years and what did that achieve? Unemployment stayed the same and inflation shot up. We gave them their PR and decentralized the Civil Service and what happened? A landslide victory for us. Politics is about survival of the fittest, Rosie my dear, and the survivors have gone over to us. They have to think of their careers like anyone else, and what sort of career is it, stuck on the wrong side of the House for years, whining on behalf of people who don't even have a vote? That's why they're such a wishy-washy bunch. Fifteen parties and not a convincing leader between them.'

113

'A lot of their leaders are in prison.'

'They broke the law.'

'You made the laws. And you took away the votes of the unpinables, after you'd taken everything else away from them.'

'I hope you're not going to write anything silly, Rose.'

'I'm paid to write silly things.'

Immediately she wished she hadn't been frank. It struck such a false note. But he looked pleased.

'There's a bit of cant in all jobs.'

'Even yours?'

He gasped with laughter, stopped pretending to do his exercises, sat on the edge of the chest and laughed again. His blood churned hotly beneath the skin of his heavily jowled face and his belly wobbled under his habit. Rose decided she preferred him on a platform and returned severely to business.

'Some observers feel you've cut us off too much by your Fortress Britain policy. Our exports have dropped by 50 per cent since you left the Common Market and it's often said that the only government still well disposed towards us is the United States.'

'I don't know about the Yanks. Personally I think they're a nation of amiable barbarians, give me the Russians any day. At least they're literate and have some stability, too much of course, but if you meet a chap one year you can be pretty sure you'll deal with the same fellow ten years later. Mind you, it's getting a bit like that over here, I'm glad to say. As for the Common Market, it's dominated by a lot of Frogs throwing their weight and their wine around. Look what they did to our apples!'

'If you look outside that window you'll see an orchard of Cox's Pippins. Look, over that wall. Best apple in the world, I'll give you some to take home. Those abominations the French tried to foist on to us were just cotton wool covered with sickly green plastic. No, believe me, all this stuff about Europe being one nation is rubbish. We have our national differences and we should be proud of them, cultivate them. The Germans always have been a humourless guzzling bunch of culture vultures, they can't help it and they don't want to help it. I'm all for leaving people alone and accepting them as

114

individuals, I've never been a joiner. I see this island as a ship, a neat, safe little ship. We've been a bigger ship and we've sailed on higher seas but for the time being we're doing all right in our own harbour.'

His voice rose on the last two words with the triumphant, assertive note that she recognized from visits to the House of Commons. He's made his speech and he wants to get rid of me, she thought, and immediately felt she'd wasted her time. A dozen questions jostled each other on to her tongue.

'How do you reconcile your defence of private enterprise with the recent tax increases?'

'Seven million people in this country can't or won't work. Someone has to pay for them.'

'But you don't, Sir Maverick. Over the last ten years unemployment benefits have been decimated while the number of jobless has increased by –'

'Rosie, you must forgive me, but I have to be at the House in three hours. I must wash and change. The English might love a lord but they've certainly never loved a monk.'

'It's been reported in the Italian newspapers that your conversion to Roman Catholicism followed a huge investment you made in a Vatican telecommunications firm with Mafia connections –'

'If you want to know more about my faith, read the book I'm writing about it. It's being published next Easter by a new little company I'm launching, Bulldog Press.'

A vast yawn broke up the smooth plain of his face into pinkish-grey caverns and yellowing fences. He was quite old and very tired. He edged towards the door but Rose followed. They stared at each other; he was nervous as she was suddenly revealed in all her determination, cold and hard, the kind of woman he loathed. She wondered if he would summon his bouncer/butler.

'When Ireland left the United Kingdom last year you were reported as saying it was the only way to end our Irish problem after five hundred years. Did you feel any regret when six thousand people were killed in the civil war that followed?'

'So sorry, must rush. Nice to have seen you. Love to Bernard.'

He almost slammed the door and she heard his sandals

flapping down the marble corridor. Rose sat in the window, where Pandora had posed so much more decoratively, and fought off the beauty of the view. She knew Sir Maverick would find time to phone her editor before he left for London. Or would he wait until he read the article, which would be so bland and ingratiating? Rose felt she'd forfeited his goodwill without preserving her integrity. Virago intactus. Hardly, she had just bared her teeth half-heartedly at him, and would butter him up behind his back. If only she could have managed it the other way round. Confused, her professional pride wounded, Rose waited for Gerry.

When he opened the door he also had a beaten look. She smiled faintly and in silence; with a noticeable lack of kisses and injunctions to come again, they went to the car.

'Hospitable old fart,' Gerry said half way down the drive.

'Very.'

'You've got to hand it to them, they know how to live. Furniture, clothes, wine – that's what I call style!'

'I'd call it money.'

'Good old Rose. Get them in the jugular. Are you going to rip them open?'

'I think he's more likely to rip me open.'

'Christ that port was strong. I'm glad I'm not driving. I got some lovely shots.'

'Of her?'

'Fantastic body. And face. Still they're funny you know, those upper-class women, somehow the signals aren't the same.'

'Did you make a cock-up too?'

'Unfortunate choice of phrase.'

> As we drove away over the mellow landscape Sir Maverick's family has farmed and loved for generations, we knew we were leaving more than an architectural monument. The man himself is a monument, to history, to the future, to pride and eccentricity. I think he spoke for most of us when he sat on his medieval manuscript chest in his flowing robes and said, smiling boyishly, 'I'm not a joiner.'

'A monumental bore. No wonder he's so successful.'

'Is he really a friend of your dad's?'

116

'They're making a lot of money out of each other at the moment.'

'Don't you get on with your family?'

'Only with my brother.'

Rose always discouraged questions about her parents. At the root of her ambition, nourishing its tangled profusion, was the need not to be their daughter. Now that Bernard, after decades of failure, had become the distinguished man he had always pretended to be, Rose's position was complicated. As a journalist, it was her job to keep tabs on his fame, but as a daughter she found him more embarrassing than ever. Still, she wouldn't speak of him with contempt to anyone except Simon, just as Bernard only criticized his children to their faces or to Madge. Freeman loyalties were odd but strong.

'Are you in a hurry, Gerry?'

'What are you offering?'

'There are some lovely roads down here. I used to be at school near Wells – do you mind if we take them instead of the motorway?'

'OK. Tried to make a young lady of you, did they?'

'They did try.'

Carried away by a passion for out-of-date school stories, Rose had demanded to go to a boarding school when she was eleven. She had been sent, because she was tough enough to take it and because Madge hoped the discipline the prospectus boasted of would blunt Rose's tongue. She felt her daughter ought to be punished for saying sarcastic, insulting things but had no idea how to set about it. Someone, usually Simon or Grandma, always laughed. Simon, who was sensitive, had stayed on at his London day-school and Rose was jealously aware that the household ran more smoothly without her.

Her school bore no resemblance to the ones in stories. It was small, mild, had central heating in all the rooms and no uniform. The stuffing wasn't knocked out of her, as Bernard had vaguely threatened. She soon dominated the school magazine and several less determined friends; when her parents attended her Open Day they realized for the first time that other people were unaccountably impressed by her.

Rose opened the window so that she could smell the baked vegetation. Hot earth, juicy trees and moist flowers crowding down to the narrow road, branches and leaves curving above. How these rich green tunnels reminded her of school, and of her ambiguous attitude to the countryside when she lived in it. On walks she could never remember the names of the plants and would write down 'blue flower' or 'yellow weedy flower with little white furry bobbles' in the nature notebook they were supposed to keep. Horses frightened her and her instinct when she played netball or tennis was to flinch from the ball. The only outdoor activities she enjoyed were walking, swimming and sunbathing.

At school she read voraciously. Her incapacity to lead the healthy, hearty outdoor life the school encouraged made her feel like a foreigner. There was no anti-semitism there, for girls from rich Jewish, Catholic and Protestant families found money was a great bond. But there was a colouring the girls were expected to take on, a robust, bright-eyed ease of manner, which enabled them to enjoy life in big houses, horsy occasions and dances in marquees. And, between social events, perhaps a little job in an art gallery where interesting people would congregate. Rose was too urban, caustic and talkative for all that.

By the time she left school Bernard was visibly disappointed that she didn't like the brothers of her schoolfriends any more than they liked her. He had his eye on an exclusive enclosure of English life that had always been beyond his reach, and he had assumed the outrageous fees at Rose's school were the gate money. But she didn't want to go inside. She wasn't ugly or gauche, but she would talk about feminism and Proudhon and come back from dances in a taxi, alone and sober, looking bored stiff. For a few years Rose had remained an outsider, despising and envying the girls who coped with it better than her. She knew her parents were waiting for her to bring them a shiny young scalp. There was always – even now – an urge to please them and a counter-urge to annoy them as much as possible.

George had appealed irresistibly to the second. He had been an old frog who liked wallowing in the mud and had no intention of turning into a prince. He had made her see how insipid princes were. Clutching his webbed and slimy fingers, Rose had jumped into a university. Bernard and Madge had

118

still called women who went to university Blue Stockings, and most of the girls she had been at school with had gone on to finishing schools or courses in china appreciation or cooking. So going to university was, strangely, an act of rebellion.

Then George, drunk and ranting his awful poetry at readings, began to seem less lovable. Rose had turned to younger and more savoury men, though none of them had aroused as much passion in her as that fraudulent, villainous old toad. Perhaps Bernard had given her a taste for aging charlatans.

'Will you have the story ready by Tuesday, Rose?'

'I'll do it tonight if we go straight back now.'

'Aren't you going to Bill's party?'

'I might come along later if I get it finished. I've seen enough people for today, though.'

'Bye, passion flower,' Gerry said later as she dropped him off at Hammersmith.

CHAPTER 13

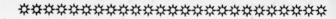

The night before the opening Madge dreamt she was a little girl again, a porcelain blonde in a pink frilly dress whom everyone stroked and tweaked, as indeed she had been. The dream was illuminated by her sense of warmth and triumph, by the certainty that she was pretty and adorable. It was so long since she had felt adequately fussed over that she woke up weeping, as if she had had a dream about a dead lover.

Bernard saw her but quickly shut his eyes and turned over. She cried too much. This was to be a day without complaints or reproaches; it was going to be perfect because he wouldn't let any imperfections in. Bernard heard the thump upstairs as their domestic monster left Grandma's tray outside her door. She wouldn't let that stunted zombie, as she called it, inside her room. Hero Ten clanked downstairs and rapped metallically at their door. Once Bernard had met it on the stairs, balancing three trays one on top of the other, and had been repulsed by its parody of human movement as it jerked out of his way. Yet it was so much more reliable than any servant. The table under the window shuddered as the tray bumped down on it, the curtains swooshed, the bath taps surged in a cheerful torrent. You didn't even have to say thank you; mornings just happened with a wonderful sleekness. Madge said you needed an almost human touch because it would be creepy to have things turning themselves on and off. Bernard inhaled the smell of coffee, new paint and clean bedclothes before he picked up a croissant from the table and got into his fragrant bath.

Merlin knocked on their door, with far less assurance than Hero Ten. He stared at his grandmother's puffy, swollen face and wondered if grown-ups would ever stop making him feel awkward. Only when I'm one myself and making other children feel awkward.

'Darling! Off to school?'

'Can't I come?'

'They wouldn't like it at school, I'm afraid. It'd be far too obvious. Our photographs will be splashed all over the papers.'

Madge sat up and practised looking radiant for photographers. Yes, she was undervalued and unloved, but life goes on, and she would wear the Italian dress with the flattering neckline.

'But I want to see all those new games. And Daddy'll be there, I haven't seen him for weeks.'

'We'll all go at the weekend. Simon too, we'll all go together and you can try all the games. Have you finished your cereal?'

'Yes. You could write a note saying it's a national event. It's only tennis and swimming all afternoon.'

'Now be a good boy. And give me a big kiss to show you love me.'

He didn't, really, though she was firmer now, less red and wobbly. He kissed her gingerly and went downstairs to the waiting car. Merlin wasn't surprised by his failure to persuade his grandmother. He had put on his uniform anyway, knowing he would go on to school. Its neat, dark green geometry sliced his thin body into circles, squares, cubes and rectangles which bobbed together out into the sunlight. He seems to float, Connie thought as she watched him from the landing window, he's too lightweight.

By ten Madge and Bernard were wrapped for public consumption. Madge wore a pink silk coat over an orange dress with a cascade of frills at the neck. Her white hat swooped mysteriously over one eye and that new cream she had bought really had smoothed away her tell-tale wrinkles with a loving hand. Or would do as long as she didn't smile, and she had no intention of smiling too much. She practised looking gracious, triumphant but not overbearing. Perhaps a hint of softness around the eyes but not enough to show her bags. She would outswan that mangy old duck upstairs.

'I'll just go and say goodbye to Grandma, darling. She'll want to share this moment with us.'

121

Bernard was dubious but followed her upstairs nervously. Madge knocked, her long red nails grated on the door. Old music, and soon that awful smell would knock them over.

'Grandma! Connie dear! Can we come in?'

'Who is it?'

'Me, darling, Madge. With Bernard.'

'It's already brought the tray.'

'We want to *see* you.'

'What for? Nobody else does.'

'Don't be childish, Mummy.'

'You were never childish enough, that was your trouble.'

'We have to go in a minute. This is a very important day for Bernard, aren't you going to congratulate him?'

'What on? Is he leaving you?'

Her malevolence came through the door in an audible spit. Madge took a step backwards and felt hot, wet anger channel down her immaculate face. Stabbing at the stair carpet with her heels, she went down to the cloakroom to seal her face up again.

Bernard followed, muttering, 'Doesn't always know what she's saying.'

'She knows exactly what she's saying. Which is why we never go near her. I only thought today –'

'We've worked so hard –'

'A milestone for you.'

'Some mothers would be proud.'

'I wish I had a son who'd achieved as much as you.'

'Will he be there?'

'I expect so. It's only next door and he hasn't got anything else to do. And Rose said she'd come.'

'Perhaps we could all go up on to the platform together. Like those American politicians.'

'That might be very nice, darling. Supportive. We're going to have to do something about Grandma.'

'I'm afraid it isn't easy, having her in the house now.'

'No. She'll have to go into a home. Joan knows of a good one.'

'As my old friend Binkie Topham used to say, "God gave us our relations, thank Him that we can choose our friends".'

'I do think she might have been a little more sensitive. Specially today.'

122

'Don't let her upset you. Not today.'

Connie crept back to the landing window to watch them walk arm-in-arm to the official-looking black car. Fat, pink, overdressed, not even young any more. And Bernard deserved her; he was as smarmy smooth as a marble egg coated with vaseline.

In the car, in a haze of perfume, aftershave and excitement, they leaned against each other. Madge gave him her hand, encrusted with rocky jewels, and he held it cautiously. As they skimmed across London the city was warm and bright, ripe for him.

The Fulham Road shone with hats, flowery dresses, little red and silver cars, pink and green powdered wigs, orange sequinned togas, turquoise hooped skirts, purple doublets, golden tights, top hats two feet high and pantomime crowns. The colours were intensified by the majestic night of the limousines and the black and white striped bureaucratic paunches. There were ticket touts, souvenir balloons, posters, badges, mugs and dolls for sale, while dozens of cameras gobbled up the crowd. A French TV company filmed the arrivals while an English TV personality interviewed a famous American news announcer. Inside the gates, children bounced and screamed on an inflatable Tower of London and Morris dancers puffed and skipped.

Above the wide entrance, in golden letters dulled by the sunshine, was written: GREAT TIME FUN PALACE. And beneath it on a huge black and white banner: OPENING TODAY. ENTRANCE FREE. At night, Bernard gloated, how those letters would flash and sparkle and trick the optical nerves and draw them in, something to do with lasers that engineer had said. Their car couldn't get through the crowd, they were stuck in the gates for ten minutes while kids clutching cans of that drink Maverick was so keen on pressed grinning faces against their windows, leapt in front of their car and danced in the middle of the road.

'They're not on drugs?' Madge asked, edging away from the powdered, transexual faces, with flittering ornaments in their ears and nostrils and sequinned eyelids.

'Just happy, darling. They'll calm down very soon. We're going to make these young people see how beautiful life can be.'

'That's nice.'

But Madge still stared at the white, leering, unnatural faces. She had read that the suicide rate amongst them was terribly high, she could never remember statistics but something frightful. She wondered how one would know they were dead, they were so like corpses now, gyrating in their *danse macabre*. Even as she watched, some of them abruptly stopped jumping around, sat or lay where they were with glazed faces. Calmed down, as Bernard had said, only somehow it wasn't calm at all. Well at least they wouldn't vandalize Bernard's lovely funfair. Rose and Simon had been impossible too of course, at that age, but thank God they hadn't looked like this. Like something in a circus but all the time, not just at Christmas; evey day they must spend hours in front of a mirror doing these extraordinary things to themselves. Well circuses made people happy and that was all Bernard wanted, his mission in life.

'Takes all sorts,' he said thoughtfully, staring at them too. He had never seen them close up before.

The police, who were there in massive numbers just in case, made way for the waiting cars. They drove past the Roman Pavilion, the Jousting Hall, the Bonk the Conqueror Arcade and the Chaucer Snuggery.

'It's so big! I've got used to those funny little models like matchboxes.'

'And our next one in Brixton will be even bigger. It'll go from Neanderthal Nora to Brits on Mars.'

They walked down a strip of red carpet leading to a platform that had been rigged up between Nelson's Nook and the On the Beaches Shooting Gallery.

'Daffodils everywhere! Lovely, darling.'

'I told them to keep it simple.'

In the splintery, rather seedy backstage shadows behind the platform, they shook hands and accepted drinks. Sir Maverick was there, with an actress, a popular historian, a pop star and a typical jobless youth supplied by the Ministry of Leisure. They had to wait until a large enough crowd had assembled and all the cameramen had arrived. Madge couldn't keep her eyes off Hieronymus Gunk, the founder of Scrapheap Rock, who looked like the kids at the gates but was at least forty, immaculately made up and was passing the time by stamping his autograph all over the bare arms and legs of the token young person. Sir Maverick's secretary was whispering anxiously that there ought to be another woman on the platform; they were supposed to have obtained a jobless female but it was too late to send him back now. Bernard and the popular historian established they had sent their sons to the same prep school. Madge was trying to remember where she'd seen the actress and the actress was trying to remember where she'd seen Madge.

When the signal came that the last TV camera was in place, Sir Maverick flooded his face with benign compassion, stepped up on to the platform and cut the symbolic red, white and blue ribbons. His voice was scarcely audible to them, huddled beneath its vast amplification.

Bernard didn't want to hear the other speeches. He was on third and desperately needed these last few minutes to memorize his lines. He didn't want to use notes because, although he wasn't an experienced public speaker, he felt he ought to be, at his age. Madge saw his panic and felt sorry for him.

'Give me your notes. I'll prompt you if you forget.'

'Would you? I can't think why I – just a few minutes – nobody listens to these things anyway.' He was sweating all over, his eyes popping.

She took his hand. It was really his weakness she loved yet she had always to pretend he was a strong man. 'This is your finest hour,' she whispered. 'Like Churchill. We'll all be so proud of you.'

'Where are they?' He looked around for his children.

'They said they'd meet us here. You know what they're like. It's your turn now, up you go, good luck.' She gave him a push and he shakily climbed the steps. She was glad they weren't there, sniggering and snotting.

At the back of the crowd, ready for escape, Rose and Simon stood deep in whispered conversation. The people around them, irritated by the disturbance, edged away until they stood isolated together.

Simon was saying, '. . . so you walk through these mauve plastic flying buttresses and laser beams clothe you in chainmail. Then lots of men on horseback come galloping down on

125

top of you. If you press the right button, they go backwards, and if you don't this inflatable axe appears and hits you on the head.'

'The one I went on was a roundabout which played "The British Grenadiers" very fast. You sat on lions and unicorns and as you went round you watched a holographic map of the world in the centre gradually turning pink. Then the music stopped and Stanley, Clive and Rhodes stood up and made little speeches. I quite enjoyed it.'

'Yes, it has a certain kitsch appeal. I'm sure it'll be a big success. I felt a bit self-conscious because I was the only person I could see over twenty.'

'The whole idea is to keep kids happy so they don't riot. They can have free entry all day every day if they want it, they only have to produce their food vouchers.'

'Why are they all drinking Neuropepsi? Is it safe? It seems to have a very odd effect on them.'

'I know but it's perfectly legal, in fact it's being distributed free all over the country.'

'Here he comes.'

Simon felt his usual embarrassment at his father's presence. Even at that distance, he seemed to emanate insincerity. No more than any other man on a platform, he reminded himself as the crowd clapped and cheered. Bernard had been introduced as 'the man who's put the "free" back into enterprise'.

'Ssssh. I want to listen,' Rose said firmly.

But within minutes they had turned to each other with smiles of collusion and shame. The whispering started again.

'He's out to get a knighthood,' Rose whispered.

'Anyone would think he'd sunk the *Belgrano* single-handed.'

'I think I can see one of Madge's hats bobbing around at the back there.'

'I suppose we ought to go and see them. Merlin might be there, I haven't seen him for ages.'

'Well why the hell not?' Suddenly annoyed with him as well, Rose turned away. 'I can't face them this morning. I'm going to the Press tent to get a drink. Coming?'

He followed her but almost immediately wished he hadn't. Rose's colleagues always struck him as being unnecessarily tough, alcoholic and foul mouthed. He didn't like to see her get on with them so well. But he kept smiling and retorting and downing glasses of wine. I'm getting more aggressive again, he noted with relief. While Rose discussed the details of her father and daughter piece, Simon stood at the flap of the tent and watched the crowd.

Apart from an occasional civil servant or business man they were all very young, with the round, unlined faces of children but without their frankness. Many of them had terrible pimples, pustules and other volcanic skin eruptions visible through their heavy make-up and, presumably, caused by it. Their clothes were touching in their baroque gaudiness. This was the age group he never saw at Smiles: the children left at eleven or twelve and went to teeny camps, which he pictured now as long rows of mirrors in the mud where undernourished, spotty kids painted and wiped and squeezed and tried to love their reflections. They must scavenge for the bright materials and then spend hours cutting, pinning and sewing their brave, pathetic costumes. Parents who tried to visit their children in those camps came back with stories of their gangs and rituals, drugs and cruelty, shocked. Smiles saw itself as a respectable, well-run camp with a low crime rate. Simon rarely believed horror stories about youth because he was predisposed to side against parents, not having accepted that he was one himself. He continued to stare, until a girl Merlin's age came up to him, put her arms around his shoulders which she could hardly reach, and asked if he wanted to take her home with him.

Simon wandered back into the tent where Rose was still talking, intense and edgy, for she had no intention of telling nine million readers what she really felt about her father. Her article was to take the form of a mutual interview, but the questions she and Bernard would ask each other had to be agreed on with her editor.

'A nine-year-old girl just tried to pick me up.'

'Child prostitution's nothing new, we did a double page spread on it two years ago. Now, Rose, do you mind if your father asks you if you feel overwhelmed by his success?'

'He's only been successful for about five minutes.' Rose smiled at Simon.

127

'Still he's always been wealthy, you must have been influenced by that.'

Rose looked puzzled. 'You should have heard him complain about money. Every time a bill arrived there was panic.'

'Really? Can we use that?'

'Yes. Go on Rose, hit him while he's up. Tell them about your school uniform.'

'Shut up, Simon.'

The editor offered Simon another drink.

CHAPTER 14

✿✲✿✲✿✲✿✲✿✲✿✲✿✲✿✲✿✲✿✲✿✲✿✲✿✲✿

Martha arrived after the speeches with her friend Dawn. They had been late because it took Martha hours to apply the layers of black and white make-up, green false eyelashes, silver stars, white lipstick and sparkly nose rings. Her scalp itched under her long purple wig and the wig itched under her green velvet turban, although, she supposed, a wig couldn't really itch. Her face burned with grease as if someone had lit a candle under it.

But Martha looked great, according to Dawn, who looked similar but more comfortable. Martha's eyes were sore where various bits of goo had run into them; she hoped they weren't red as then they would look even smaller. She was painfully aware that her eyes were too small and the rest of her too big. She took small steps so as not to burst out of the tight yellow brocade trousers she had made the night before. She had intended them to be baggy and oriental but somehow nothing ever billowed on her, however much material she used. Dawn walked ahead, thin and pretty and knowing. Martha followed anxiously as she had ever since she left Smiles two weeks ago. She was too nervous to take in her surroundings, she just kept her eyes on Dawn's small, tight, confident buttocks. Her baggy trousers had come out brilliant. A man handed them each a canned drink and they smiled, relieved that someone had noticed them.

Martha drank hers very fast and felt the cold, saccharine gas bloat her stomach. They paused to drink and for the first time she looked around her. It was a kind of fair ground, full of flasheroos like them; she couldn't see many wrinklies or dowdies. Martha looked around for Hieronymus Gunk; she had heard he was going to be there and had expected him to be on a revolving stage high above everyone else. Lowering her gaze and her expectations she saw Simon, standing outside a tent on the other side of the river of people. He looked back without recognition and she felt a curious thrill of loneliness because she wasn't Martha any more, who he had told stories to, who Christy had shouted at, who had hung around that stupid playgroup until she was far too old to play because she and her mum got on each other's nerves in their tent. They wouldn't look for her because kids always disappeared at her age, except for bunglebums like Peter who stayed with that disgusting old gran, who couldn't even walk. Maybe I'll change my name, a lot of kids at the camp done that and I never liked Martha. Sounds heavy and slow. Jackie, Linda. A petite name.

Then, for the first time in months, Martha stopped worrying. She had followed Dawn into a kind of tent with pictures all over the walls of big ships landing on a beach and lots of soldiers getting off. She saw by the flickering light that Dawn was wearing a muddy green soldier's uniform, and looking down Martha realized she was wearing one too. This was so funny that she started to laugh, couldn't stop, heard her shrill laugh above the waves and guns and seagulls. They had to press buttons to keep the soldiers away, but the soldiers kept coming and Martha kept laughing. Dawn nudged her to belt up but she was smiling and giggling herself. Two blokes were staring at them, in scrapheap rags. They were wearing Viking helmets with little mirrors all over their faces, arms and legs. Martha wondered how they stuck them on. Through their green soldiers' uniforms you could see their long pale skinny limbs sparkling. They must look great in the sunlight, real flasheroos. They moved in beside Dawn and Martha and started to press the same buttons, then they left that tent all together and went to another where men were galloping on horseback. Martha saw that she and Dawn and the two boys were all wearing suits of armour. They drank some more fizzy drinks and Martha felt really happy, she smiled at the two blokes and at Dawn. Friends, she had friends now. One of the blokes was fantastic looking with blue eyes and a nice tidy nose and a small mouth like she had always wanted. He kept looking at her, once when they were going into a tent he kissed her on the back of the neck. She liked that. She liked the way he'd stuck his mirrors on, careful. He didn't pick his nose or scratch his balls all the time like a lot of the blokes in the camp.

None of them had spoken since the two boys had joined them. In a brief patch of daylight Martha and Dawn smiled at each other and knew they both liked these blokes. They would go back to their camp for a few days. They all exchanged names, the two blokes were called Ron and Dave and Martha said her name was Jeanette. Maybe they would be kind, Martha thought, like that rich old geezer who took them back to his house last week, gave them food and let them watch films. There was a woman and some little kids living in the house most of the time. While he was asleep she and Dawn went round opening all the doors. One room was full of toys, like a toyshop, and another had a golden bed and pink cupboards full of clothes in plastic bags. Wrinkly clothes but really expensive, about a thousand pairs of shoes too. Dawn wanted to try them on but Martha was too scared, the house gave her the shivers. It was so big and clean and silent, anyway she didn't want to sleep with that bloke again, he was fat and hairy and made them do yucky things. Even after an hour in his turquoise bathroom she didn't feel clean. So they took two bottles of perfume and a box of chocolates and left the house.

Ron and Dave wouldn't have a house like that or nice food, they'd live in a tent like them. But at least they were young and skinny and Dave had lovely eyes. She wondered if he took his mirrors off when he went to bed. She didn't like the things he would do to her when she took her clothes off. Dawn said she liked those sex things but Martha didn't believe her. Her mum used to mutter about men but she didn't tell Martha anything really, maybe she didn't know. Dawn said it was all right as long as you went along to one of those vans and got your insides fixed so you didn't get babies. That girl in the next tent to Dawn had one, it cried all the time and she couldn't go out, just had to sit there like a dildo and none of the blokes fancied her. Martha decided she'd stay with Dave till he threw her out, then she'd find one of those vans.

Rose and Bernard sat over strawberries, gins and tonics in the Chaucer Snuggery, making notes for their interview.

131

Madge sat and listened, prepared to act as umpire, while Simon tried not to listen.

Bernard examined Rose's notes suspiciously. 'What does this mean? "School uniform".'

'I wasn't sure whether to mention it or not. But I think I will. When I first went to Hedgley you saw the uniform list and said it was rubbish, a complete waste of money. You said I didn't need half that stuff. So I never had the right clothes, I had to wear my tennis dress for gym and netball and I had to go on wearing my winter uniform until I boiled because I only had one summer dress.'

'My heart bleeds for you,' Bernard said acidly.

Madge felt the anger flow up to her ears and forehead, a pleasant sensation, like being mildly drunk. 'Do you really think millions of people want to know the trivial details of what you wore or didn't wear when you were thirteen?'

'Yes. It's just the sort of thing people like to read about.'

'They don't want to know about you at all, my girl. It's your father who's distinguished himself, not you.'

'Well they'll know now because I've just recorded it. And I'm writing this article.'

Bernard looked at her pocket nervously.

'I expect they'd like to read about your carryings on, too.' Madge looked at her cool, smart daughter with dislike.

'I have nothing to hide. Anyway I carry on about as much as a dead rattle snake.'

'And you're about as warm blooded,' Madge said hotly. 'And while we're on the subject of school uniforms, we've just had to fork out a fortune for another one. I didn't hear Merlin's doting father or aunt offering to contribute.'

They all looked at Simon expectantly but he refused to be drawn into this Christmas scene in midsummer.

'I must get back to work. I shall look forward to your article.' He grinned at Rose who didn't smile back. She thought, he always forgets which side he's on. 'Bye. I'll be in touch soon about Merlin. Well done, Bernard.'

They all sighed as he wandered off, briefly united in disapproval of his woolliness.

Simon felt a terrible, gnawing loneliness which led him away from Bernard's rape of time, back to the cemetery. But

132

he realized, as he sat on a bench in the crumbling stone colonnades that curved through a forest of grass, weeds and broken graves, that the peace he used to find there was shattered forever. From behind the high wall came military marches adenoidally whined on electric organs, shouts and giggles and screams of excitement, a background whir of machinery. Over the top of that wall, which had once been so comfortingly blank, he could see red, white and blue flags bobbing, the tops of pink and yellow towers, domes, spires and flashing neon signs.

Simon forced his eyes and ears inwards. He had meant to go to work, as he had said. But it was too late now, it would be lunchtime before he got there. Monday and Tuesday had been so humiliating, waiting for Christy at Smiles, then going home to wait for Ellen to phone. Gutless, he told himself, yes my guts feel literally frozen, locked in need. Waiting for her to come and thaw me. She's more likely to shout at me because the children will have been miserable without us both. Sean's no fun for them, he just stomps around looking dutiful. Now she won't be back before Monday, I suppose. Four and a half days. I wish I'd had more to drink while it was free, then I could sleep through the rest of today. Oh God! Why don't I learn? Jessica reduced me to this, this quivering jelly of love, then when I saw how repulsive she found it I solidified, hardened, became in the end quite cruel in fact. It's the height of my ambition to love and be loved by Christy. Love just isn't supposed to be a full time occupation. Not for a man, Madge would say. And certainly not for a woman like Rose. Yet somehow or other with me it's an obsession. Until I feel secure about her I can't do anything at all.

Later that evening his phone rang. A girl's voice, breathless, with a party or pub behind it.

'Simon?'

'Who's that?'

'Me, Ellen. She's back. Do you want to talk to her?'

'No. I mean, where is she?'

'With me. We're having a drink.'

'You didn't tell her –?'

'Don't be so coy. Are you sure you don't want to talk to her?'

133

'No. Yes, I do want to.'

'Hello? How are you, Simon?'

'All right. Will you be at work tomorrow?'

'Yes. I missed you.'

'Did you? Really? Well I missed you.'

'See you tomorrow then.'

'Yes. Goodbye.'

Later, in bed, as the conversation echoed for the twentieth time, Simon thought it must be the flattest climax ever to weeks of suppressed passion. Yet he felt wildly happy.

CHAPTER 15

✿✿✿✿✿✿✿✿✿✿✿✿✿✿✿✿✿✿✿✿✿✿✿✿✿✿✿✿✿

At dawn Martha wriggled out from under Dave, pulled on her damp yellow brocade trousers and red clogs and launched herself through the tattered flap door into the fresh air. It stank even out here but not as bad as in the tent, four of them rolling around in their own muck, disgusting really. Cold, damp, hungry, Martha ran blindly away from the camp. She didn't want to go back, not even for Dawn who was supposed to be her friend but behaved like an animal with blokes whenever she got the chance. Martha felt so miserable that she even thought, I could go back to Smiles, to Mum; but it's disgusting there too, and lonely. I wish I'd stayed with that rich geezer, real platinum set-up. She was at South Kensington, having run all the way from Dave's camp in Fulham. Must be beautiful, living up here. Creamy houses like wonderful cakes full of steaks, wine, jewellery, perfume, hot water, chocolates, central heating. Cars outside all shiny fast and sleek. Martha started to cry because life up here was so brilliant. Her wig had fallen off, her head felt greasy and her eyes were gummed up with stale make-up. Maybe if I sat on one of their doorsteps and waited until they opened the door, took me in with the milk. I heard a story once about a girl who did that, got to live in one of them houses, as a maid of course but still you'd wake up there every morning, get clean clothes and plenty to eat. No wages of course because you couldn't legally employ unpinables. Martha's legs ached from all that running. Cautiously she sat on the doorstep of a pale house in a wonderful plaster crescent. But she was scared a policeman or security guard would catch her, so after a few minutes she jumped up again. She stared at the rows of milk bottles. I'm so hungry. But you can get taken into care for pinching milk, well, maybe care's not so bad.

Then, Martha saw a black oblong between the wheels of one of the beautiful cars. She looked around again to make sure nobody was watching, dove down, grabbed it and sprang up again, not daring to look at it. It must be a wallet, and it was hard so it had something in it. Giggling hysterically, she stuffed it into her trouser pocket and looked around for somewhere she could examine it. She crossed the road to a fancy coffee shop which was still closed – there was nobody sleeping in the doorways up here – turned her back on the road and looked.

Inside the black leather wallet was a golden plastic square. And the pin? Shaking, Martha turned the wallet inside out and dropped a scrap of paper with a number scrawled on it: 62007542. Up to 20K as soon as the shops open. Food, clothes, car, a flat in one of these houses. She stuffed the wallet back in her pocket and ran down a side-street, have to keep moving, it's only seven. People like that don't get up early. I could go to a hotel but they wouldn't let me in like this. I'll go to the hairdresser soon as they open, get a facial, manicure, new make-up, clothes, all the breakfast I can eat. Maybe I'll buy presents for me mum, go over there in a taxi looking like a Scrapheap princess. Nah, then they'll guess. Better not have anything to do with Smiles or with Dawn or any of that lot. I always knew I was special, that's why I never fitted in. I'll find friends now, platinum blokes, they'll all be after me.

Martha didn't dare show her Britcard until she looked glamorous enough to live up to it. Between eight and nine she skulked past hotels, brasseries and cafés, slavering at the aroma of toast, bacon and coffee. She went for a walk in Hyde Park where she looked with contempt at the shrivelled grimy bundles asleep on the benches and with admiration at the men in crisp suits and women in smart dresses striding through the park. She knew they couldn't see her, she didn't exist yet, she was waiting to be born.

As soon as the boutique in Knightsbridge opened Martha went in. They think I'm just looking, afraid to let me try anything on case I've got fleas. I probably have but I'll get rid of them now. That's real flasheroo and so soft, must be silk, I dunno what size I am. I never bought new clothes before. I wouldn't mind doing their job, even: nice clothes, coming up here every day, where nothing's dirty and no one stinks.

Martha watched another customer. Easy. You just handed over the card and tapped out the number. She bought six dresses, four sweaters, two blouses, three skirts, a belt, a handbag and three pairs of shoes. Martha tried them on again and again, dancing in front of the mirror. Only her dirty face and hair spoilt it, that and the sour faces of the other girls.

'Shall I put your other clothes in a bag?'

'Nah. Burn them.'

She'd taken everything off, stark naked under her green spangled low-backed mini-skirted folly. The girl, who was only a few years older than Martha, said without expression, 'Can I see your card please?'

Martha produced it with a flourish from her new black velvet bag. For a moment, as she tapped out the number, she felt sick. What if it was only a telephone number? But the card was accepted, she swept up her parcels and staggered out of the shop into a café next door where she ordered coffee, scrambled eggs, toast and marmalade, pancakes with maple syrup and chocolate cakes.

'I see you're not worried about your figure,' said the waiter, a smirking skinny boy she quite fancied. Martha grinned at him between mouthfuls, stretched her legs and held her breath inside the green dress which was too tight over her hips. She wished she had a flat to invite him back to. But she wanted to feel the morning sun on her bare back: she was off, having left the chocolate cake to show that she could afford to. There were so many bags that she could hardly walk but why complain? She'd known old tramps laden with hundreds of bags and nothing in any of them. She might have ended up like that.

The beauty cave was the most wonderful place of all. It was like sex ought to be but wasn't, or maybe it was when you were rich. Soft hands caressed, massaged, waxed, washed, dyed, plucked, squeezed, brushed, polished, spread, sprayed and painted the beauty on to her. She lay back on a succession of chairs in dark alcoves while the hands worshipped and served her. Martha wallowed in her semi-nakedness, wondered if they noticed she had no knickers on. Things like that don't matter now, I can do what I like. All the dirt had been seduced out of her, she would never stink again. Above the hands the faces were friendly, respectful. They said she had nice skin and hair. She said she had a flat down the road and a boyfriend in Scrapheap Rock.

At the end of her ritual cleansing Martha stared at herself in the mirror for a full minute before paying. Her hair was very short, layered and sort of bubbly, purple shaded to mauve around her neck, her eyebrows and lashes were orange and she had acquired a tan. There was lots of brown flesh, too much. She wondered if she could go to another cave where hands would make her skinny. She put down the gold card again like a child playing Snap and tapped out the pin. It flashed up on to the telescreen and the card jumped back at her through a slot. Martha wanted to tip them all but she had no cash. She smiled round at them; their hands were on other girls now. She wanted to say, thank you, you made me, you gave me what I always wanted and never thought I'd get. But it was best not to speak except when she had to, her voice gave her away. So she smiled again instead. Her teeth gave her away too, so yellow and rotten. She practised smiling with her mouth shut.

Martha staggered, swayed, floated across the road and into a hotel. There was an old geezer in uniform who saluted her, a door like a roundabout she nearly got stuck in with all her bags, a marble hall encrusted with flowers. An arcade of sumptuous shops curved away, a vista of perfumes and wonderful clothes. She could hardly wait to get into them but first she had to get rid of her bags. A man leaned towards her over the desk and she stared back, not frightened any more.

'I want a room, please.'

'For how many nights?'

'For a week.'

'May I see your Britcard please, Miss –?'

'Smiles.' She handed over the card and was seized by a fit of giggles. She stuffed her hand over her mouth and kicked herself painfully with her new spiky sandals, but she couldn't stop the waves of laughter. She'd meant to say Miss Kensington or even use Peabody, her mother's name. Martha tried to smother the giggles in a cough but they burst out again as violent hiccups.

138

The man behind the desk ignored her attack, gave her back her card and gave a key to a boy her age who carried her bags up in a lift. Martha had recovered her dignity; she bit her tongue to punish herself, looked straight through the pageboy and pushed past him into the room. It was huge, white, domed like the inside of an eggshell. As soon as the boy left she flung herself around and bounced on the circular white bed until she nearly hit her head on the perspex chandelier. She arranged her beautiful clothes in the wardrobe and drawers, inhaling the sumptuous smells of new clean leather, cotton, silk and wool. In the black marble bathroom there was soap, bubble bath, a toothbrush and towels. As if they'd known she'd arrived without luggage. Inside the fridge, which was built into the wall like a safe, Martha found champagne, cheese, salami and fruit juice. She couldn't open the champagne but wandered around the room, naked, munching the food.

All this for one person, for me, forever. I don't need a flat, it's more fun here. If I press that button by the bed there's videos, as much as I like. I could lie in bed all day and watch them, eat as much as I want and never go out again. Then one day I'll go over there in a taxi and get Mum, bring her back just for one night, spoil her. Nah, she'll only start nagging, call me a thief, a whore and that. Anyway they'd never let her in the door. Even the maids in the corridors look smarter than what she does, they're clean, nice hair. It's disgusting that life, I hate it, I never want to go back. It's stupid to live like that, like animals in the mud when up here there's all this up for grabs if you're clever enough to grab it.

It took her a while to work out how the bath worked. Then she stood in the bathroom and watched the water pound down on the white billowing foam. Six baths a day if you wanted. At Smiles, once a week, we went over to the washhouse with a damp towel and a slimy cake of soap, stood shivering under a dribble of cold rusty water. The taste of garlic from the salami mingled with the hot pine fragrance. Martha turned off the taps, fingering the gold in amazement. With her foot she broke the crisp froth, like snow but so warm, and lowered herself until the soft bubbles tickled her neck and the water lapped her body gently, washed away all spots and smells. It washed away her make-up too, that beautiful tan; she watched the foam break up into archipelagos and then dissolve into the water, which was now pale brown. She didn't dare lie back in case she drowned but sat bolt upright, her face white again, her small brown eyes mesmerized by comfort. Every few minutes she ran some water away and turned on the hot water again. She stared at the toilet, black and gold like a magician's hat. A bathroom for people who never got dirty. Lifting one hand she saw furrows in her fingers and sat up hurriedly; maybe Mum was right, it's bad for you to wash too much. I'm drying up, melting. She reached out for the soft white towel. Small shreds of grey and brown fell from her arms and legs as she rubbed them. I've washed meself away. Ten more minutes in there and great chunks of me'd've started dropping off.

I wonder what you can see from the window. Trees, fountains, flowers, grass. Better get dressed in case there's a proper princess out there, she won't want to see me in the nude. I've still got no knickers. It's gorgeous this red dress, I could wave to the princesses and they'd never know the difference. Fucking awful these blinds, shit that's not right, oh Gawd –

The room was flooded with mid-afternoon sunlight as a cord broke and the blinds zipped up to the ceiling. Three floors down, traffic swirled in a heat haze and well-dressed people strolled past beautiful shops. Opposite, she could see the café where she had had breakfast, the boutique and the beauty cave. They aren't frightening any more, I can go down and walk into them any time, just like I owned them. Martha knelt at the window and inhaled the beauty of her clean skin, new dress, new world.

Downstairs at reception the microchip alarm on P E Marshall's Britcard started to bleep. The bleep was immediately picked up at South Kensington True Brit Information Agency and ten minutes later an armoured car full of men in riot gear stopped with screeching brakes outside the hotel. Brandishing shields and grenades of puking gas, they rushed up to Room 205 and broke down the door, which was unlocked.

140

CHAPTER 16

✿✿✿✿✿✿✿✿✿✿✿✿✿✿✿✿✿✿✿✿✿✿✿✿✿✿

Christy's last lift took her as far as the Putney Bridge Road. It was early evening, Wednesday; she remembered this was the night when Ellen, Beatrice and the others had their weekly booze up in a pub near Smiles. She didn't feel like going straight back to her caravan to face Sean or the wall and decided to go straight to the pub. She hadn't been there for a few months and it had been tarted up in the interim: there was now a holographic games room and a disco/barbecue area at the back. At the bar the publican glared at her as if her rucksack and muddy jeans represented a threat to the bright summer dresses and light jackets of his clientele.

'We don't like your lot coming in here any more.'

'What do you mean? What lot?'

'Don't take cash no more. Too much trouble.'

Mortified, Christy walked out. All the fizz of her holiday evaporated, the evening felt flat and sour. As she walked towards the Thames the late evening sun bled visionary beauty into it, ripples of gold and flamingo pink. Angrily she reminded herself that its beauty was an illusion; the river was really as ugly a symbol of division as a barbed wire fence. North of it the city was a rich ghetto, with only a few unpinable corners. But here in South London the camps stood in an expanding chain – Putney Common, Smiles, Clapham Common, County Hall Gardens, Southwark Park, Ruskin Park, Blackheath. They almost touched hands, they were growing fast and this terrified the people who had bought property in between, struggling for gentrification. The Residents' Associations signed petitions to get rid of them, the schools rejected their 'disturbed' children and the pubs and shops refused their cash.

You don't need laws to create outlaws, Christy thought bitterly. Then she grinned with relief as she saw Ellen, Beatrice and Rita coming towards her, arm-in-arm, with Ellen in the middle. She looked perky because for once she was free of Jack. Like Rita, who towered above her, Ellen wore shapeless trousers and one of Ted's remaindered T-shirts. Beatrice was elegant in a white, backless, silky dress. The other three women looked and felt like boiled potatoes beside an exotic, swaying flower. Beatrice's glamour would have been unforgivable if the fires that kindled her sensuality had not also stoked a molten furnace of anger at the conditions they all lived in. But they knew, and Beatrice knew, that she would get out of Smiles and forget its existence as soon as she got the chance. And she will get the chance, Christy thought, watching the tiny bones of her spine ripple beneath purplish black skin, we won't. She half listened to Rita and Beatrice bickering.

'Dressed for business, I see.'

'What exactly might you be dressed for, Rita? Saying Hail Mary? Ain't nobody else gonna hail you looking like that.'

'I heard you stopped giving Neuropepsi to your kids. That right?'

'That drink's part of the whole fucking conspiracy against us. You want to sleep for a hundred years, you just carry on drinking it. Hope your prince comes quick.'

'I just can't cope with the twins without the Neuropepsi. And they really like it, you know? It seems to calm them down.'

'Course it calms them down, that's how they want us, intit? My kids was just the same. Now Douane's real hyper, bin pinching stuff from all the shops. They took him into care again. Christy, I meant to ask you, will you help me get him out?'

'I'll see what I can do in the morning.' She walked behind with Ellen. 'Where are we allowed to drink, then?'

'We're going to that place in Battersea. It's a long walk but its the nearest place'll still let us in. How was your holiday?'

'Good. It seems a long time ago.'

'There was a bloke here asking for you.'

'Who?'

142

'Simon. Was he the one you told me about?'

'Probably.'

'He's really nice. One of Nature's gentlemen, a bit soft but you could do a lot worse. Here's his number. It's a bit sweaty, I've been carrying it round for days.'

Christy unscrewed the barely legible scrap of paper and memorized the number. London, which had seemed so unwelcoming, at once looked warmer and more real, like a photograph developing before her eyes.

Two hours later the four women sat on benches in a pub so stripped of comfort that it looked like a bombed out station waiting room. The landlord, unable to afford to redecorate it, made money on the side out of the black cash economy. Zonkies, small-time crooks and prostitutes met there and junkies shot up in the lavatories, which stank as vile as the ones at Smiles. Every few months the place erupted into a savage and often fatal battle, fought with broken glasses, bottles and knives, which was reported with distaste in the *Morning Glory*. It was also frequented by occasional journalists and tourists who wanted to catch a glimpse of 'real people'.

Christy's head was pleasantly fuggy, her cheeks burned and her bladder swilled with tepid beer. They had treated themselves to some of the pickled eggs which floated like anaemic rabbit turds in a vast jar on the counter. Protein, Christy thought hopefully as she bit into the acid flab. They gossiped about Martha's arrest and Beatrice told her a new, embellished version of the battle against Ted's Neuropepsi supplies.

'He's got it coming to him, that little bugger. Next time we'll get the whole lorry, him and all, drive it straight into the river. Had enough of being pushed around.'

Beatrice's eyes were ruthless, charged with anger. Looking around at Rita and Ellen, Christy saw the same hatred reflected in their less expressive faces. There was no need for them to lower their voices, they were all unpinables here. Even the landlord was some kind of outsider, who left copies of the *Prodigal Bum* on all the tables and listened to the buzz of fury with a grim smile. There were no visiting voyeurs that night, they had been put off by a particularly vicious fight which had been reported the previous week.

In a corner of the pub was an old fashioned box-shaped

colour television which still worked. Somebody turned it on for the news and they all stopped talking for a few minutes, jeered and spat as Felicity, the computerized nation's darling, announced through a curtain of orange hair and eyelashes that a baby chimpanzee had been born at the zoo. Felicity was shown fondling the little creature, which was unnerved by her electronic tenderness.

'Aaah! Isn't he gorgeous! Tomorrow I'm going back to the zoo to see how Clarence the camel's getting on. And it looks as if we might get some more nice sunny weather tomorrow, isn't that yummy? But now I'm afraid we've got some less happy news. Here's Bill to tell you about it.' Felicity coyly waved goodbye and William, a seasoned father figure computer with a rich baritone voice, directed his kindly baggy eyes at the camera.

'Yes, Felicity's right. Those of you at home who are mums and dads know that children can't always do just as they like. Well, the United Kingdom may not be as united as it once was but we all like to think of it as one big happy family. Recognize this place?' A picture of the Isle of Man flashed up on to the screen. 'I expect many of you have spent happy holidays there. Today I'm sad to say they've declared UDI. Here's what they think about it in the House of Commons . . . '

The baying and roaring of MPs rose above the cat calls and screams of laughter in the pub. Christy could hardly hear what followed and soon the publican turned it off.

'Got to go soon,' Beatrice said.

'Picked up someone in the toilets again, did you?' Rita sneered.

'Wouldn't be seen dead with any of this lot. I got a date down in Brixton, real classy guy, plenty of pin money. He'll buy me a meal, wine, steak – you coming?'

'You'd be less disgusting if you didn't act like you enjoy it. Degrading, that's what your life is.'

'Rita, I sometimes wonder how those twins of yours got born. You get immaculate conception or something? Course I enjoy it, and I'll tell you something else, I enjoy it a helluva lot more since I stopped drinking that Neuropepsi.' Laughing, Beatrice left the pub, left the other three feeling dull and old.

144

Christy thought bitterly, she's the only one likely to find out whether sex is better with or without Neuropepsi.

'Phone him,' Ellen said, watching her narrowly. And in the end it was Ellen who dialled Simon's number, standing beside Christy in the damp, fetid corridor outside the lavatories.

A fight had started outside the pub. When a brick came through the window the three women took it as a signal to leave. They picked their way through and around the battling men and women and walked back to Smiles, where Ellen picked up her sleeping child from Rita's tent. The twins, Dimelza and Beatrice's baby were curled up in a heap like puppies.

Christy stared enviously at the soft, warm bundle, wishing she had something half as comforting to hold in the night. The three women kissed, still charged with the exhilaration of their evening out. Christy turned and walked home over the mud, trying to keep to the hard ridges which had been baked by the days of sun. The slimy ruts were still foul ditches of garbage, soapy water, urine and shit, where rats swarmed. Briefly, at her mother's, Christy had been free of the diarrhoea that was one of the rewards of life at Smiles.

The lights of the pub and the desire in Simon's voice soon faded as the camp swallowed her up again. A party near the washhouse was ending in a fight; she could hear screams as bottles broke and a woman sobbed. The tents rumbled with coughs, moans, muttering, sighs, rasping breath, curses, children crying even in their sleep. Few people slept well or soundly. The fragile canvas structures shook as people tried to writhe into comfort on the lumpy ground, as couples made love for a few seconds of oblivion and the children listened with all their bodies to the adults' alien grunts and snorts. Because there was no electricity the night sky was always darker above Smiles, not a London sky at all. Christy looked up and saw the sleek, complacent knob of a full moon regulating their rising passions.

There was a light on in her caravan although she had left it padlocked. Either a friend had left the lamp lit to welcome her, which was dangerous, or Sean was waiting for her. She wasn't frightened. Already her eyes wore a veil of city tough-ness, behind which she could walk alone down unlit streets,

145

tread on dead rats and push her way through crowds of drunks. Christy wriggled her shoulders out of her backpack and swung it against the door to open it. Sean's face was tight, sullen and miserable, an expression which had once moved her very much.

'Hello! Thanks for putting the light on,' her voice breezed against his stony ruins.

'You stayed a long time.'

She sat on the floor, as far away from him as was possible in the tiny space. 'It was wonderful, I really feel as if I've had a holiday. Glorious walks and long talks with my mother – have an apple.'

She handed him a small, crinkled russet, the kind he loved, perfumed after a winter in an outbuilding. It was all she could give him. He thought so too as he ate it in five bites and waited.

'Well. What's been happening here?'

'The playgroup's fallen apart without you, so you'll be glad to know you're indispensable. Most of the kids have been playing down by the river, and your friend Simon hasn't turned up for days.'

'Really? What's the matter with him?'

'He lost his incentive for philanthropy and slumming. I expect he'll be back now.'

She looked down at the floor, away from his bitter face. He would attack me like this, she thought, making me feel guilty about the children, not mentioning any feelings he might have about me. *He* would never say, I missed you. She began to talk very fast, about anything but Simon.

'I heard a ridiculous thing on the news in the pub. The Isle of Man has declared UDI! I thought it was a spoof at first but they had all these extracts from speeches in the House of Commons, you know, the enemy within and the traitor at the gates, though how anyone can be both I don't understand. And then a marvellous man ranting at something called the Tynwald about tyranny and fighting for their ancient rights – Sean? Don't you think that's funny?'

'You didn't mind my coming in?'

'Of course not. It was rather nice to find the light on.'

'You weren't expecting anyone else?'

146

'Who?'

'Ellen. Or Simon?'

The name was like a mosquito in his brain. And the only way he could relieve the itching, red, ugly bumps was to think, talk, brood about him. Sean hadn't intended to mention him but the mosquito had just injected fresh poison into him.

'As a matter of fact I thought it was you.'

He reached out and put his hand on her bony brown fingers. Every night since she had left he had dreamt about her. She looked at him steadily but gave him no encouragement. On the way back from Devon she had decided that if she slept with Simon while she wasn't sleeping with Sean, it wouldn't be a betrayal. Her body had already entered into this pact and stiffened in nervous defiance.

Sean felt himself propelled back to the furthest corner of the narrow bed, the bed they had fallen off so many times in the middle of the night. It wasn't just her loss of sexual interest in him that hurt, that was an old story. But that she could want that nebbish, that droopy middle-class greyhound – one day soon her caravan would rock with their lust and he would have to lie alone listening . . . Sean thought of the fights between men and women he had seen and heard every night for years. He had intervened in some of them, but not recently, not since the screams of rage and disillusion echoed something in his own heart. He knew he ought to go home but he couldn't move.

Christy watched his muddy wall of a face. She felt cruel, greedy for change, glad that he had so little power to express his emotions. In the vacuum of his feelings hers flourished; she wanted to stride around big rooms and talk all night. But not to him. She got up and moved two paces to the tiny stove where she made them both some watery soup. Her fists were clenched again, the lines had dug themselves back into her forehead and she pushed her lips backwards and forwards between her teeth. Oh yes, she was back.

'Sean?'

'Christy?'

'I'm so tired. Please let me sleep.'

We used to talk until four in the morning, he thought as she handed him his consolation bag of apples.

Peeved but not heartbroken, Christy thought with relief as she slid under the blankets, fully dressed and unwashed.

The next morning was blue and gold with optimism. Crystal sunlight warmed and flattered the streets that drifted past Simon's bike. Sallow faces felt the sun awaken the blood beneath their skin and turned up like flowers to the benign sky. From the top of the North End Road market Simon could smell tableloads of strawberries bleeding sweetly. Windows glinted, children in bright cottons ran to school and the river was shot with silver and fluid turquoise. Above it gulls screeched and mocked, cynical urban birds swooping down on the swift current of garbage and dead fish. The river was dying though it still looked good in the right light. Simon's feet danced on the pedals, his eyes shone blue and he felt a tight thumping in his chest that was so unfamiliar he wondered if he was going to have a heart attack. No, he thought, I'm going to have a happiness, I'm going to see Christy and tell her I love her. His suddenly youthful eyes hunted out the details of the scene to record the image of hope.

Even in that light Smiles didn't shimmer, though the mud, corrugated iron and grey canvas looked a few shades lighter and the ragged washing strung between the tents more flag-like. He cycled straight to the playgroup and let in the four children waiting outside. The UN sacks had already been pulled to the door, which he took as evidence that Christy was around. As he mixed powdered milk in the big, red, plastic jug, the children watched in silence.

Simon's eyes were sharpened, either by love, hunger or by his few days' absence. He saw how inadequately the children were dressed, in shrunken ragged T-shirts and underpants full of holes. Only Lily's feet were covered, by fluffy yellow slippers that stuck out like boats. The others went barefoot though the mud bristled with broken glass and nails. Of all the children, only Dimelza, who hadn't arrived yet, was usually elaborately well-dressed in gaudy nylon frills.

The four little faces around the table were stained with their last meal before they went to bed, their eyes were coated with sleepy dust and their hair was tangled. As Lily smiled at him Simon noticed two rotten teeth. Soon they would have to delouse them again. The room, which seemed palatial to the

148

children compared to their tents, looked decrepit to Simon in the ruthless sunlight. Children's paintings and drawings half covered the huge patches of damp on the walls and the rotting lino floor was encrusted with paint, food, vomit and urine although it was scrubbed with disinfectant every day. The decay was like an insatiable fungus. Every piece of furniture and improvised toy was broken, the patches of cardboard and sellotape on the cracked windows had spread and the open plan stairs were a death trap for the smaller children.

Christy walked in while he was still in this mood of heightened awareness, and her face was the most vivid thing of all. Her skin was creamy and clear from her holiday and her greenish eyes were infinitely friendly as they held his. Then the children closed in and she was only visible from the waist up, doling out bread and caresses and orders. He kept his eyes on her face long after she had looked away from him. Once, her warm look as she came in would have been enough to keep him going for days. Now he wanted far more, he was prepared to follow her round all morning like the children, quieter but no less insistent. Simon extricated himself from the tiny wooden chair and went over to her for the pleasure of being close enough to smell her hair, to see her nostrils and dark lashes. She looked amused, then took a step backwards. She was as tall as him. It was as close as they'd ever been, a layer of children had always separated them.

Christy felt self-conscious. She knew he was staring at her all the time and tried to avoid looking back. She clenched her body as she passed him, but all the time his blue eyes were on her and he was smiling. He looked younger, rounder, happier. His face was a planet beaming light, the centre of energy in the room, again and again her eager eyes were attracted back to it.

Downstairs, Simon opened the door and the children, thirty of them now the word had got round that Christy was back, poured out in a screaming torrent. The big rectangle in the middle of the towers was baked mud with yellowing sprigs of grass trodden into it, like a head that pretends it isn't bald, Christy thought as she sat on a concrete slab that had dropped off one of the buildings. She moved up to make room for him, knowing he would come.

149

They sat there side by side watching the children and, surreptitiously, each other. Their legs stuck out, four shabby blue cotton parallel lines. It was strange to sit like that, within touching distance of a woman he had once thought unattainable. To test the point, Simon took her thin brown hand and spread it out in his heavier ones to examine her square topped fingers with their dirty nails. She sat back and watched her hand as if it was a toy he was mending. She didn't want to be openly affectionate to him here, in front of the kids and unknown eyes at the blank windows. But touching him was so natural and inevitable, she put her other arm around him and felt his sinewy back sweating through his shirt.

'As I was saying on the phone, I did miss you.'

'I thought about you a lot while I was away.'

'Where *did* you go?'

'To see my mother, in Devon. Didn't Sean tell you?'

'He didn't seem to want to, and Ellen didn't have your address. I was so afraid you weren't coming back.'

'It's not so easy to get away from Smiles.'

'Do you want to?'

'Not really, I've nowhere else to go. It was idyllic at my mother's, for a few days, but then I found I was thinking about this place all the time. About you. So I thought I might as well come back.'

'I want to see more of you, Christy, not just your Mother Earth side.'

'Hardly that. More like Old Mother Hubbard.'

'Well whatever. Without any children around.'

'I've thought about that too but I don't see where we can go. We can't go to my caravan because Sean will be next door listening to every sound we make – you can hear everything through those tinny walls. And I can't go home with you.'

'Well, we'll have to go – out.'

Remote memories stirred of taking women out to cinemas and restaurants. He couldn't imagine Christy in either. 'Anyway, why can't we go back to my flat?'

'Well, because of your wife. And your son – he must live with you sometimes?' She thought he might have one of those legendary, excruciating open marriages. That woman with the little round glasses ushering her into a smart bedroom.

'But my wife's dead, and Merlin's still with my parents.'

'When did she die? She came here last year.'

Simon was still sufficiently impressed by Jessica's powers to drop her hand and gasp. 'Oh. You mean Rose, my sister. I asked her to come and explain when I was ill.'

'Terribly chic and sharp looking?'

'That's her.'

'So there's no reason to hold back and look over our shoulders all the time and feel guilty?'

'Well. There's Sean.'

'Oh, I don't feel guilty about him.'

Christy kissed him with enthusiasm, keeping her eyes wide open to see how he would take it.

A loud wolf whistle came from one of the abandoned buildings.

'I can't say I feel altogether comfortable here.' But he didn't let go of her.

Dimelza came up to them. The awful thing about her, Christy often thought, is that at three she probably has seen it all.

'Izzy your boyfriend now? Izzy gointer take his trousers down?'

Simon sighed as Dimelza climbed on to his knee and he and Christy withdrew back into their own bodies. 'What's the matter?'

Dimelza was weeping, hot salt trickling down her chin to her chest.

'They come and took Douane away.'

'Oh. Did he pinch things from a shop again?'

'Only sweeties. They put him in prison.'

'No, it's not a prison. It's like a big house with lots of toys and children. I'll take you to see him.'

'They gointer beat the shit outavim, my mum says.'

'No. They'll be kind to him, he's only seven.'

'Yeah? They got a lot of toys there?'

'Millions.'

'They send me there, next time I take sweeties?'

'You can't go, we'd miss you. But I'll take you to see Douane in a few days.'

She ran off. Christy frowned. 'Now a rich kid could loot

half Harrods' toy department without being taken into care.'

'I know.'

'His mummy and daddy would just pay for him to have analysis.'

'Yes,' said Simon, remembering how Madge had almost forced Rose into going to see a psychiatrist when she was twelve and kept telling her mother she didn't like her. 'It's an excuse to get kids away from mothers like Beatrice.'

'She's not so bad. She doesn't hit them much, and she does feed them and keep them fairly clean, when she's there.'

'Which is never, at night.'

'If she was a high class whore with a flat in Chelsea the authorities wouldn't mind.'

'We're the authorities. I'll phone Jill, see what I can do. Say I think the three children are better off together.'

'Then they'll take them all in. Children's homes are about the only growth industry at the moment. I read a report on them last month; the government's afraid of a generation of criminals and subversives being bred in these camps, so they're herding kids into homes to teach them traditional values, whatever they might be.'

'It would help if they'd just let them into the schools.'

'Can't have them contaminating the hearts and minds of true little Brits. How's your son by the way?'

'That was a snide association, Christy.'

'I can't help it. When I'm looking at this lot I always start to wonder about the budding elite, privileged little sods like him.'

'He is and he isn't. Privileged.'

'I suppose he can afford to have emotional problems.'

They sat in silence, further away from each other than before. Christy felt bitter and Simon was exhausted at the prospect of all the justifying he was going to have to do to her. In a way he wanted to lay himself down in front of her and let her judge him. But it would be such hard work – he felt her hand on his again and grasped it.

'I'm steeling myself for your disapproval.'

'Of what?'

'Oh, of most of what I am.'

'I don't even know yet. When are we going to meet properly?'

152

'Come home with me this afternoon.'

'I've got a meeting at four. About these ridiculous antics on the Isle of Man, everyone's really angry about it.'

'What's happening exactly? I haven't been following it.'

'I bought the *Morning Glory* today for the first time in months. You know the island's a Crown Possession but has its own parliament and has always made its own laws and collected its own taxes? Well the government's revoked their rights and tried to close down their parliament, the Tynwald. It's a terribly rich place, if they had to pay standard taxes there'd be pots of money in it for the government. Anyway, they had a big ceremony at the Tynwald a few days ago to declare independence. There was a picture of all these dignified-looking men, like druids, sitting outside a tent on top of a hill. They've mined the waters at Peel and Douglas and closed the airport at Ronaldsway, cancelled all holidays there and deported the Lieutenant Governor and all non-residents. They've got full employment and one of the highest per capita incomes in Europe so, they say, who needs Britain?'

'Great,' said Simon, vaguely approving of bloody mind-edness.

'Only there's probably going to be a war. The government's threatening to send the fleet.'

'You're joking?'

'Well, actually there are only two ships left in the Navy, but they are talking about sending both of them, with some very fancy missiles they've been dying to try out.'

'I'll come to the meeting with you,' Simon said hurriedly as they heard screams of pain. One of the twins had stepped on a rusty nail and had to be carried to the first aid box.

153

CHAPTER 17

✿✿✿✿✿✿✿✿✿✿✿✿✿✿✿✿✿✿✿✿✿✿✿✿✿✿✿

When he saw them come into the portakabin together, as a couple, Sean flinched and looked at Christy so reproachfully that she wished she hadn't decided to brazen it out. But he was, of course, chairing the meeting and his eloquence was far too professional to be disturbed for more than an instant. He's got what Martin, who had it too, called the gift of the gab, Christy thought, watching that elastic and expressive feature.

'. . . Look at this headline in today's *Evening Hope*: KNOCK KNEED KNOCK-E-DOONEY SWINE. And a picture of some people clutching old rifles and sticks and breadknives. Then on page five there's a competition with a "Britannia Rules The Tynwald" T-shirt if they print your joke about the Mangy Manxies, as they insist on calling them. Do you know how much their gunboat diplomacy's going to cost, even if they don't invade or nuke them as people were demanding outside the Commons at lunchtime? Enough to rehouse us all and feed us for the rest of our lives. . .'

Simon was surprised at the anger he saw and felt all around. He had always been saddened by the apathy at Smiles. If people were able to tolerate such conditions, their spirits and bodies diminished but not actually broken, how were things ever going to improve? But today there was fire in the air, he sniffed it with relief and stared at the man who had kindled it. Rivalry apart, he would never have expected that Sean, so sour in private, could be such a powerful speaker.

There were faces at the window and more people crowded in at the door. All their eyes were wide with that feverish vitality that comes to people who suddenly realize there is something they can do. When he saw how many people there were Sean, with real showmanship, ushered them outside

154

where he stood on a table and let them surround him. He felt hot, light, elated with the joy of righteous indignation. He saw he was influencing them, even those two sneaking their arms around each other. The words pounded, swift and rhythmic like hoof beats in his brain.

'. . . I can see new faces all around me. You've woken up, haven't you? Well, are you going back to sleep, are you going to lie there snoring while the government kick you again and waste millions intimidating a few people on a tiny island?'

'No!'

'Shall we go to the House of Commons now and tell them what we think? They're marching from all over London, from the Squattery and Eel Brook Common and Tent City. They're stopping the traffic and blocking the roads, reminding all those fat politicians what poverty looks like. Reminding them we've got opinions too, and we don't live with mud and rats and empty bellies because we like it, and when the money that should be spent on us is spent on a stupid, pointless, hysterical little war, we know what to do about it. Shall we show them that?'

'YES!'

Ellen thought, as she yelled with them, we sound like children at a pantomime. We're so used to letting things happen to us that we'll accept any leader, whether it's Sean or some creep from the Ministry of Leisure doling out Neuropepsi and sympathy. Ellen jumped up, cheered by Christy, Beatrice and Rita. She looked very small and waiflike. As she spoke she clutched Jack and played with his fingers.

'I don't think marching's such a good idea. They don't care what we think, those platinum shits in the House of Commons, none of them does. We can't vote, we've no pinability, no rights. Until we get Britcards, until we're people again, we can't fight them. It's been tried before, I've seen it, I've been here longer than any of you, since I was ten. When the camps started, in the late eighties, there was marches and fires and riots all the time. My dad died in one of them. Then they introduced rations and Neuropepsi and Britcards and we all went quiet.'

'So what are we supposed to do? Carry on sitting here like idiots?' Sean felt their energy and anger grow diffuse again;

155

already people were wandering away, he wanted to drag them back and galvanize them into the action and violence his soul longed for. He quick-witted fury contrasted with Ellen's slow doggedness.

'No. But we've got to be clever this time, and clear about what we want. I think this war's a red herring, they wouldn't spend the money on us anyway. If we go marching up to Westminster now there'll be street fighting, arrests, tomorrow we'll be back here and they'll forget about us again. I think we should move the camp out there.'

'What?' Sean asked incredulously. A few people laughed, others moved forward to hear what she had to say.

'Otherwise they'll never see what it's like, will they? I think we should take our tents, kids, cripples, babies.' She hugged Jack and smiled at her idea, which surprised her as much as anyone else. 'Set up a sort of replica Smiles. Squat in front of the Houses of Parliament, what about those gardens by the river? Go up there quietly, a few at a time so they don't get too suspicious.'

'Use Ted's lorry to move the tents and babies and the old geezers as can't walk,' Beatrice yelled gleefully. She had it in for Ted, having eaten his rotten vegetables and fruit for years, and led a dozen women over the rubble to his lorry. Ted had heard the unaccustomed shouting and excitement; he had been scared ever since they smashed up his supplies of Neuro-pepsi and when he saw them rushing towards him he tried to drive away. But a group of them had already broken into the back of the lorry. He saw them in his mirror, looting and wrecking. They seemed more interested in his lorry than in him, and although it was his only source of livelihood he knew he was lucky to escape. They're tough, these Smiles women, he thought as he jumped down from the cab and ran away. Castrate you soon as look at you. And he ran towards the bridge, ignoring the jeers of the women, to warn the True Brit Information Agency at Fulham Broadway that there were subversive, unpinable goings on at the camp. They would get his lorry back for him and compensate him for riot damage.

Laughing uncontrollably, the women shared out Ted's rotten goods and filled the back of the lorry with tents, sleeping bags and people too old or too young to walk. Beatrice scrawled 'Whores against Wars' with a felt tipped pen on the side of the lorry. They were all whooping with laughter and triumph because they were going to revenge themselves on their enemies, they were on the move at last, they were going to show them.

When Sean saw the way things were going he shrugged and joined the group around a radio an ex-engineer had rigged up. They crowded around it to hear snatches of the Manx debate in the House of Commons, interrupted by news bulletins announcing arrests and traffic jams. Sean, suddenly very quiet, hunched over it listening to the voices. Although it was called a debate there seemed to be no difference of opinion between the government and the opposition voices. Their voices rose together in a crescendo of jingoism.

'. . . Lords of Man have been English since Edward the Third took the islands in 1333 –'

'Crown Possession –'

'. . . Our kith and kin turning on us –'

'. . . audacious and unreasonable demands –'

'. . . interests of national security –'

'. . . and setting up their own tinpot dictatorship over sixty-five thousand people –'

'. . . didn't let Hitler get away with it either –'

'We're interrupting this live debate to tell you that Victoria Street and Whitehall are still impassable. Back again to the House of Commons where the Right Honourable Member for Chalk Farm East is telling the House about his experiences as a tank driver in Tobruk.'

'Order! Order!'

'. . . and as the fleet sails from Llandudno let our hearts go with her –'

'. . . forget at last our differences of party –'

'. . . one nation –'

'. . . traitors –'

'. . . defeatism –'

'. . . we need no lessons in patriotism –'

'. . . Britain's resolve.'

Some courageous MP (Sean couldn't hear his name or party) appealed for calm in a breaking voice. 'I'm not a unilateralist or a defeatist or anything like that, but I don't think we should go to war over a little issue like this. It's not as if our national survival is threatened. Killing's wrong, people are going to die if those ships land on the island.'

A baying and growling and thumping, as if a pack of pedigree dogs had smelt blood, emanated from the loudspeaker.

'. . . Spreading alarm and despondency –'

'. . . lightweight liberal intellectuals –'

'. . . not a game of croquet!'

(And, bellowing above the rest:)

'You're a disgrace to your school, your regiment and your country!'

A few more voices spoke up against the invasion. The debate became an inaudible uproar punctuated by a voice begging for order.

Someone turned the radio off and Sean found himself transported from the corridors of power to the pits of jealousy. He watched them pretend to quarrel about something, use the mock argument as an excuse to brush against each other and laugh. The next time he looked their arms were around each other. They were cut off from him in a floodlit bubble. *She never flirted with me like that. The trouble with desire is it's beautiful to the participants but brutal and ugly to the beholder. The trouble with being the beholder is that you see too much, you're always in the way as you flounder on the sharp slimy rocks of wounded dignity and self pity.* Sean turned and stumbled away from them.

After the wet spring it had been dry and sunny for weeks; flowers and decorative weeds were sprouting all over Smiles and people lived outside far more than usual. Simon thought, *this mood has fallen on them since the somnolence of Neuropepsi lifted like a curse, since the sun came out. The flowers and the lively faces give Smiles a Neapolitan look. Although why a slum in southern Italy should be more attractive than a slum in South London I can't think.* He stood with his arms around Christy, who still thought they were being discreet. She was aware of Sean a few yards away, crouched silently over the radio, and something in her triumphed at his defeat. She was glad the people in the camp were acting for themselves at last, glad for them and also because Sean's pseudo-

158

bureaucracy had ruled long enough. He glanced up at her, saw the spleen in her face, flinched and quickly took shelter in the radio again. Christy was relieved when he ran away and stopped watching them, judging them like God.

Many people had already drifted over Wandsworth Bridge. Children were rushing around with plastic bags full of clothes and broken toys as if they were going off on holiday. Dimelza and Lily had jumped off the lorry as it lurched towards the river and now followed Mick who wore his clown costume and played a melancholy tune on his trumpet. Sarah stood behind her grandfather in his cumbersome rickety pushcart. She was exhausted because she had already pushed him up to Sloane Square and now he was nagging her to go back again north of the river, something to do with the government. Sarah didn't know or care what he was on about but wished he'd lost the use of his voice instead of his legs. Then she saw the lorry had stopped again, and rushed over to beg for a lift. Hands reached out of the back and hauled up her astonished grandfather in his pushcart. He was another scar to exhibit at Westminster. Sarah's frozen little face thawed as she saw him disappear, she turned and rushed over to Dimelza and Lily, danced off with them over the bridge.

Caught up in the anarchic carnival gaiety, Christy and Simon also wandered towards the bridge. All around them people danced, ran, walked, surged towards the centre. Christy thought, it's as if, as Sean said, we really have woken up, only to abandon ourselves immediately to another dream-filled sleep, a more spontaneous and active one. It's so unreal anyway, to be walking with Simon like this. Our arms around each other; I can't separate one fantasy from the other. It's dangerous up there, it must be, riot police and street fighting. I'm scared of violence, I'm sure we're walking into some kind of a trap. But the city's on the move, it's my city, I've got to go. On the bridge she turned back and looked at Smiles, empty now, shining in the late summer afternoon. Even the zonkies had left their island.

On the other side of the bridge they passed Ted's lorry, which had stopped again. Beatrice waved at Christy and offered her a lift but Christy shook her head. After a lot of argument about how to drive the lorry, which way to go and

159

what to do when they got there, the hijackers decided to go through South London and to stop as close as they could get to Lambeth Bridge. Rita, who was driving, performed a wild U-turn and shuddered back over the bridge.

All the shops in the Wandsworth Bridge Road had closed early and from the gentrified flats on the upper stories terrified faces peered out. Cars had been abandoned in the middle of the road when their owners had heard on the radio news about the hordes of scroungers, zonkies and unpinables invading central London.

Simon wondered if at the end of the Roman Empire, when the Franks and Visigoths looted and destroyed the last Imperial villas and decadent cities, there were people whose sympathies were split: the offspring of Roman matrons raped by Frankish warriors, perhaps. People who despised the clapped out remnants of an exhausted civilization but also feared the destructive force of new blood. People like him, who really wanted to duck beneath the ruthless waves of history but who were instead swept out into the open sea to be battered by hidden rocks. Simon caught himself wondering if his windows would be broken by this crowd he was a part of. Just in front of him a group of men whom he recognized from Smiles walked four abreast with their arms around each other, chanting:

'Which side are you on, boys,
Which side are you on?'

The rough, jeering voices reminded Simon that there were only two sides that afternoon.

There was no organized marching or slogan chanting and, strangest of all, no police although they could hear sirens in the distance. They turned into the New King's Road and met another human river flowing east. On Eel Brook Common people were hurrying out of their tents and shacks to join them and here too the shops and houses were locked, barricaded against a violence that had not so far been unleashed. All these people moved silently, swiftly, their faces made impersonal by a fury they were not even conscious of. Many carried iron bars, bottles and sticks. Christy thought, if someone fell over now they'd be trampled at once and none of us would notice the squashy mess beneath our feet. Nothing can stop us now.

160

Above their heads a police helicopter hovered; infra-red cameras surveyed the long snake winding from Putney Bridge to Westminster and photographed the faces twisted with fear and hatred, turned up towards it. The streets were empty, they possessed the streets at last.

A jeep drove towards them very fast, honking continuously on the four opening notes of 'Rule Britannia'. It bristled with union jacks and angry men who stood on the seats waving their arms and shouting through loudhailers. Just in time, people in their path realized the jeep wasn't going to swerve out of the way and ran screaming to the pavements. As the jeep drove towards them Christy heard a high-pitched man's voice scream: 'Scum! Traitors! We spit on you! We shit on you! Go back to the sewers where you came from! Black bastards, go back to the jungles! Breeding like rabbits in your filthy slums . . .'

The patriots' jeep tore a ragged hole in the crowd, drove straight through it so fast that there was no time to do anything except get out of its way. Then there was a lot of shouting and running about to establish that no one was hurt. Later that seemed to Christy the one auspicious event; the bloodshed could so easily have started then. The patriots would have been glad to mow down a few traitors and some of the marchers would have pulled them out of their jeep and beaten them up if there had been time to grab them.

The wide empty road ahead was no longer reassuring now that they all expected some kind of ambush. Their feet rang on the hot tarmac. Simon was surprised to see so many shops boarded up. How had the authorities known they were coming when they hadn't known themselves? The stagnant heat of the early evening held a menace, a foreknowledge of violence. He wished it would get dark so that they could hide, disperse. At Sloane Square they were joined by another huge crowd, coming from North London. All traffic on the way to Westminster had been diverted, Central London had been turned into a stage for them, a deserted, artificial setting for their drama.

Now that they were so many they were packed closer together and moved for a while as a procession. Rumours hissed through the crowd like fireworks: the armed police were

161

waiting for them at Victoria, they would never get through to Westminster, the helicopter above their heads was about to discharge grenades of puking gas. With no leaders to bellow instructions or give them a sense of identity, the tension built up to an unbearable pitch.

Then at Pimlico the human river divided again into many tributaries as people fled to the Embankment, through the Royal Hospital Gardens and down side-streets towards West-minster. Outside houses in Belgravia armed guards stood ready to shoot at the first sign of violence from the mob. Christy and Simon followed the main flow of people down the main roads to Victoria Street. The crowd surged on to the pavements, conscious of its power, no longer silent. Individual men and women screamed battle cries which were quickly taken up by those around them: 'Britcards, shitcards!' 'Burn the Pigs!' Verbal violence swept them forward, made their hearts pound, their breathless voices choke with excitement and fear. A few streets away they could hear screams and breaking glass. They knew the police were waiting for them. Their anger was inflamed by the sight of people huddled together in shops and in Victoria Station, staring down from upper windows, waiting in fear for the tempest of collective hatred to pass.

Christy was almost relieved when the destruction began. Above Victoria Station there was a huge holographic ad for Neuropepsi. Children held hands around a giant can of Neuropepsi, laughing and dancing up towards the sky, singing their angelic, moronic jingle twenty-four hours a day:

'We are the Neuropopsies
Full of joy and pep.'

Beneath the ad the crowd stopped, so abruptly that Christy and Simon were nearly crushed. Then people started to throw their weapons up at the image in the sky, although they must have known it was indestructible. The source of light and sound was hidden away somewhere, probably in the roof of a building opposite. They ran out of missiles, overturned a fruit barrow and started to hurl apples and tomatoes, most of which hit the onlookers sheltering in the station, who shrieked and moved further inside. The shrill voices of the Neuropopsies warbled on, an unsatisfactory target. People looked around for more concrete ways of unleashing their anger. The remaining

162

fruit was handed round and Christy and Simon munched apples, just as, a few minutes before, they had screamed, 'Burn the Pigs!' Around them people ran off to loot shops in the arcade and in Victoria Street. Those who had been sheltering there, thinking it was neutral territory, scattered in terror. As the crowd broke up Christy felt lucid again. It was as if her own will had been paralyzed by the epidemic of violence.

She turned to Simon who also looked dazed. 'We've got to get to Westminster. See if the others are there, help them put up the camp if that's what they want. I don't want to get involved in all this looting, it's pointless.'

'We'll never get through to Westminster now. We might as well go home – will you come home with me?'

'Not now. We've got to find the others.'

As she spoke a helicopter flew low over their heads and a cloud of puking gas blinded them, forced their stomachs and guts inside out. With the sickness came a fiery headache. Blindly they ran in the direction of Victoria Street where they found more puking gas, screams, sirens, groans, thumps, shattering glass and the gentle buzz of a helicopter swooping down to puke on them again. Christy was almost certain that she could hear bullets from the new police guns whip through the air, and that some of the screams came from their victims.

After that they only ran, only wanted to escape from the acute discomfort of their own bodies. Sometimes the blindness is permanant, Christy recalled as she ran, her arm locked in Simon's. Together they barged into parked cars, lampposts, other stumbling nauseous figures. The smell of vomit was everywhere, the taste of it was in her nostrils. Imprinted on her sightless eyeballs was the image of Sean, arrested and beaten up, a crumpled heap in a cell.

Outside the main entrance of the House of Commons a circle of MPs and policemen surrounded the babies and cripples of Smiles who lay in a filthy heap on the hot tarmac. Most of the babies were crying but the older eyesores just stared back. Sarah's grandfather was enjoying the attention and the change of place, and wondered if they'd be offered a drink. They were too young and too old to be arrested. Several of the onlookers resisted the impulse to pick up the babies and cuddle them, remembering the danger of infection.

CHAPTER 18

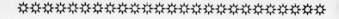

When they recovered their sight and balance they were leaning on the Embankment wall, their arms around each other. Christy had always been irritated by the phrase, they know not what they do. She liked to think that she knew exactly what she was doing and therefore required neither forgiveness nor serious doses of guilt. In this case, she was walking away from Sean, who might need her help, with Simon whom she loved and desired. They were going to consummate their desire in his flat, which she still pictured as a rich man's, pied-à-terre, that was the phrase. With a huge corrupt bed, a flashy bathroom where everything worked and lots of new expensive furniture. Nothing about her companion (certainly not his clothes) suggested this kind of tasteless lifestyle. Perhaps it was something she had imagined as a schoolgirl, her seduction by a rich man. Or perhaps it had to do with the fact he had been an architect and carried with him the confident aura of a man who has never slept out or gone hungry or regarded those conditions as more than the subject of anecdotes. She was sure he had a Britcard, at least a gilt-edged one, although he had never mentioned it or flashed it around. Yet all that time he'd helped at Smiles . . . Smiles wasn't to be thought of just now. Christy made an effort to focus on the real Simon beside her.

But for all her resolve to fall in love efficiently the night made its own terms. They walked beside the river where patchy white clouds like cobblestones with silver light cementing the cracks shimmered in the dark waters and leaned together on the wall opposite Battersea Park.

'The kids are always asking me to take them to that theme park they've built in the old gasworks.' Christy was surprised to find it was so difficult not to talk or think about Smiles. 'Didn't you say your father builds those things?'

'Did I say that?' He had certainly had no intention of telling her so much, yet.

'Well does he?'

'Yes. He built that new one in the old Chelsea football ground. Almost next door to where I live.'

'Don't look so ashamed. You can't help what your father does, mine might be a murderer for all you know.'

'Really?' he asked hopefully.

'He buggered off when I was twelve, I don't really know what he's been up to since.'

They stood and watched the river. It was high tide and the water was at its most domineering, lapping at the bottom of their wall and sweeping fiercely out of the city. He looked at Christy to find out what she felt, if she felt – she was staring down at the river with great concentration. Her thick dark frizz of hair hid her eyes, so he pushed it back to see them. They were quite dark that night, tabby grey with brown flecks and only a hint of green when the street light shone on them. Swimming in her face like tail-less fish over her stumpy pier of a nose.

'Is it all right if we go back now?'

'Yes. Let's go.' But her face, even her big, expressive mouth, was unnaturally still.

'Are you worried about leaving Sean there?'

'Yes. It puts him in the right, you see. Never mind. We'll go now.' She turned away from the wall, gave him her hand and they walked slowly along the Embankment. Christy kept staring into the shadowy depths beyond the last houseboat, towards Wandsworth. The rest of her was with Simon and happy to be there.

Christy was surprised and reassured by the shabbiness of his flat. It was a natural extension of him, worn, kind and a bit neglected. She liked the sitting room overlooking the garden, specially when Simon disregarded the warm night and lit a fire. But she couldn't sit by it, she picked up the glass of wine he'd poured her and wandered down the corridor opening doors.

'What are you looking for?' Simon asked nervously.

'Bluebeard's wives.'

'There was only one.'

'And where is she?'

'In the garden, most of the time.'

'We'll see about that.'

She stared at Merlin's room, struck by the wealth of toys. Not since she was a child, before Martin left, had she seen a room so suggestive of comfort and security and indulgence. Then she felt sad because it wasn't really so, not for this child either. For a few years he had been a little prince on his rocking horse with his Winnie the Pooh wallpaper. Then his mother had died and his father had dumped him; who knew what he was suffering now? Simon switched the light off.

'You're keeping the room for him?'

'He's coming back soon. When I get things sorted out.'

'When will that be?'

'Not tonight.'

He guided her into his bedroom. She was the first woman to stand there since Madge's visit just after Jessica's death. To him it was the most haunted room of all but she thought it utterly bleak, as desolate in its way as the shacks at Smiles. One uneven door swung from the cupboard, the empty dressing table had a thick fur of dust, the curtains didn't draw properly and leaked a sickly yellow light from the street. His clothes hung in the half-built cupboard all crooked, like corpses dancing gawkily on an improvised gibbet.

Gravely they sat on the bed and kissed. With some bitterness Christy thought, it's all going to end up with the usual fumble and rush. Clothes off and at each other. It was one of her complaints against men that they didn't give her enough time to enjoy sex. She had always felt Sean was fitting her in between meetings and now, more than ever, she needed time to filter her impressions of Simon's flat, his body and soul and the curious new world they were entering together that night. She wanted to enter it gradually, not with competitive gymnastics.

To her surprise he only took off her shoes and his own and lay back on the pillows with her.

'I'm out of practice.'

'Let's just talk. Is there some way we can keep that horrible

166

bilious light out? It makes you look like a skeleton with jaundice and I hate to think what I look like.'

'Like an angel of light come to cleanse the tomb. I'll light some candles.'

'Couldn't we go into the other room? It seems – friendlier,' she said as he found and lit four candles which he arranged in brass candlesticks on the dressing table. 'Now it's like an altar. You're not religious, are you?'

'Not in any orthodox way. But I have a strong sense of ritual.'

'I'm not sure I want to be that much of a cult. Are you Catholic?' she added suspiciously.

'I'm half-Jewish, but we'll go into that another time. Is the light less off-putting now?'

'I feel I've come out of the morgue and into the chapel.' They lay down side by side again. Effigies, she thought.

'Don't worry, I'm not a religious maniac. But I need all this before I can talk to you. This is the room my wife died in. I can't make love to you until you know more about her.'

'When did she die?'

'Two and a half years ago, a few months before I first came to Smiles.'

'How?'

'She took an overdose of sleeping pills and half a bottle of brandy.' He was surprised she couldn't still smell the brandy on the sheets. He could.

'Where were you?'

'At my parents', they had a party there and I stayed the night. She didn't believe me, she thought I was having an affair, she was always waiting for me to fall in love with someone else.'

'Did you?'

'I slept with one other woman while I was married to Jessica. A very bright young architect, Dicken, I met her at a conference in Bath. But it wasn't – serious.'

'Would it have been if Jessica had done it?'

'I don't know. I couldn't have told her though, she would have over-reacted.'

Christy sighed. And Simon nearly got up to put the light on, he found her tone so unsympathetic and professional. But they forged on.

167

'Why wasn't she at the party?'

'They always invited her but she didn't like it there. She thought they patronized her. Maybe they did. She was always very quiet and nervous with them.'

'What about your son?'

'Oh, he came along with me, he's always got on very well with them. They're good grandparents.'

'Had she ever tried to do herself in before?'

'I don't think so. But she talked about it a lot, it was her way of hitting back at life. And funnily enough – I don't mean it's funny, but you know what I mean – now it seems to me inevitable. She was the type who dies young. She never bothered to learn from her experience, as if she knew she wasn't going to need it.'

'People's deaths always seem inevitable, you know, when they're dead. Who found her?'

'I did. I came back early the next morning with Merlin, to take him to school.'

'So he saw the body?'

'Yes.'

'And how long after that did your parents take him away?'

'There was no force involved. I think he was glad to go there – to such a comfortable, orderly household – and frankly so was I. I couldn't cope with myself then, let alone with a child. My sister Rose said I was like a tree that had been shrivelled and blasted but was still standing. In the space of a month Jessica died, Merlin went to live with my parents and I left my job.'

'Why did you do that?'

'I'd been losing interest for years. My idealism peaked when I was a student, it never seemed such a glorious vocation once I was doing it. Pretending to beautify and improve when really I just made cities even uglier, never got a chance to build an original house or, at the other end of the scale, houses for people who really needed them. Never built anything I was proud of.'

'So it wasn't accidental, your coming to Smiles?'

'I couldn't live here alone without working, so I went to a volunteers' agency. They asked me what my interests were and I said architecture and children. I missed Merlin so much. So they sent me there – rather imaginative of them really. As a matter of fact, for the first few months I did have a crazy idea I'd rebuild the place, lead and organize a community that people could construct and run themselves. Then I saw I hadn't the ability, and nobody would follow me even if I knew where I was going. So I stayed for the children. And later because of you.'

Her silence was terrible. He began to dread that his self-exposure had made her despise him. She wasn't touching him, she lay parallel and quite separate.

'Is this the way you interview your cases?'

'I'm not usually in bed with them.'

'I mean the cool, detached manner.'

'Semi-detached. I think your story's very sad, but I hear sad stories every day. I feel sorry for your son.'

'Now tell me something that makes you feel guilty, any memory that makes you squirm. Go on.'

She saw him glaring at her and the passion in his eyes finally aroused some in her.

'All right. I'll tell you something I've never told anyone. When I first came to London I was eighteen, I was very lonely and I didn't have any money. My mother didn't have any either so I couldn't ask her for help, anyway I desperately wanted to show her I could look after myself. Quite soon I ended up in a hostel near King's Cross, a great concrete barn of a place with huge dormitories. Every room stank of disinfectant and the lights were never switched off, so that the warden could come quickly when he heard screams.

'You were only supposed to stay in the hostel for a month but if you found a job they sent you on to another organization that gave you your own room. Me and six or seven others used to get up at dawn each morning to go and queue for kitchen jobs in restaurants in the West End. They would only hire you by the day, you got eight pounds which covered the hostel and meals and left something for the following day, in case you weren't taken on again. About once a year someone would get a full-time job in one of these restaurants, that was our highest ambition. Though we all hated the work, everybody in those filthy kitchens did, you wouldn't believe the foul language about customers. If anyone

169

complained about their food we'd spit on it and send it back.

'Anyway, I used to work about four days a week. We walked everywhere to save fares, I remember setting off through the shiny dark streets, there were so many of us we sounded like horses. When I got back to the hostel in the evening I had to rush to the warden's room to get him to put the money in his safe before someone stole it. It was really violent there, much worse than at Smiles. A couple of people were killed in fights there. I think it was because they were all solitaries, most of them on booze or drugs or whatever they could get.

'The worst time was at night. There were twenty women in our dormitory, me and four other girls who tried to work, and a lot of much older women. Some of them must have been about the age I am now but they seemed decrepit, ancient stinking bundles of rags that didn't eat, just drank meths and stuffed themselves with pills and coughed and swore. They hated us, and I see now we hated them because we were terrified of turning into them. We were always asking the warden to put us in a separate dormitory but there was no room and of course the more we complained the more we were hated. There was no privacy at all, at work or at the hostel.

'Most nights the men came into our dormitory. It was all supposed to be segregated but there was only one warden, who must have been exhausted, he only came in the night if he heard screams. We didn't scream, we were too frightened. So I suppose it wasn't rape. All those men were violent, I'd seen them fighting downstairs in the canteen. I just used to lie there and hope it was a young one, who wouldn't smell too much or be so heavy. Someone different every night and you couldn't even hide because the lights were on. I think if it had been in the dark I would have pretended it hadn't happened. All under the neon lights in complete silence, except for the grunts and wheezes and coughs. And one of those women used to screech with laughter.

'In the morning we all had breakfast together. Those girls were my friends but we never talked about it. You might find yourself buttering a roll opposite a man who had stuck his cock down your throat the night before and he wouldn't even say good morning.

'The warden said I could stay another month and then get

my own room if I was taken on full time. I didn't want to stay there but I couldn't think what else to do. I think I had a sort of breakdown, I shook all the time and cried, and I couldn't eat or sleep properly. I couldn't get up to go to work so the warden said I'd have to leave. One night I was sick all over one of the men when he got into my bed and he hit me.

'The next morning I got up, put my clothes in a carrier bag and hitched to my mother's. I took a knife and I was really going to use it if anyone touched me. My mother could see I wasn't well, she fed me and calmed me down. I told her these stories about poverty in London, but as if I had been watching it from the distance. She believed me and went on and on about how wonderful I was, helping people. I began to believe in this marvellous girl we'd invented together. I thought I could even go back to London as long as I knew Rachel was still there, imagining me to be happy and good. She's very puritanical and perhaps I am too. Then after two weeks in Devon I missed a period. I couldn't face telling her, or going to our GP who'd known me since I was a child. So I asked her for some money to do an evening course in social work, though I knew she didn't have any to spare.

'She borrowed some from a friend and gave it to me, of course. Most of it went on an abortion. That was a great relief, I felt it hacked out of me those nights in the hostel. I got a full-time job as a waitress in a restaurant in the Strand and managed to rent a room and pay for a part-time Playleader's course. I felt rich. I went to judo lessons too, I became really good at it and used it on any man who grabbed me.

'When they closed down the hostels and the camps began to form I had plenty of work. I ran a playgroup at a camp in Southall before I went to Smiles. I worked bloody hard, everyone said how dedicated I was and it was true. But I could only work like that because I was driven by my terror of sinking down there again, being like the people I was supposed to help.'

Simon was looking at her, she knew, with far more warmth and sympathy than she had given him. He saw her face was flushed and tearful, that they were at last open to each other, receptive and vulnerable like two mussels whose shells had just opened to reveal a quivering, naked centre. He blew out the candles, took his clothes off and slid into the bed. Christy took off her clothes and turned to hold him very tightly, burying her mouth in the smooth salty flesh of his shoulder. He's so warm, she thought, I'll never be cold again.

CHAPTER 19

✿✿✿✿✿✿✿✿✿✿✿✿✿✿✿✿✿✿✿✿✿✿✿✿✿

They hardly slept. All night long they jolted back into consciousness because time was too precious to waste sleeping now there was somebody else to share it with. Again and again they made love, muttered words of love, told stories of old love. Even in their jerky bouts of sleep they turned together, wrapping limbs possessively around the astonishing fact of their love.

In the garden Jessica walked away and dissolved into the weeds.

In their anxiety not to let go they occupied about a third of the double bed. The next morning Christy woke up just as stiff as she usually was after a night in her narrow bunk. But there was too much space around her, she was too warm and her aches and secretions were in long forgotten corners of her body. She opened her eyes and saw Simon's face, thin, with a fuzz of greyish blond stubble, peaceful beside her. He was still grasping her shoulder. She knew she couldn't leave him, even to make a cup of coffee, and felt a surge of helplessness. As if the grimness of her solitude had been a kind of floor beneath her, which had suddenly caved in. The children are waiting for their breakfast. Then, with a huge effort of calculation – because the previous night had lasted at least ten years and probably an eternity – she remembered it was Saturday morning. She usually worked weekends but was under no obligation to.

Two days stretched ahead of them as an immense luxury. They truanted from everything, hardly dared go out in case they saw a newspaper or met a friend. Eventually they shuffled to the shop on the corner to buy croissants and coffee. As soon as they were out of the house, Simon found it necessary to share with her all his associations with that area of London: the cemetery, the theme park, the years with Jessica and Merlin and his period alone.

They listened to music, talked, made love, talked, sat in the overgrown garden indifferent to eyes at surrounding windows. In between they ate a never-ending supply of food from his fridge. To Christy his life seemed improbably comfortable.

'Is this how you spend every weekend?' she asked late that afternoon as they sat on the shaggy grass, their backs supported by an old and very determined plane tree. Its leaves spread flat green shadows across three gardens, giving them a subterranean light and atmosphere.

'No, because you're here. Doing all these things alone is rather a melancholy business.'

'But so calm and civilized. It reminds me of my mother's life, only she has no relief and hardly any company. I just can't imagine spending two days like this and then getting up on Monday to go back to Smiles.'

'We will. And a good thing too, if we spent too long sitting here we'd become so precious we'd disappear up each other's arseholes. Mind you I can't think of a nicer place to disappear to – what do you usually do at weekends?'

'The same as during the week, really. The children don't stop coming. More people get drunk on Friday and Saturday nights – I don't know why when most of them don't work anyway, but the pattern survives. So more kids get thumped and sometimes really hurt. If someone's hammering on my door I can't say, go away I'm shut.'

'Is it a condition of the job that you live at Smiles?'

'I don't think it's ever occurred to the agencies that hire us that we could afford not. We couldn't possibly pay rent.'

'But you want to live there?'

'No. I'd be mad if I said I enjoy being exposed to people's misery, twenty-four hours a day, seven days a week, pissing into a bucket in a leaky caravan with walls so thin it's like a biscuit tin. I wouldn't *choose* discomfort like that, who would? It's just the way the job's evolved. I don't really mind because it's so much better than the life I had in London before. Exhausting but not humiliating. And, being there all the

174

time, I do a better job than I could if I was living somewhere comfortable and just commuting in at fixed hours.'

'Like me.'

'Yes. And since we've ended up talking about it, I'll have to go over there tomorrow to see what's happened to Sean and the others. For all we know he's been arrested and they've bulldozed the camp. Like they did to those Born Again Christians at Mile End, you know, when they occupied all the local churches saying they had more right to them than anyone else.'

'But tomorrow's Sunday,' he said foolishly.

He welcomed her ability to stir him, even though he resisted it. He waited for her to seize on all the loose threads in his life, pull them, examine them, snip them cleanly as he had failed to do. The nicest moments with her, he thought, are when her ruthless incisiveness wobbles. As it had done when she told him about the hostel. In bed, at first, Christy was passive and cautious, listening for certain responses. He didn't know if he had pleased her or not and could only assume that if he hadn't she would have got dressed and left.

She slept heavily that night, until lunchtime the next day. Simon got up early and pottered around, pausing frequently to watch her. As she slept she looked defensive. Her arm shielded her eyes and mouth, as if all her dreams were about struggle. Her body, accustomed to the restrictions of a narrow bed, moved so little that she didn't even look relaxed. Simon wanted her to stay; it was unbearable to think of returning to an empty house again. Haunted by two women instead of one. After a few hours Simon began to resent her sleep, which encroached on what might be their last few hours alone together. He put on a Telemann record, very loudly, in the sitting room and when its booming trumpets roused her brought in a feast of eggs, sweetcorn and toast he had prepared.

She wondered again at the comfort of his life. Already she felt fatter, sleeker, cleaner.

'How often do you see your son?' she asked as he sat on the edge of the bath she was wallowing in.

'Not regularly.'

'I'd like to meet him.'

175

'Yes. I'll phone him later, we'll arrange something for next weekend.'

But he didn't ask her to come and live with him. He really couldn't tell if she wanted to and felt it would be a mistake to put pressure on her to do anything. If she wanted to return to Smiles that afternoon he wouldn't protest. But she didn't go, and he didn't phone Merlin. Gradually he realized that this was her way of being happy, that they were both immensely happy and scared of change. When the telephone rang that evening they looked at each other with the paranoia of new lovers. It rang five times.

'Nobody knows I'm here,' she said nervously. 'Go on. Answer it.'

She pretended to look at his records and cassettes, listening jealously to his half of the conversation.

Bernard: Hello my boy! Isn't it marvellous about the *Cronk*?
Simon: Oh, hello. What Cronk?
Bernard: Haven't you been listening to the news? We've been glued to the telly since Friday morning. The *Excalibur* has sunk the *Cronk*, that wretched little ferry boat the Manxies were so proud of. We're expecting them to surrender any minute, they haven't got a chance now. And we've taken Chicken Rock.
Simon: Do you mean people are getting killed in this stupid business?
Bernard: I knew you'd take that line. Rose is the same. I suppose you'd have let Hitler walk all over us. Well, I think it's terrifico, shows we've still got some spirit in this country. I'm getting on to a designer tomorrow to do a Chicken Rock Victory tent. I suppose you –?
Simon: No I wouldn't
Bernard: Anyway it's a great break for your grandmother.
Simon: Really? Are they going to drop her from a fighter jet?
Bernard: Now don't try to be clever with me. They're putting on a big show at the Palladium next Friday, Showbiz's Tribute to our Boys at Sea.
Simon: But surely they'll be back by then? It's only a couple of hours from Llandudno.
Bernard: For your information they're occupying the island.

176

For at least a month. And they've asked Connie to sing some of her old songs. She's absolutely thrilled. It's the biggest thing she's done – well since you were born really. She's getting herself a new stage dress made, I can hear her practising now. It's given her a new lease of life.

Simon: Madge must be furious.

Bernard: What? Yes, it'll be a golden evening. They're going to get Royalty – we don't yet know which one – and Dickie Diamante's going to present it. The Brighton Belles are coming, one of the sisters popped off last year but Yvonne and Vera are game old things. 'Taking a Shine to my Sunshine Boy', you must remember that? And some of those pop chappies, a few comedians. Maybe Mustafa Brown though he's not really a Brit and some of his jokes are a bit dirty for Royalty – so will you come?

Simon: Can I bring a friend?

Bernard: Male or female?

Simon: Um – female.

Bernard: You don't sound too sure. Ha ha. Yes of course, splendid, we'll look forward – Rose is coming.

Simon: Good. Can I speak to Merlin, please?

Bernard: What now? It's a bit late – I'll ask your mama – just a minute. He's just getting out of the bath. Madge is wrapping him up in a towel so he doesn't catch cold – oh, dear, his Ovaltine was too hot, burnt his mouth poor little fellow –

Simon: Hello? Merlin?

Merlin: Hello.

Simon: Would you like to come and stay with me?

Merlin: All right. When?

Simon: You can come back here with me after that show Connie's in, if you like, on Friday night.

Merlin: Am I going to live with you then?

Simon: If you want to. I'd like you to.

Merlin: Live in our old flat and go to my old school?

Simon: I suppose so. We'll arrange all that when you come. Is that OK?

Merlin: Yes.

Madge: What is all this, Simon? Upsetting the child. And at bedtime. You know how sensitive he is, now he won't sleep at all. Just when he was settling down. You should have come

177

over to ask us what we thought, sat down quietly to discuss it. You're always hurling these bombshells.

Simon: I asked Merlin if he wants to come back to live with me, and he does. So that's it.

Madge: Oh, is it really? I suppose it doesn't matter what we want, your poor old father and me. We're just the suckers who took him in for two years while it suited you. I suppose now you've found yourself a girlfriend you're going to use her as a babysitter. Who is she?

Simon: I'll see you on Friday. Bring Merlin's pyjamas, please, we'll come over one day to get the rest of his stuff. Is that all right?

Bernard: No it isn't. Madge is in tears now, and Merlin looks bewildered – why can't you be more tactful?

Simon: I've been trying to think of a way to take Merlin back for over a year and this is the best I can do.

Bernard: Well it's not – oh dear, Madge don't – Merlin, bedtime now –

Simon: Bye. See you on Friday.

Christy was now beside him with her ear as close to the receiver as she dared, watching and listening in amazement. Simon looked panic-stricken and the voices at the other end sounded hysterical. She poured two glasses of sour white wine from the bottle in the fridge.

'Come and sit down. Is it always like that when your dad phones?'

'Oh God – I didn't know I was going to. It came out all wrong. I'm sorry.'

'What are you sorry about? He's your son, isn't he? Why shouldn't he come and live with you?'

'But it shouldn't happen like this.'

'It was rather astonishing to do it over the phone.'

'Sheer cowardice. It was the only way I could face them, I mean not face them.'

'Your mother's got a voice like a buffalo, I could hear her over by the fireplace.'

'Can you face this awful show on Friday? You'll have to meet them all.'

'I'd better start practising my judo.'

178

'And Merlin? It's outrageous to demand so much of you –'

'I'll cope.'

As the terror always aroused by scenes with his mother receded, Simon felt some relief that he had exposed himself so utterly to Christy.

'I used to worry because I didn't know anything about you,' she said thoughtfully.

CHAPTER 20

✿✿✿✿✿✿✿✿✿✿✿✿✿✿✿✿✿✿✿✿✿✿✿✿✿✿

As Christy had no bike they walked to Smiles on Monday morning. It was odd to retrace the route of the march, to see the streets, which a few days before had seemed marked forever, looking so calm and unchanged. They were surprised and disappointed to see the camp was the same as it had been on Friday: as if their egotism demanded that the revolution in their inner lives should be reflected in the outer world. As they crossed Wandsworth Bridge they dropped each other's arms and marched with an officious working rhythm.

'I'm going to see if Sean's all right.'

'I'll get the supplies.'

Simon stopped at the edge of the pavement where the UN lorry was still unloading crates and sacks. He wouldn't turn to look at her or ask if she was coming home with him that afternoon, although the flatness of the morning chilled his heart. The camp looked so grim and ugly and she belonged to it so much more entirely than he ever would.

Christy went straight to Sean's caravan and knocked.

'What?'

'It's me. I wanted to make sure they didn't arrest you.'

He opened the door in his usual jeans and murky sweater, still fastening his belt. 'You took your time to find out.'

'What happened at the end of the march? We were hit by the puking gas and couldn't get through to Westminster. Your face looks a mess.'

'The whole of Victoria Street was one big street fight. They wouldn't take us to hospital without Britcards so we patched each other up here. There was a lot of looting, and hundreds of us got carted off in police vans. They squeezed us all into one of those giant riot cages over by Crystal Palace but they had to let us go a few hours later because they needed the space for a huge gang of kids who'd forged Britcards. They probably won't even bother fining us because if we don't pay up – and none of us could – they'll have to lock us up again. Oh, and I might lose my volunteer's allowance. But I don't give a bugger one way or the other, I'm sick of being in some kind of position of authority when I have no power to go with it.'

Listening to him, Christy felt childishly left out and, more painfully, ashamed of the comfort of her weekend. It made her aggressive towards Sean and undermined her happiness with Simon. She stood in front of him, very tense, in clothes that for once smelt clean (Simon had a washing machine) and refused to look at Sean's gaudy array of cuts and bruises.

'What about Ellen and Beatrice and the others? Did they get to their gardens?'

'They did, amazingly enough. Dumped their kids and disabled dependants in front of the House of Commons – they wanted to leave them in the lobby but they weren't allowed in. Then they put up their tents and spent the night in the gardens. There were so many cameras and journalists down there, lapping up the squalor, that I don't think the police dared move them on. You should have seen the headlines: Slum Mums Ditch Babes. But in a way, I have to admit, they made their point.'

'Where are they now?'

'They came back in the lorry late last night, very pleased with themselves. At least there's some fighting spirit around here now. And how was your weekend?'

'Good. I stayed with Simon.'

'Oh yes. Where is he?'

'At the playgroup, I'm moving my stuff out of the caravan.'

'Going to set you up in comfort, is he?'

'Oh, don't be so old fashioned.'

'Money doesn't date. Has he got a nice flat? Full of antiques and potted plants? And a gilt-edged Britcard?'

'The trouble with you is, you take stereotypes seriously. You'd have everyone with an income of more than twenty thousand a year striding around in top hats and frock coats brandishing whips.'

'So when are you going to resign?'

'I'm not. I don't have to live in the camp, I can do a perfectly good job if I just come in every day. Someone else can have the caravan.'

'Right. I'll phone the estate agents then, tell them it's available.'

'I've been worrying about you all weekend.'

'I phoned every police station in London to find out what had happened to you. Though I might have known you two would avoid any trouble. I'm sure he has a good solicitor.'

Christy turned and left, rather glad, in a backhanded way, that he hadn't been noble. She didn't want a pretence of friendship between the three of them. Sean was entitled to feel aggrieved and she liked him for showing it. But she wanted to like him from a distance, back him up at meetings and then go home to Simon.

When she opened the door of the playgroup and saw him sitting with Dimelza on his knee, Christy felt so much love for him that it was like an attack of sickness; her legs were weak and her heart jumped. She held on to a table and laughed because the symptoms were so absurd, so much more violent than she had ever imagined. It was such a shock to her system to be happy.

All that week they enjoyed their double life. During the day they were sedate together and gave more attention than usual to the children. Christy attended almost every meeting in the camp, just to make sure that her back was available for stabbing. But nobody there was interested in her private life, except Sean, who never confided. Ellen and her child moved into Christy's old caravan.

In the evenings they went back to Simon's flat, ate and drank and talked and slept together, still amazed that they were free to do all this.

CHAPTER 21

✿✿✿✿✿✿✿✿✿✿✿✿✿✿✿✿✿✿✿✿✿✿✿✿

Connie sat in her dressing room and inhaled the smells. Not the old greasy pancake but a feathery, artificial perfume; it just floated on your skin and didn't melt under the lights. Flowers everywhere too, as many as a funeral and probably more. Telegrams, one from Dolly who she'd thought had died years ago, probably surprised to find her still going too. Strong. She took a swig of brandy and soda, nobody had said she couldn't, and thought how strong she would be if they would let her do this every night. The brandy put the dark velvet back into her voice, not too cosy, a bit of enigma on those long drawn-out notes. The troops went mad when she sang it in Cairo.

She leaned forward to examine her mirror image. They hadn't let her do it herself. She had turned up with her old box of Leichner and she knew every stroke of her stage face, though she was a bit shaky. That girl had done a good job; she didn't look a day over sixty-nine and quite sultry, all things considered.

I've never arrived less than an hour before. The theatre's still empty except for journalists outside and nobodies in the corridor. Stars nowadays probably just get out of a taxi and go straight on stage, they certainly look like it. Bernard promised champagne first but it would be just like him to forget, still he has sent flowers. They'll be here soon but I don't want them, I want the young ones, they've never seen me as a real woman. Show them not all women are walking nylon puddings like their mother. Staying power, that's what you need, maybe this'll be the start of a second career. Talent doesn't age. And fancy Hitler still being alive and fighting us again, you've got to hand it to the old bastard, he has got guts, must be a hundred if he's a day.

'Shall we put the dress on now then, love?'

That dresser is a mistake, she sounds like a nurse. And she's putting too much soda in. Ah, that shiny black, it's like a snakeskin, fits perfectly though the workmanship's not the same. It'll fall apart after tonight, not that that matters. I wasn't sure about the slits but they're still the same legs, thinner if anything. I ought to give them what they remember and they will remember, I know, I still get letters. There was that one a few years ago from that man in Worthing who'd named a new kind of delphinium after me.

'Don't mess my hair!' It was in gleaming copper snake coils.

'Never mind, love, we'll do it again in a minute. There, aren't we smart?'

You're not, you crumpled fat yellow thing.

'Oh Mrs Freeman how nice, visitors! She's just putting on her finery.'

The zip slid to the top of her spine. Maurice used to say she had a back like a snow-covered precipice; he had his moments. Connie stared with frenzied admiration at the reflection of her brilliance before turning petulantly to the harbingers of dreariness.

Madge whispered to the dresser behind the flowers, 'How is she, Caroline?'

'Blood pressure up a bit but not too bad. We'd better get her straight to bed after she finishes her little piece.'

'What on earth is she drinking?'

'Just brandy snap flavouring with soda. That bottle your husband's holding, it's not –?'

'De Luxe Apple Frizzante. Do you really think you could come back and look after her? It would be such a help. We're trying to get her into a Slumber Home but there's an enormous waiting list.'

Bernard, a union jack in his buttonhole, opened the bottle with a flourish and poured out eight rather mean glasses.

'To a fabulous old lady! And to our brave boys in Douglas.'

Connie spat it out. 'Really, Bernard, can't you afford a decent champagne? Catspiss!'

Simon and Rose kissed her dazzling cheeks and pushed Merlin forward.

'You look well, Grandma. I'd like you to meet Christy.'

'Who's this? The child's au pair?'

Merlin giggled and Christy thought, I hope I die before I get to the stage when I think it's funny to say whatever comes into my head. Old monster. Christy had put on her only skirt, which had been made even worse by ironing, and felt awkward. Simon put his arm around her and Connie realized she must be some kind of girlfriend.

'Better than nothing,' she muttered.

Standing beside his father, Merlin tried to believe he would sleep in his old room that night. He wondered if the woman in the old clothes lived there too. He never seemed to get his father all to himself. But she was smiling at him quite nicely; tentatively he smiled back. The old witch was making horrible faces at him and touching his new suit with her claws, which tonight had purple talons.

'This is how you must remember me, little one. Do you understand? Not as a stale old hag locked up in a room.'

'No one's ever locked you up, Mummy,' Bernard said, looking nervously at Caroline.

Christy thought, if she didn't have any money she'd be raving in doorways and cherishing old newspapers. The rich can go gaga in style. She was grateful when Rose approached. Christy liked her compact, intelligent face which was, just then, friendly.

'Five minutes please.'

Connie swept to her feet. Her relatives enthusiastically kissed her and patted her on the back as Caroline led her away. Christy thought it was all very strange. So much politeness, so many kisses and such obvious mutual dislike. Simon's mother kept looking at her as if she was a cockroach suffering from herpes and then, whenever Christy caught her eye, smiling effusively. Christy stuck to Simon and to Rose, who seemed fairly trustworthy. The little boy kept looking at her too. Christy wanted to take his hand but wasn't sure how to respond to such a well-dressed child. He looked like a miniature bank manager.

'I need your help,' Rose said as they walked to their seats. 'I've heard there are people, children and adults, who make a living out of scavenging in the sewers and down by the river at low tide.'

'That's right. Mudlarks and toshers, some of them live at Smiles. A little kid drowned near us last month when there was a storm and the sewers flooded. Some of them do quite well, find Roman coins and things. It's terribly dangerous though.'

'I'd like to write about them. Will you take me along there one day so I can talk to them?'

'All right.'

'Thanks. And will you and Simon come and have supper with me one night next week? And Merlin?'

'Yes, I'd like that.'

Someone called Frankie had invited them too. Simon seems to come with a lot of ramifications, Christy thought, exhausted. Within a few days she had acquired a flat, a bike, various honorary friends and some kind of stepson.

The theatre was decorated with balloons, flags and banners reminding God whose side He was on. A brass band was playing a medley of pompous marches. The Front of House Manager made a brief announcement that sales of the vast souvenir programme had already raised ten thousand pounds. Almost everyone was in evening dress and, it seemed to Christy, knew everyone else. They fell upon each other with shrieks and whinnies. In the front row, a few feet away from them, the backs were stiffly military. Above her the Royal Box was unmistakably illuminated by camera lights. Sean would have said at his most violently anarchic, one bomb now would get them all. It was so improbable to be sitting here talking to Rose about sewers. Long before the curtain (appliquéd for the occasion with lions, unicorns and manx cats) rose, conversation had died down, as if the strain of this temporary and expensive alliance between Royalty, the military and the media was unbearable. It was a relief when they had to stand up for the anthem.

Connie lay in the wings on her blood red brocade upholstered chaise longue. There had been quite a debate, at rehearsals, about whether she should tango across the stage to it or be wheeled on already lying seductively on it. When she had fallen over at her second attempt to tango it was decided that Dickie Diamante, after introducing her as the woman who broke a million Tommy hearts, should raise his arms as a signal to Caroline, who was to give the chaise longue a forceful push. Runners were to glide it to centre stage. It was the one moment of her act Connie was nervous about. What if it didn't quite get there, overshot the mark and crashed into the orchestra pit? Still the girl was muscular enough.

Dickie came up, in his pear-shaped quilted velvet claret suit. 'All right, darling?'

'Fine. I just thought I'd wait here, I'm not in the way, am I'?'

'Mrs Freeman shouldn't be moved around too much,' Caroline whispered loudly.

'Lovely atmosphere. Like Dunkirk,' Connie murmured and shut her eyes again.

'Can't you get her back to the dressing room? She's not on for forty minutes, we'll all be falling over her.'

'It wouldn't be wise to move her now.'

'Christ, all these old crocks. We've got another one that hasn't been seen in public since Waterloo. Keeps asking for Turkish cigarettes. I'll say this for the fellas, they have the grace to die off before they're museum pieces. There goes the anthem.' He stood quivering with nervous energy, reminding himself to turn his best profile to the Royal Box.

Connie felt a charge of nostalgia at his malice. But she wouldn't snarl back because he was still a big name and you never knew. She beckoned to Caroline who bent over her. Connie croaked in her ear, 'Years ago, when he had his first face lift, they used to call him the Queen of Diamonds.'

It's so lovely just being here, surrounded by funny, glamorous people (glamorous by today's abysmal standards anyway) with hundreds more waiting out there in the dark. Millions, they're doing it on television. There never would have been any insomnia or illness or being difficult if I could have kept on doing it. Here everybody's difficult so it doesn't matter, we spit and scratch and drink together. I was never alone when I was young. Always out to a restaurant or club after the show, all the waiters loved me. A boiled egg and a Horlicks if Madge is feeling permissive.

'Connie!'

'Delilah!'

They fell upon each other so noisily that the Stage Manager, who had never heard of either of them and had been seething ever since Connie first appeared on her chaise longue, told them to fuck off, which made them both feel years younger.

Escorted by their dressers they went to Delilah's dressing room, which was smaller than Connie's and had fewer flowers. They sat down on a couch and examined each other, comparing greedily.

'I'm just going off to get a sandwich, Mrs Freeman,' Caroline said and disappeared.

'It was Angmering.'

'No Brighton. The Royal Albion.'

'Maurice died, didn't he? So did Teddy, years ago.'

'Now maybe we'll marry again.'

They both laughed. Glancing in the brilliantly lit mirror Connie saw two happy faces, a brunette and a redhead, ageless really. Delilah didn't look too bad at all.

'Still drinking?' Connie asked hopefully.

'When I can get it. Brandy?'

As soon as the fragrant fire singed her throat Connie knew it was real and she hadn't tasted it for years. That girl had cheated her. She swallowed it in two gulps and held out her glass.

'You old devil! Haven't they put you on the wagon yet?'

'What wagon? Oh, do you remember "Bandwagon"?'

'Wasn't it gorgeous! So romantic. Which number are you doing?'

'I'm doing three. "There's Another Woman", "Don't Torture Me" and "Fascination Tango". And you? I know, don't tell me, "RSVP in Heaven".' It had been Delilah's only big hit, terribly schmaltzy.

'Absolutely right! Do you think they'll remember us?'

'How could anyone forget us?'

Connie's pushiness and confidence, that ruthless air of always knowing what she wanted, were less detestable now. Delilah remembered with a shock how she had hated her forty years ago. Connie had always been ahead, more famous, richer, better dressed and aggressively ready to point all this out. Her style, though devastating, hadn't been at all English. Delilah remembered how on one occasion Connie had stridden

188

into a restaurant in a new black dress and had stared at the pianist – was it Bunny Haskins? – until he stopped playing for her entrance.

'What happened to that boy of yours?'

'Bernard? Oh, he's out front now. Married, two children, never made any money until last year. His wife makes my life a misery.'

'You don't look miserable, Connie.'

For twenty minutes her vitality fed them both. She sparkled, alone with the mirror and a woman she had always been able to upstage. And who, she was now quite sure, was wearing a wig, swept up on top of her head like a black nylon broom. The drinks kept coming until Caroline returned and reminded her it was time to go on.

The two old women looked at each other with terror and exhilaration, kissed and exchanged phone numbers.

As she supported her to the chaise longue Caroline smelt the brandy. Damn, she thought, now her daughter-in-law won't give me a reference. Caroline knew Mrs Freeman wouldn't last more than a week or two and she wanted to apply for a job looking after Hieronymus Gunk's five children in Eaton Square. She'd had enough of geriatrics.

Connie lay panting on the chaise longue. My heart's going like an ack-ack gun. My voice'll be down half an octave, growl it, I wonder if I'll get any reviews. A star is reborn, they don't write lyrics like that any more, a living legend graced the stage of the Palladium last night. My God that boy is strong – it's not going to stop – smile –

'First of all I'd like to sing for you a song that some of you will remember and some of you will be hearing for the first time. I first sang this song in 1939:

> There's ano-other woman
> Stroking that brown hair
> Ho-olding your sweet hand dear
> But darling I don't care.
> I know that other woman
> Is mee-eee.
> I'm with you when you wake dear
> I'm with you when you're sick

I help you strap your gun on
And your uniform so slick.
You know that other woman
Is mee-eee.
Some day when Hitler's beaten
How happy we will be
Two lovebirds in a cottage
And later maybe three-eee.
Till then that other woman
Is mee-eee.

Christy, Simon and Rose had whispered and fidgeted through the extract from Henry V, Hieronymus Gunk's Schrapheap Rock version of Land of Hope and Glory and Mustafa Brown's insinuations about the Manxies' virility. Sitting together in the dark muttering sarcasms, they drew closer. Then Connie shot forward on to the stage, red and white and black, and in her husky voice spoke-sang her song, arrogantly flat and almost a beat behind the music. As a performer she still had power. Simon and Rose realized that, decades ago, she must have been really talented. All their lives they had heard that song, crackling away behind her locked door, being hummed or whistled by Bernard when he was feeling filial.

'Marvellous for ninety-five,' he muttered now.

'She's been drinking.' Madge made a mental note to sack Caroline.

Christy found the face and the voice grotesque, a skeleton doing tricks. The strain at the back of the throat was horrible and at the end of the last, drawling 'meee-eee' there was a rasping, croaking sound like a d—.

'Why isn't she getting up and waving her arms around?' Merlin asked as Connie continued to languish on her chaise longue. The applause became hesitant. Bernard attempted a feeble 'Bravo!' and the conductor reached up with a bouquet for Connie. But she didn't accept it.

'Ungracious old thing,' said Madge, who knew exactly how she would smile as she took a bouquet.

'No darling, I think there's something wrong.'

'In a drunken stupor, I suppose.'

'I think she's dead.' said Christy, who had seen a lot of people die.

The word made Madge shriek, the military-looking people sitting in front turned round to glare in disgust and Bernard hoped this new girlfriend of Simon's wasn't going to be a troublemaker.

'Well people do die,' Christy said apologetically.

The curtain was lowered. Dickie Diamante and Mustafa Brown came out dressed as a sergeant and corporal and did some gags. An ASM bumbled down the rows looking for someone.

'Is Mr B Freeman here?'

'I say I say I say av yew polished those boots today?'

'Are you Mr B Freeman?'

'No I'm not. Sit down.'

'What's the difference between a pair of dirty boots and a Manxie boat?'

'I'm over here. What is it?'

'One stinks and the other sinks.' (Laughter.)

'Please could you come backstage? It's your mother.'

'Knock knock ooze there?'

'Douglas.'

'Douglas oo?'

'Douglas Yew Knighted Kingdom.' (Wild applause and cries of 'Hear! Hear!' directed at the Royal Box.)

'I suppose we'd all better go,' said Madge, and they stumbled after Bernard.

Connie was laid out in her dressing room, still on the chaise longue. A doctor was examining her and Madge saw with irritation that she didn't look at all peaceful. Her mouth was open, as if she was about to snore or sing that awful song again, and her eyes glittered with amazement. Creakily, Bernard knelt beside her.

Simon, who thought Merlin had seen enough death, suggested a drink and they went to the bar with Christy and Rose.

Madge turned on Caroline. 'How many drinks did you let her have?'

'I just went off to have some supper. I'm allowed a half-hour break, the agency said so. When I came back she'd been drinking with that friend of hers.'

'Who? She didn't have any friends.'

'De Lulu I think her name was. One of the performers. About the same age as your mother-in-law.'

'Delilah Potzenberg. RSVP in Heaven,' said Bernard, still on his knees.

'Oh do stop praying and get up. We're not religious for God's sake.'

'Respect, Madge.'

'Would you like the certificate now, Mr Freeman?'

'Well goodbye Mrs Freeman – Mr Freeman. Sorry it –'

'It's no use sneaking off, I shall phone the agency in the morning. You as good as killed her.

At the door Caroline met a crowd of journalists.

'Any suspicion of foul play?'

'So sorry to disturb your private grief, Mr Freeman, but could you describe your feelings at this moment?'

'Would you say your mother was a deeply patriotic old lady?'

'Good evening Mr Freeman, Mrs Freeman. My condolences. Not an intimate way to pass on. But perhaps the loved one would have wished it? I know she was a very great star. Do you think she would have wanted teak or pine? We have a selection outside. Teak? Satin lining or rayon? Most certainly. There is an extra charge for evening calls. Terribly sorry to rush you but there are a lot of clamps in this area. Perhaps we could come and see you tomorrow morning to discuss the funeral arrangements? When the first reefs of your grief, so to speak, have healed.'

'Reefs can't heal,' Madge said sharply.

'Of course not, Mrs Freeman, these wounds go very deep.'

Later they all met on the pavement outside the theatre.

'At least she'll get some obits,' said Rose, before kissing them and hailing a taxi.

Merlin stood between Simon and Christy, firmly holding their hands. Madge realized with a seizure of loneliness that she and Bernard were going back to an empty house.

'Don't cry!' said Bernard and Simon simultaneously as she started.

'Poor old thing. She was very gutsy really. I shall miss her – and now Merlin's going off –'

'Why's Grandma crying?'

192

'Death is sad,' his father said.

'Even in a war? When soldiers die in this war on the Isle of Man will it be sad?'

'It isn't a war it's a crisis,' said his grandfather, and stooped to kiss him affectionately before ushering Madge into a taxi.

CHAPTER 22

On Saturday morning Merlin came into their room and sat on their bed. Christy reached out to hug him sleepily, as she had always hugged the Smiles children when they came into her caravan. Stiffly, shutting his eyes as if in fear, the child rolled on to the bed and into her arms. He had never been sure, at his grandparents', whether or not he was supposed to do this. He used to get dressed before going into their bedroom and had, anyway, been embarrassed by the sight of the huge porpoise-like monuments in bed. Their house was too big, it discouraged cuddling. Now the scale of this flat, and of his new parents, was more manageable. And a stepmother was nearly as good as a witch in a castle, though she didn't seem particularly wicked.

'Now I suppose we're a family,' Christy said at lunch after a formal and awkward morning.

They all felt more or less miscast, rushed into an intimacy that should have been acquired over years. Yet there was no doubt of their need for each other. At odd moments they acknowledged it in sudden caresses and bursts of three-cornered laughter. They weren't confident enough to leave each other alone and so all day long they ate, talked, played and shopped together, putting a strain on their solitary personalities.

Christy stood in the doorway of Merlin's room and watched him ride his rocking horse, cautiously, as if it might bolt or throw him any minute. Rachel's got her grandchild at last, she thought. Then she ran into the living room with an idea.

'Simon! Let's go and stay with my mother. All of us. We'll have enough space there, and some time to think.'

'Will she want us?'

'Yes.'

'But you've just had a holiday.'

'I know. I'll have to say she's ill, I know it's a lie but one of us will be soon if we carry on like this.'

'Like what?'

'Locking ourselves up in a prefabricated nuclear family.'

'All right. We'll go.'

'I'll go to Smiles tomorrow and try to arrange it.'

'Shall I come too?'

'No. You're a volunteer, you don't have to ask permission for a week off.'

So he let her go, on Sunday afternoon, and tried not to agonize over whatever scene took place between her and Sean.

Merlin took the prospect of a holiday seriously. 'I've got nothing to wear. All my clothes here are too small and the others are at Grandma's.'

'Just take what you're wearing now.'

'But it's my best suit.'

'Merlin it doesn't matter. Clothes don't matter.'

'How are we going to get there?'

'We'll hitch.'

'But that's begging. Grandma said –'

'Look, you're going to live with us now. We all have to accept each other. And we do things differently here.'

Later, as Simon put him to bed, Merlin said, 'I don't really mind being poor.'

It was still light. He shouldn't start worrying about her until it was dark. She must be having a long conversation with – the bell rang three times with the shrill, hearty note that could only be Bernard or the police. Simon went into Merlin's bedroom to see if it had disturbed him, and then into his own which overlooked the street. He peeped out through the curtains. He had perfected this technique of not being at home during the months after Jessica's death and was ashamed to find how easily he reverted to it.

A few feet away, to his right, Madge stood on the steps with a large basket and a suitcase, looking puffy and hurt. Bernard stood beside her holding her arm, frowning, reproving the door. They lowered their voices for discretion but Simon could still hear them through the window.

195

'Gone out,' Bernard grunted.

'I hope they haven't left him on his own.'

'Give him a ring tomorrow.'

'He'll have to go back to that awful rough school.'

'Well. We've done what we can. Let's leave the suitcase on the step.'

'But someone might – it's not like around us, you know.'

What am I afraid of now? Simon thought angrily and went to open the front door.

'Hello. Sorry to be so long, I was just putting Merlin to bed.'

'We brought his clothes. And there's a chicken and a banana custard in the basket, his favourite supper.'

'Thanks, Madge. Have you had a hard time arranging Grandma's funeral?'

'It's all been very harrowing for your poor mother. But they've squeezed us in tomorrow, Golder's Green Cremat-orium at nine fifteen. On the early side I'm afraid. Will you all –?'

'Oh yes, we'll come.'

'Very sad.' And for a rare moment Bernard's face lost its patina and looked utterly sad, old and lost. Simon saw that he had been hit by his mother's death. But almost immediately he regained his optimism. 'Still, what about the Giant's Grave, eh?'

'What about it?'

'Don't you ever buy a newspaper or watch television? They're flying the union jack from it. And there's an inscrip-tion in ogham script saying "Rule Britannia". But I suppose you think all that's nonsense.'

'Yes. Nasty, violent, dangerous nonsense. Anyway we'll see you in the morning. Thanks for bringing Merlin's clothes.'

Madge's offended kiss reproached him for not inviting them in. A few minutes later Christy let herself in and caught him at the curtains.

'Simon? What are you doing?'

'Waiting for you.'

They embraced in the dark room. She wanted to ridicule his devotion but it touched her. 'I got my week off.'

'Good. Then we'll leave tomorrow, I'm afraid we have to go

196

to my grandmother's funeral first – you don't have to come, of course.'

But they all turned up, in anoraks, with rucksacks and flowers.

'Not many mourners. Just three of the seven dwarfs,' Madge said acidly to the man who let them into the scrubbed pine, secular chapel. You could have any religion or none, and Connie had stipulated none. There were only ten of them, dotted around on the benches, including Bernard's account-ant Sammy, his wife and Delilah, who was still weeping from her shock that Connie wasn't, after all, indomitable. She kept reminding herself that poor old Connie had been eight years older than her. All the women except Christy wore black, despite the secular nature of the ceremony, and all the men except Simon wore dark suits.

A man who had never met her unctuously recalled Connie's star quality, her dazzling beauty, her sweetness and light as a wife and mother, her long struggle with a painful disease and her heroic insistence on serving the country she loved yet again at the last. Rose and Simon tried to avoid each other's eyes but Rose let out a snicker when the man referred to Connie 'ending her days in the bosom of a close and loving family'. Madge turned round to glare at her.

Then they all waited, staring nervously at the pine sliding doors set into the wall in front of them. There was a grinding sound somewhere under the floor, horribly reminiscent of goings on in hell in a medieval painting, Simon thought. When at last the doors opened Connie's casket shot out, reminding them all of her chaise longue a few days before.

They went out again into the misty sunlight and Christy sniffed the smoke that made the process so uncomfortably down to earth, like cooking. Hundreds of thousands of boxes neatly stacked.

'We're having a little, er, party at home, if any of you would like to come.' Madge stared hard at her son and daughter.

'I'm afraid I have to go back to work,' Rose said.

'And we're going off on holiday.' Simon picked up his rucksack and put it on his shoulders.

'Hitching,' Merlin added defiantly.

'Holiday? Where?' Madge demanded.

'We're going to Devon to see my mother.'

'Whereabouts in Devon?' Madge asked suspiciously.

'Near Bodmin. She has a very isolated house on the edge of Dartmoor.'

'Years ago I knew an old actor called Oliver Ponting who had a marvellous house on the outskirts of Exeter. Drank himself to death there,' Bernard said thoughtfully.

'Awfully bleak, Dartmoor.' Madge disapproved of people who lived in the middle of nowhere.

'I'll give you a lift to the Cromwell Road,' Rose offered.

They all exchanged kisses – again Christy marvelled at the amount of kissing that went on among them – and trudged off to the car park.

'At least Jessica was pretty and had some dress sense,' Madge commented, looking after Christy.

'They're all the same,' said Joan, Sammy's wife and Madge's confidante. 'Alex turned up at Ruthie's wedding in a short red tunic, white ballet tights and a jade bracelet. And he was such a nice little boy.'

CHAPTER 23

Rachel lay in bed and listened to the strange morning sounds downstairs: doors banging, a child making discoveries and demanding attention, crockery and cutlery clonking and ringing on the wooden table. It was a little like a recording from her own past, only they sounded more cheerful. Perhaps it was only because she wasn't there, with her resentment of the drains and strains of domesticity. It was lovely to sprawl here above it all like God. Her happiness in Christy's new situation was almost guilty. She had never been a woman who said, or thought, that what her daughter needed was a man and children; in fact she had been proud of Christy's independence. But Rachel liked Simon and couldn't help seeing how much more alive Christy was than before. She responded to the waif in Merlin, as he responded to the matriarch in her. If I'm to die let it be like this, in the knowledge Christy's safe, she thought.

She heard Merlin shuffle painfully upstairs with her cup of tea. A wobble and clatter at the door.

'Can I come in?' He didn't know what to call either of these new women, though he liked them both.

'Thank you, Merlin. Help yourself to a biscuit.'

It struck him as the height of decadence that she kept a huge tin of biscuits under her bed. There in the dusty, fluffy darkness between the springs and floorboards were also shoes, books, pens, pencils, notebooks, socks, cups, glasses, newspapers and blankets, quietly rotting away. She was in her way as squalid as the old witch but she reigned in the middle of it all, a big, white, strong thing like the moon. He took two chocolate biscuits and sat on her bed.

'Shall I pour it back into the cup?'

199

'I don't mind it in the saucer. Where are you going today?'

'Somewhere called Princetown.'

'I'll come with you. I have to collect my pension.'

'What's that?'

'Money they give me for being old.'

He walked with Rachel most of the way. Behind him, he knew, his father was kissing Christy and putting his arm around her all the time. Merlin felt ashamed for them. Sometimes Rachel took his hand, in a dry sensible way, to help him over ditches.

As soon as they entered the town the war was upon them. There were posters in many of the windows saying 'Pax! We only want your tax', and advertising concerts, jumble sales and wine and cheese parties to raise money for 'our boys'. After she had collected her pension Rachel bought them all sandwiches and a drink in a pub where they overheard a loud conversation about the strategic wisdom of taking Chicken Rock.

'Those countries in South America,' Simon said to Christy, 'probably become military dictatorships because people admire soldiers' uniforms so much.'

'I don't understand what's happening,' Rachel said sadly. 'I walked miles to Angie's house, just before you came, to watch the TV news and see what was going on. But they'd censored all the news, all I saw were some still photographs of ancient looking battleships and postcard shots of the Isle of Man and some druids. It all seems quite mad to me.'

'It is. There's nothing else to understand.'

Christy smiled at a man who was listening to them and frothing over his beer. She felt an urge to outrage people like him, to express her anger at hatred and chauvinism masquerading as noble patriotism. Perhaps it was because she had sat so quietly through the Palladium concert. She raised her voice:

'Ever since I can remember this country has been nostalgic about the war. Look at all those TV programmes romanticizing prisoner of war camps and concentration camps, best-selling glossy books with lush photos of weapons, war films still being made now, half a century later. It was the last time people in England felt secure about being goodies. And it's always The War as if there haven't been dozens since. The

memory doesn't die, either, it's passed on down the generations, like your grandmother still singing her song, Simon. So a
bit of bloodletting like this stupid Isle of Man adventure is
necessary every few years to keep up the national fantasy that
we're heroes and it's only the rest of the world that's wrong.
Then I suppose the troops who used to be in Ireland got restless.'

Within minutes the pub divided like a beery Red Sea and
they found themselves in a very small minority.

'Too damned young to remember the war.'

'If we hadn't fought Hitler you'd have been born in a
concentration camp, my girl, if at all.'

'Were you born over here? Looks foreign to me.'

'That's half the problem nowadays. All these wogs with
British passports, but they don't think like Brits.'

'Might as well live in Calcutta.'

'Blacks in the army now.'

'Those Manxies, they're not really British either.'

'Lot of French blood.'

Rachel had now been recognized as a member of the old
CND group.

'Still marching?'

'I would do. I'd march against this idiotic war if anyone
would join me.'

A young woman said, 'I quite agree with you. I think we
should at least have a public meeting for people who think it's
wrong.'

Amidst the general laughter a man spluttered, 'I'll lend you
my cloakroom if you like.'

'I should think you could squeeze into our pigsty.'

'I'll come to your meeting. I don't hold with fighting and
killing. If everyone as didn't pay his taxes had to go to war
there'd soon be an end to us,' said the publican.

'I'm a printer,' said a middle-aged man. 'If we can fix on a
date and a time I'll get some posters up.'

'They won't stay up for long,' said the man who had made
the pigsty joke.

'You can have the room upstairs, Mondays or Wednesdays,'
the publican offered, unperturbed by the rate at which his pub
was emptying.

'Next Monday at seven, then,' Rachel said, her old organizational flair restored. 'We'll call it, "Don't fight the Island, Fight the War." I'll try to get some speakers along.'

'I'll speak all right,' said the pigsty man.

'It'll be a public meeting,' Rachel said calmly, and arranged to meet the printer the following afternoon.

'But if we don't fight the Russians will come,' Merlin explained to Rachel as they left the pub.

Rachel smiled at him. Christy was struck by the power that had returned to her mother. Her flesh was firmer, her eyes a brilliant green instead of a sagging olive colour. They shone like that because Rachel was close to tears; Christy saw she was moved and astonished to find there were still people in the town who thought like her. On the pavement Rachel stopped by the Estate Agents and hovered.

'What are you doing, Mum?'

'Just looking. There, three bedrooms with outbuildings and an acre, that's less than I've got.'

'You've not moving?'

'Well it's ridiculous, all that space just for me and living on carrot soup. Anyway I've had enough of being isolated. I'm thinking of buying a flat in the town, it'll be a lot cheaper and I'll be nearer – things.'

'Of course it's up to you.' Christy was surprised to find herself so upset.

'You can still come and stay.' Rachel glanced at them all, felt unaccountably responsible for them, specially the child. Odd how you could go on in perfect selfishness, quite happy for years, then suddenly, bang, people mattered again. She wasn't private any more.

'What will you do with your lovely goat?' Merlin asked anxiously.

'Keep him if you like. Disgusting senile old stinker.' Sentimentality about animals was the last refuge of the lonely.

This provoked a discussion about whether you could keep goats in London gardens and whether a goat would be an aid to hitchhiking.

While they were waiting at the stop for the rarely sighted bus that went within a mile of Rachel's house, a Land Rover stopped. Christy recognized Steven, the farmer who had given her a lift on her last visit.

'Can I drop you off?'

On the way he asked, 'Did it come to blows in The Phoenix?'

'I didn't see you there,' Rachel said.

'I wasn't, I just heard about it from Jim.'

'Well. How the word spreads.'

'You're out of it, you don't know what gossip's like in a small place like this.'

'I will do soon. I'm thinking of moving into town.'

'Good idea. I daresay my wife'll be along to your meeting.'

'Really?'

'I think she's crazy but there you are. It's all mixed up with her Christianity. Be careful what you call yourselves, won't you?'

'What do you mean?' Rachel asked.

'I mean, if you're going to form a group consult a lawyer before you choose a name. Nothing political, subversive, that sort of thing: "for peace", "against war" "campaign" – they dissolved the Friends of the Earth in Exeter recently, said "earth" had pagan, anarchic and anti-social connotations.'

'That doesn't leave much choice,' Rachel said.

'Call yourselves a knitting circle,' Simon suggested.

'Be careful,' Steven said again when he stopped outside their door.

That evening, while Merlin helped Rachel to make supper, Christy and Simon talked in their room. It had been Christy's room for so long that it was strange to share it with anyone, even Simon.

'Your mother's an enterprising woman.'

'Do you like her?'

'Aren't I supposed to? What's the matter?' He sat beside her on the bed.

'I keep thinking, this might be the last time I come here. I've got so used to the idea that my mother and this house are always here, a permanent refuge. And I suppose I don't like her changing, in a way I feel she ought to be the same, just go on being my mother, only existing when I'm here. Is that awful?'

'Fairly outrageous. After all, you've changed.'

'It's a pity we have to go back on Sunday, I'd like to go to her meeting. I wonder what'll happen.'

'Nothing, probably. Lots of talk, and she might a find a few fellow spirits.'

'You're cynical about political activity. I think that's the way things change: little groups of people all over the country get together and agree that what the government's doing is wrong. Once you start criticizing this farce on the Isle of Man you can't just stop there. Think of all the disaffected people who would join a group like that. I've often felt at our meetings at Smiles, people would like to say or do more, if only they weren't so tired and hungry and frightened. Most people around here have a bit of time, and full bellies and the confidence to say what they think. That's when change begins.'

'Well, I hope you're right. I'm not cynical,' he added, hurt. 'Not about Smiles or about you. But as soon as things become organized, with meetings and agendas, I lose interest.'

'You are an idealist, in your way, I suppose. You would have been perfectly happy in an aristocratic age, building marvellous follies for some rich man. As it is you have to survive in a civilization that's on its last legs.'

'I've got you.'

'Me and Merlin, your follies.'

As they came downstairs they saw Rachel and Merlin bending over the radio together.

'I'm trying to get the news,' Rachel said.

'Yours must be the last radio in England that has to be tuned in.'

'Your father and I bought it second hand when we moved here. He didn't believe in buying new machines because it encouraged the consumer economy, so nothing ever worked. Here we are.'

They bustled around laying the table, half listening to the bland, reasonable voice until his words made them all start:

'A ceasefire was agreed one hour ago between British troops and guerillas on the Isle of Man. A spokesman at Downing Street said that the island will now be regarded as a normal part of the United Kingdom and its population will pay tax at the full rate of 45 per cent. Ferry services between Douglas and Liverpool, Androssan, Fleetwood and Llandudno will be resumed tomorrow morning and so will all flights to and from

Ronaldsway. Crowds in Trafalgar Square are rejoicing tonight. The ten day campaign is regarded in military circles as a triumph, with only forty-two British soldiers reported missing. Seventy-four Isle of Man guerillas died in the fighting and Douglas has been severely hit by missiles. Good news for one of our brave boys on the island – two hours ago Sergeant Pete Murphy's attractive wife Valerie gave birth to twin girls in a Liverpool hospital. The sergeant, who is being flown out by helicopter, is reported to be over the m . . .'

As Rachel turned it off they looked at each other, shrugged and raised their glasses.

'Did we win?' Merlin asked.

'Nobody won,' Simon said. 'But they've stopped killing each other.'

'So much for your meeting.' Christy smiled at Rachel.

'Not at all. We'll just rephrase the poster – a public meeting to express concern about the recent Isle of Man campaign.'

'If you have regular meetings,' Christy said, 'we could send you a monthly report from Smiles. Just to tell people what it's like.'

'We could arrange guided tours,' Simon suggested.

'You can arrange one for me. Could you put me up if I came up to London in the next few weeks?'

'You can have my room,' Merlin said.

'Thank you. Then I'll come soon.'

Whenever they were all in a room together, they planned. They were infected with a wild optimism which made all things seem possible. It was as if, sealed in their four solitudes, they had accumulated years of energy which now burst out in compulsive activity. Simon felt it in the love he and Christy made, frenetically, in her chaste room whenever they were alone, in the way Merlin rushed around, in Rachel's new political galvanism. They had all been sleeping for years and the same promiscuous prince had kissed them all.

On the last morning Christy woke up early. She lay in the bleached light and tried to induce the mood of silent melancholy that usually overcame her before she left this house. But even when she shut her eyes it wouldn't come. Simon was between her and the silence. In a few rushed weeks enormous changes had taken place inside her, certain states of mind were lost to her and she had experienced others for the first time. She was something like a wife, something like a mother, those female roles that had always seemed unnecessary and faintly absurd. This anxiety to plan, to turn every conversation into a manifesto, came out of her need to believe the change was permanent. Simon did it too, and Merlin kept asking when and where and why, like a much younger child. With every answer she gave him she felt more bound to him, which was of course what he wanted.

There was so little time, whereas before there had always been too much. In a way Christy wished things would stop happening so that they could drift again, but together; pause and think and absorb each other. This house was the closest they would get to a desert island and it was exhausting – well what am I for, anyway? she thought impatiently. She had almost always believed she was for work, for struggle, in a life that wasn't too complacent. Downstairs she could hear voices. She pulled on her old red slippers and went down to them.

CHAPTER 24

✿✿✿✿✿✿✿✿✿✿✿✿✿✿✿✿✿✿✿✿✿✿✿✿✿✿✿✿✿

All week Simon had been looking forward to the lunch with Daniel and Frankie. They were fixed in his imagination as a good couple, the best he knew; he wanted to exhibit them to Christy and her to them. His own proud attempt at good coupling. Then he wanted Merlin to play with their attractive children, perhaps be invited to parties or whatever the local social circuit for kids that age was. His last meeting with them had been so comforting. He often thought of them in their beautiful room, solid and sane. He kept trying to describe them to Christy, who looked sceptical, and to Merlin, who thought their children sounded revolting; he was often, as an only child, invited to play in families where the children either played him off against each other or left him out of their games. Simon strode ahead of Christy and Merlin.

At first Simon thought Daniel must be ill. When he opened the door his face was flabby and white, the features seemed to have shrunk and he greeted them abruptly, without warmth. Simon had known him for so long that his loss of charm and bloom was inexplicable. But of course there must be an explanation, so they trooped upstairs to the huge bright room, which today looked shabby and untidy. Frankie, tense and with bags where none had been before, sat as usual on the couch, flanked by her children. The light that filled the room so generously played cruel tricks on her face.

But Simon was kissed and plied with drinks, Christy was greeted as someone they had been wanting to meet and Merlin welcomed as an old friend. Then there was a long silence. The children were too old to be dismissed. They sat beside their respective parents and apathetically exchanged lists of possessions.

'Why don't you *show* Merlin your computer, Toby?' Eventually the three of them trailed upstairs.

'Well?' Simon looked at them together on their couch, not enthroned today but clinging to some unknown wreckage. He couldn't keep a peevish note out of his voice, because they hadn't lived up to the high standards of his fantasy about them.

'I've lost my job, that's all,' said Daniel.

'I've still got mine. But it means we'll have to move.'

'We'll have to put the flat on the market next week. I'm afraid if our income goes down too much we'll lose our gilt-edged card, they'll only let us have a green one, and you know that makes it so hard to do anything.'

Christy and Simon, neither of whom had a Britcard of any colour, said nothing.

Frankie went on, 'It's so upsetting for the children too, having to leave this enormous garden and change schools. They'll probably have to share a room.'

'I'm not likely to get another job, not in England anyway.'

'And if we have to go abroad I'll lose mine. Oh dear, sorry, have another drink.' Frankie jumped, flushed with shame to hear herself complaining instead of comforting.

Christy found her nicer than Simon's description of her. Though she was mystified that all these middle-class people were convinced they were poor. Surely it was only the difference between owning a vast flat and a medium-sized one, between holidays in India and in Devon, between good wine every evening and an occasional bottle of plonk? But she tried to sympathize and to forgive them their expectations.

'I suppose you think we're making a fuss about nothing?' Misery hadn't blunted Frankie's perceptions.

'Yes, when I think of people in the camp where I work,' Christy admitted. 'I'm afraid I can't see a room like this without thinking it could be partitioned off and used to house four families.' Daniel winced.

She talked mainly to Frankie while Simon gently persuaded Daniel to tell him what had happened. Out of the corner of her mind Christy was uncomfortably aware of the dark man's anger, his bitter incredulity that he had been ejected from a club he had belonged to as a birthright. There was about him the stumbling clumsiness of a man who has just been wounded and caught off balance. Christy thought, how sure he must have been of his place in the world to be so utterly displaced now. Simon was shocked to see his friend's monumental confidence had had such a fragile base.

'It's not just the job, though that matter's a lot. Architecture's been my only real interest since I was – oh God – about eighteen. And it's not as if you can go off on your own and be an architect, not without a lot of capital. Well you know all about that. I really don't think I will be able to get another job. You see there's been less and less for me to do over the last few years. And last year they didn't make me a partner though I was expecting it, nobody said anything so I thought – well I did what I had to, did a good job. I know there's more opportunity outside England but there's Frankie's job to consider as well. There's just no building going on here. The firm's been reduced from fifteen to six since I joined it.'

The children came back for lunch. Christy saw how Frankie's eyes followed Toby and Lisa, even though she was busy talking and had been glad to get rid of them earlier. She wondered if she would ever feel that close to Merlin, who was behaving with his usual composure. In every situation she had seen him in he held his own. She thought, he must have been through a lot to have acquired all that poise at nine. As he passed her chair Christy reached out and held him, so that he half-sat between her knees. She felt his ribs beneath his striped T-shirt, his bones long and fragile as she pictured his father's, a little too fragile. She was aware that this public hug was partly for Frankie's benefit, but Frankie was still almost blinded by disappointment.

'That boy wants to know if you're my stepmother.'

'His name's Toby. No I'm not.'

'What are you then?'

'I don't know. What do you want me to be?'

'I'm not sure.' He freed himself and ran off.

'It's lucky you get on so well,' Frankie said absently. She could remember when Simon's and Merlin's happiness had seemed quite important but now a dense fog of humiliation hid them from view.

'He's a nice kid. And he seems to like yours, perhaps if you stay in this area they can play together again?'

'We won't be able to afford anything near here.'

'It's a lovely flat,' Christy said, though she knew she was pursuing a tactless course. 'I've never seen such vast rooms in London. And the original fireplaces and cornices and shutters – have you got those in all the rooms?'

Surely, Christy thought, she must be pleased that her house is beautiful. It's a privilege to live in rooms like this, even for a few years. A house or flat is only like a hotel room that you pass through and leave your mark on. Then the next transient occupant resents your mark and tries to erase it.

'We restored everything. There were gas fires in here, we stripped the fireplaces down to the original marble and opened them up again. Most of the cornices had crumbled, we got someone in to remould them. You see that ivy in the middle of the ceiling? That took a week. And the shutters were in a skip down the road, covered with pink paint and riddled with woodworm.'

These people are obsessed with the past, Christy thought, Simon's just as bad. As if by living in nineteenth-century rooms they'll bring back the security their class had then; but she looked at Frankie with genuine sympathy, which prompted an outburst:

'I just haven't the energy to go through all that again, put my heart and soul into doing up a house. Fussing about every doorknob – we'll never find so much well-proportioned space again. I suppose Toby and Lisa will have to share a room – oh well – I'd better do lunch.'

Christy followed her into the kitchen, another graceful room, overlooking the back garden. There was a marble topped table, tiles everywhere, a good cook's array of chopping knives and boards, grinders and mixers.

'Who are you angry with?' she asked Frankie.

Furiously she stabbed the baked potatoes on to plates, shook the lettuce and hacked at the chicken. 'Not with Daniel, of course, it's not his fault. Though perhaps we ought to have seen it coming. It's happened to so many people we know. I just feel cheated. Every time someone on TV talks about rewarding hard work and valuing home-grown brains I want to throw a brick at the screen. And I feel a hypocrite now when I

210

tell the kids they've got to do their homework and pass their exams and go to university. What for? I just hope they're tough and don't fall for the same stupid dreams as us.'

Christy stared at her powerful, beaky face, at her slim, energetic body and thought, a woman like that will always survive. In a way she was glad she had met Frankie in this moment of uncharacteristic weakness. It would be difficult, otherwise, for two strong women like them to need each other.

In the sitting room, where they ate on their knees, the tension between Simon and Daniel had built up to an explosive silence. For so long they had been ensconced as the irresponsible drop-out and the exemplary father and provider. Now Simon felt that he ought to be chastising his friend and, not knowing where to begin, he had begun badly.

The seven of them perched and crouched uneasily over their food.

'Simon thinks I ought to visit his camp, darling.'

The use of endearments between them had always added to Simon's sense of inadequacy. Never had he found it possible to call Jessica or Christy darling or love, even though they were. Yet now it sounded brittle.

'Good idea. I'd like to come along,' Frankie said firmly to Christy.

'I seem to be setting myself up as a tour operator for London's underworld. Next week I've promised to take Simon's sister round the sewers.'

'Oh yes that *would* be up Rose's street, or should I say down her street.' Frankie laughed.

'Colour photographs of turds, rats, people up to their necks in shit, all beautifully reproduced of course.' Daniel smiled and the children giggled with delight to hear their parents talking dirty.

'Can we come?' Lisa asked.

'Certainly not. You children are quite anally regressive enough,' her mother said.

'Quite what enough?' Merlin thought these people were quite interesting.

'Obsessed with our bums,' Toby explained, and the three of them collapsed into helpless laughter.

211

After a few more glasses of wine and jokes at the expense of a fifth person their parents also relaxed.

'Do you like her?' Frankie asked Daniel as soon as they had left.

'Yes, I think I do. She's very clean and straight, and seems to have resurrected Simon. Amazing the way she's taken on that child.'

'He's got sticky-out ears,' said Lisa, hoping for another giggling bout.

'She wears horrible clothes,' Toby added.

Frankie sometimes wished she hadn't encouraged her children to be fastidious. 'I think she's the most honest woman I've met for years, I'd like to see more of her. If we manage to stay in Central London.' Then the sick misery engulfed her again, because outside Central London lurked the wastelands of friendlessness, philistinism, bad wine and meagre salaries.

'Did you like them?' Simon asked later that night after they had made leisurely love, naked on the warm bed.

'Much more than I expected to. I don't think I would have liked Daniel before, though, when he still had that professional man's complacency.'

'He's a very talented architect.'

'I'm sure he is but it's a sort of assumption of grace, a grabbing of the best as if you had an inalienable right to it. They all do it,' she said vaguely.

'You've as much class prejudice as I have.'

'More, perhaps. I don't feel as guilty. But I do like Frankie, she's very warm and generous.'

'Good.' Simon drifted off to sleep on a cloud of security. He had never felt so well loved.

Christy lay wide awake in the dark. It was speckled with floating amoebalike shapes, seething with flecks of shadow, drifting islands of consciousness; memories of the afternoon, all the changes of the last few weeks shifting slowly into a mosaic, Simon's passion in and out of bed.

'I love you,' she whispered in the dark.

He didn't hear but his body did, for he rolled over and held her tightly. She stayed inside his embrace though his shoulder was knobbly and her mind danced with wakefulness.

212

CHAPTER 25

✼✼✼✼✼✼✼✼✼✼✼✼✼✼✼✼✼✼✼✼✼✼✼✼✼✼✼✼

'Don't make it too downbeat and sordid, Rosie,' said her editor, pausing to yell a few obscenities at a subordinate who had put the wrong caption on a photograph. '"Loos Through the Ages", that sort of thing, light and a bit facetious.'

'I was going to concentrate more on what goes on under them. "Life Down Below?"'

'Great. So I'll expect it on Thursday. Are you sure Gerry'll be all right?'

'He's not exactly wild with enthusiasm. He went out yesterday and bought himself a sort of diving suit with a built-in deodorizer.'

'I could let you have that bloke who covered the war in South Africa? He's got a strong stomach. Must go now.'

'So must I. Bye.'

The early morning light from the river crystallized the big, creamy room. Rose drooped her lids like a cat and felt her skin glow in the reflected sunshine, then poured herself another cup of black coffee from the blue enamel pot on the low glass table in front of her. Her flat was spacious and comfortable; she rarely gave parties but when she did they were spectacular. The huge sitting room was designed to look good when it was full of people. Yet she was happiest in it on her own, writing or spending whole mornings, like this morning, on the phone.

She wondered if Christy would seem more approachable on what was, Rose supposed, her own territory. At the theatre she had seemed, to her credit, severe and uncompromising. Rose imagined her striding through the sewers, her great bush of hair standing up on end as an alarm whenever the build-up of gases was unacceptable. Rose was puzzled by her. She could just about conceive of the idea of living for other people, but there was no aura of sanctity about Christy. And now she was involved with Simon, an old solipsist if ever there was one. Rose still thought that her brother had bumbled into Smiles for occupational therapy and had just happened to stay on.

Rose hoped that there would be time to talk to Christy that morning. More and more, she found that her friends were people she worked with, and that her interests either became sucked up into her work or faded out. A fellow journalist had once said to her, 'I'm the opposite of an alchemist; I take other people's gold and turn it into lead.' Lead, cement, dirty newsprint that was thrown away the next morning. Yet it did all have some value, if only as a way of channelling her own burning curiosity about how things worked and what people were. If I didn't write, Rose often said, I wouldn't know what I thought. She knew she could write better but there wasn't time: books paid so badly and there was so much ground to cover. Now her affectionate curiosity about Rose and Simon had directed her antennae towards Smiles. Rose knew that sooner or later she would descend on the camp, with her tape recorder, photographer and most sympathetic manner, to try to wring from it the last drop of human interest.

At midday she packed the waist-high rubber waders she had bought at Lillywhites in a chic red canvas bag with a plastic-covered strip of chemically treated paper and a spiral safety lamp. It was part of the deal that she should buy them all lunch first.

They met outside a pub in Battersea. There were five men aged between about eighteen and sixty, a woman in her forties and Christy, who looked amused and detached. She introduced them all and almost immediately turned to go.

'Won't you have lunch with us?'

'No. I have to get back to the playgroup.'

'But you're coming with Simon on Monday night?'

'All right.'

Rose was disappointed. She had hoped to find in Christy an ally and guide to Hades as well as a new friend.

In the pub Gerry sat at a separate table with a bottle of wine and a plate of shepherd's pie, his enormous bag of equipment held tightly between his knees. Rose bought the toshers drinks and food, switched on her recorder and negotiated a price for the story. She had hoped Christy would do this for her; now she would end up paying them too much.

It was obvious that most of the talking was going to be done by Steve, a black cockney in his early twenties with thin sharp features, and by Bridget, the group's comic, who had a round, florid face and a huge, muscular body.

'You all look very well,' Rose commented.

'Oh, the air's great dahn there,' Bridget said as she tucked into her macaroni cheese. Rose laughed. 'Nah, really. You never do meet a sickly tosher. We either get the Rats' Piss Fever or the Yepatitis early on, or we live forever, bloody near – 'ow long'd yer farver go on for, George?'

'Ninety-six. And I'm sixty-four. Been dahn there since I was sixteen. Work it aht yourself, forty-eight years.' George poured a pint down in a steady stream to show how strong his lungs were.

'There's one fing we wanted to get straight first. 'sall against the law, you know that don't you?' Steve stared at her with quick, suspicious eyes.

'I know. So we won't take any recognizable photos or mention names or where we met. Why is it illegal?'

'Toshers is. Flushers wasn't,' George said enigmatically.

Bridget lowered her voice, which still boomed. 'Five years ago, we were flushers. Cleanin' aht the sewers, shovellin' the muck inter skips, all legal an' above board though the wages wasn't much. Then they made us redundant, see? Stopped spendin' money on the sewers alonga everyfink else. George was our ganger then, we worked in a team of five same as all the flushers, 'cos of the rats. Not to mention the wild pigs.'

'The what?'

'They was spendin' a fortune dahn there till a few years back. Bloody great plastic bubbles like Durex linin' the tunnels.'

'Keep it clean, Bridget,' George said.

'Then it all stopped. No more closed-circuit telly, no more restoration and no more jobs for us. And some of us – me and George – 'ad never done anyfink else.'

'So we carried on, freelance like,' Steve said cheerfully. 'Invested in metal detectors – I fahnd a Roman coin not long back, and George got a ring from Queen Elizabeth's reign.

215

The old one, fifteen somefink. When we get valuable stuff like that we share it aht. Course, there's always been toshers dahn there. We used to be on the uvver side, so to speak, shoppin' them ter the police. I'll tell you somefink else: since they stopped all that work dahn there there's bin tunnels cavin' in all over the place.'

'The whole fuckin' city'll be in the shit soon,' said Jamie with evident satisfaction.

'Doesn't that make your job very dangerous?' Rose asked primly.

"tis dangerous,' Bridget agreed. 'And disgustin'. My kids've never told their friends what I do. My son-in-law still finks I'm an engineer. But it 'as its moments and it 'as its rewards. That Roman coin Steve spoke of, we sold it to a collector in Knightsbridge for two fahsand quid. Anyway we could be worse off.'

'Like the mudlarks,' Steve said contemptuously. 'I used ter go dahn the beaches at low tide wiv 'em, when I was a little kid. Me mum died of AIDS and Dad went off somewhere. There was four of us kids livin' at Smiles in a tin shack. We used ter play by the river and when we 'eard there was money to be made we'd stay six, seven hours at low tide, 'untin fer antiques and money and old cloves as gets washed up there. Never made more'n the price've an 'amburger.'

'Mudlarks wouldn't know a hobjet dah if it bit 'em. Just a bunch of kids an' old women.' George stood up ponderously after his third pint. Rose thought they had better go while they were all still fairly sober.

They followed the toshers to an abandoned tower block between Battersea Bridge and Wandsworth Bridge. The car park in front of the block had become a small camp where Jamie lived, and the toshers used a ground floor room in the tower as storage space for their working clothes and equipment.

'Nobody ever seems ter nick this lot,' Bridget remarked as she pulled on her stiff overalls with their huge pockets and her muck caked gauntlets and waders, an outfit which looked as if it could walk by itself.

Gerry folded his clothes nervously into his leather bag. He hadn't enjoyed an assignment so little since the Hackney

216

Football Riots. Rose kept flashing smiles at him, like a hostess jollying along a difficult guest. When he was zipped into his shiny black skin Gerry sat on his bag and sulkily cradled his camera in its waterproof and, he hoped, rat- and wild pig-proof carrying case.

'Slinky,' Bridget remarked in her pooftah baiting voice.

The men sniggered. They had resisted making jokes about photographers in the pub but now they were near the lid of their world. Rose wished Gerry hadn't made himself look such a twerp.

Outside the block, George raised a manhole cover and lowered himself ponderously into the pit. They were all carrying seven-feet-long poles with hoes at the end and either metal detectors or spiral lamps, which made climbing difficult.

At first, when the cover was replaced, Rose couldn't see anything. She was blind in a cold, dark place, wading knee high in icy water that chilled her feet despite her rubber waders and thick socks. Her boots sank into a layer of sand, shingle and sediment that felt oddly like a beach. She remembered a seaside holiday in Italy when she was eight, Madge endlessly calling her and Simon back in case they swam near the open sewers.

As the blackness faded to misty grey Rose was able to see they were in a brick tunnel. She and Gerry could stand up but all the toshers except Jamie had to stoop. They carried their lamps very low and shone them on the brickwork, where coins were often wedged. In the yellow lamplight their six figures threw grotesque, hallucinatory shadows on to the brickwork and the gleaming muck at their feet. The toshers used their poles to test the ground ahead of them and rake the slime for any objects.

Gerry's legs were shaking and he wished he'd stayed safely above. Rose could have taken some pix herself, she was hard as nails and twice as sharp. The smell wasn't quite as appalling as he had expected but just the fact of being there – Gerry was almost sure he was going to be sick. His mind had jammed on the words of a song he had heard years ago:

'I've been livin' in this river of shit
For nearly twenty years and I'm gettin' tired of it.'

George asserted himself as ganger. Rose and Gerry were

217

happy to let him push ahead; they never moved more than a couple of inches away from the toshers and had no need of their injunctions to stick close to them. They walked in single file.

George's voice was loud and confident. 'Now there's rules to observe dahn 'ere and you'd better listen 'cos they're safety rules. Number one, there's brickwork crumblin' all over the place and if you so much as tap the roof you could cause an avalanche. Number two, the law don't like us. They say they don't want us ter get suffocated dahn 'ere and then be 'eld responsible. Touchin' innit? Doesn't matter bein' responsible fer us starvin'. So when we pass man'oles an' grids an' that, put the lamps aht. I'll tell you when there's one comin'. Then, number three, there's the wevver. We don't get forecasts no more like when there was the van up there and the two-way radio and the shahs. That was luxury though we didn't know it then. If a storm comes sudden we'll get swept right dahn ter the river, fancy cameras an 'all. Keep yer voices dahn.'

They trudged forward in absolute silence. The brickwork tunnel continued for miles and the sludge hardly varied in depth. The cold and wetness seeped through to Rose's bones and every ripple in the muck looked like a rat. She didn't dare to ask about the pigs just yet. The toshers moved very slowly, diving their arms down up to the elbows, groping for lost objects and scraping the crevices in the wall. Anything they found was examined wordlessly and either tossed behind them or thrust into one of their capacious pockets. Half-heartedly, Gerry took a few photographs of them. Rose had nothing to do but endure the discomfort and soak in the atmosphere, of which she had had quite enough. She switched off the tape recorder in her pocket and rehearsed her article, which was already partly written in her head. For once the chatty, blithe tone of her own writing comforted her.

> *Medieval London valued its cesspit cleaners, or gang-fermors, and paid them well. Maybe they were right! If my friend Alf (as I'll call him) is to be believed, our sewers are just about ready to collapse from neglect.*
>
> *Ever wondered who invented the loo? It was Sir John Harington, a cousin of Queen Bess, who built two of them in*

218

1596 and wrote a book that just must have been a Tudor best seller: The Metamorphosis of Ajax, a New Discourse on a Stale Subject. Cousin Bess liked it so much she kept it on a chain in her own loo at Hatfield. Here's a piece of advice that certainly hasn't gone stale: 'Item, that children or busie folk, disorder it not, or open the sluice, with putting their hands, without a key, you should have a little button, or scallop, to bind it downe with a vice pinne, so as without the key it will not be opened . . .'

But Harington suffered the fate of so many great inventors and his idea wasn't taken up commercially for two hundred unhygienic years. Poor old Pepys could have done with it when in 1660 he wrote from his address in (seriously!) Seething Lane: 'Going down to my cellar . . . I put my foot in a great heap of turds, by which I find that Mr Turner's house of office is full and comes into my cellar, which doth trouble me, but I will have it helped –'

Steve and Bridget shone their lamps on the two aliens to see if they had clammed up, as they hoped, out of fear. In the gaudy light their own faces were reflected, a pasty globe and a narrow black shield. Rose caught in both a glint of mockery and triumph that, underground, they were on top.

'Course this is one of the cleanest, innit Steve?'

'That's right. Under the City now there's medieval sewers 'asn't bin cleaned fer centuries. Old arches collapsin', that's where we got that Roman coin. Yer offices 're rahnd there, aren't they?'

'They used to be,' Rose said. 'Now they're in Dockland but I live in the City.' She would never feel quite the same again about her elegant grey marble bathroom.

''arf a million gallons a day comes dahn 'ere.' Bridget chuckled and all the toshers shook their heads and clucked, as if they took credit for this wonderful fact.

Suddenly the dreary tunnel opened out into a glorious space like a cathedral. There were gleaming vaults, buttresses, pillars and, high above their heads, a metallic weir shot needles of water down into yet another tunnel. It was both mystical and industrial, a reminder that religion and technology had once had faith in each other. Rose thought, I must

219

ask Simon about that. Her feet were still freezing but she felt exultant, as if she had just taken deep breaths on top of a mountain. Perhaps they were right about the healthy air? Or perhaps there was a spontaneous joy in being either far above the world or deep in its bowels, a heaven and hell condition – Rose smiled at Steve, who walked beside her, still trying to impress and frighten her.

Gerry revived and took some photographs. Bridget plunged her arm into the water near the wall and the other toshers helped her to drag out a huge conglomerate of metal. It was a great sputnik of lost nails, coins, iron bars, rings, pipes, keys, knives, forks, spoons and spanners; an infernal sculpture three feet in diameter and so heavy that the six of them could hardly support it for a minute. They posed with it on their shoulders like pall-bearers, and Gerry clicked with enthusiasm. After-wards, briefly, there was a picnic atmosphere when he produced a flask of brandy from his bag and they passed it round.

Then they branched off down another dark tunnel, in single file again, though this time they could all stand upright. All sounds except the splash of their footsteps and the echo of their voices were sealed on the other side of the bricks. So, Rose thought, nobody out there will hear us if we scream as a tidal wave or some hidden danger sweeps us off –

'Underneaf Nine Elms Market now,' George said cheer-fully, and added in the same tone, 'And 'ere's where the rats got Charlie.'

'Nah, it was the next on the left,' said Bridget.

'Bloody stoopid, goin 'orff on 'is own like that. Always was a stoopid git, Charlie.' Jamie sounded as if the rats' piss had poisoned his blood long ago. He was the only tosher Rose didn't like.

It was the boredom she would remember. They moved so slowly, every monotonous stretch of wall held dozens of crevices to prod, and in the dark Styx there were endless pockets of slime to poke and grope. It's a monstrous job, Rose thought, awful and poetic and fascinating, yet in its details as repetitive as most jobs. Including mine.

In the eighteenth century Sir John Harington's bright idea still hadn't caught on. All those elegant, cultivated people in

220

powdered wigs had to duck as they walked down the street,
whenever they heard the cry of 'Gardez l'eau' (gardy loo).
Then, at the end of the century, the first water closets were
built. And their cesspits overflowed into the sewers, contami-
nating the city's water supply.

London just got smellier and smellier until the 'Great
Stink' in the summer of 1858, when the curtains of the
House of Commons had to be soaked in chloride of lime and
both the House and the Law Courts were nearly evacuated to
the provinces. On the Thames, boat traffic came to a halt on
the 'aqua mortis'.

Then along came Joseph Bazelgette, a brilliant engineer
who built a hundred miles of intercepting sewers, enabling
Victorian London to expand without collapsing. We still use
his sewers. But, according to 'Alf', they are wearing out and
the government's recent attempt to privatize the metropolitan
sewers and launch a share issue in them has not been
successful. Come again in Bazelgette!

Steve was behind Rose again the dark, whispering.

'See that tunnel? Runs due norf. We don't go up there, not beyond St John's Wood.'

'Oh I'm sure St John's Wood's all right,' Rose said with a private giggle.

'It's 'ampstead you 'ear the stories abaht,' Bridget said without turning round.

Rose couldn't see either of their faces and really didn't know if they were making fun of her or not. 'What stories?'

They all paused while George stooped to scrape the wall. 'Not so much a story as a legend. Like King Arfur. My farver worked wiv a bloke 'oo saw one of 'em, and 'e first 'eard abaht 'em from 'is farver –'

Rose switched on the tape recorder in her pocket and George relished their attention.

'People say they first got in at 'ighgate, when it was all fields and farms rahnd there. There was this pregnant sow, right, got into the sewers when they was open. Well pigs'll eat anyfink as you know, so she 'ad a good feed, lay dahn in the muck an' gave birf. Only the little ones, bein' quick to adapt an' that, soon grew bristles like thorns and scales and loominous eyes

221

like cats. Charged arahnd the tunnels like bulls they did, feastin' on rats an' frogs. The rats didn't like that did they, and some of 'em was six foot long. So they formed an army. Rats is 'ighly hintelligent as you know. There was this 'orrible battle atween the rats and the wild pigs. When they was buildin' the Tube they 'eard the screams and the shrieks. A coupla the old toshers got mixed up in it and the rats picked ther bones.

'Well after that, uv course, nobody'd come dahn 'ere. Then after a year or so they comes dahn again – me grandfarver 'eard this when 'e was a little kid – an' it was quiet as anyfink. But every few months or so a man'd get lost dahn 'ere and the body'd be washed up. And it'd either be a white skeleton – that'd mean the rats'd got 'im – or there'd be jest an 'ole in the neck and anuvver 'ole where 'is 'eart 'd bin. At first they fought there was a murderer dahn 'ere, a sorta Jack the Ripper cum Dracula. Then they sent a famous nat'ralist dahn to 'ave a look.

'Well what'd 'appened was this. After the big fight atween 'em the rats and the boars, as they was by then, 'ad divided the tunnels. The boars was to stick to the Norf and the rats could 'ave the rest, seein' as there was millions of 'em. The boars didn't breed so fast but they was 'orrible. Rats'll only attack a yooman bein' if 'e's alone but the boars, after a few generations, grew big as bulls and twice as ferocious. Nobody 'oo met one ever lived to tell the tale.'

'Then how come you're telling it?' Gerry asked sceptically.

'Oh, they've bin seen an 'eard often enough. I've often seen great scaly creatures gallopin' past at the end of a tunnel,' Bridget said complacently.

'You do often 'ear 'em,' Steve agreed. 'Roarin' an 'snortin'.'

'Listen!' George raised his arms portentously.

To their right, on the other side of the bricks, something rumbled, bellowed, grunted and snuffled. It wasn't a human sound and it echoed through the tunnel.

'It's the Tube!' Rose cried out in fear.

Gerry's arm was gripping hers. 'Don't you think it's rather odd that in all these years – nearly two centuries according to you – not one of these wild hogs has been washed down into the river?'

'They'd 'av to go dahnstream, wouldn't they? And pigs can

222

only swim against the stream,' Steve said conclusively.

'Well, I think it's absurd. And, as George said at the beginning, it's a legend, so why do you tell us as if it was history?'

'It's both, innit?' Steve said.

'But I don't see –' Gerry argued on and on but the toshers only shrugged. Rose thought Gerry's prissy, rational voice sounded rather silly in the dark sewers.

Soon after they turned around and walked back, quite fast as the toshers had already filled their pockets, which bulged like panniers. Rose asked them a few last questions but the wild hogs stampeded in her brain, and were still there when they pulled each other through the round hole into the incongruous summer afternoon.

CHAPTER 26

The day Simon received a solicitor's letter telling him Connie had left him Freeman Castle, Bernard phoned.

'I suppose I'd better congratulate you?'

'On the house? Yes, it was nice of her.'

They had just cycled back from a long, hot day at Smiles. A baby had died of cholera in the camp the day before and two new cases had been confirmed by an unemployed doctor who lived there. A van had come round, offering free vaccinations. Simon and Christy had gone along and had had Merlin vaccinated as well, by his school doctor. But many people in the camp had refused, out of apathy and automatic suspicion of doctors and of vans that claimed to give things away. The panic had begun; already several people with children had left the camp. The solicitor's letter, with its engraved heading and pompous greed, was like a stuffed leather couch abandoned on a bomb-site.

'That's a matter of opinion. It's not particularly nice for your mother and myself. Some people might consider we had a moral right to the house.'

'Really? Who?'

'We've lived here all our married lives. I've lived here since I was three years old, as a matter of fact.'

'That's not bad, without rent.'

'Were you intending to charge us rent?'

Simon could hear stifled shrieks in the background. Here I go again, he thought, having hysterical scenes with them on the phone. Christy came, clutched his arm and tried to listen in to the conversation. Merlin picked up the extension in his father's bedroom.

'No. I assumed you'd want to move.'

224

'Oh did you? Rather a convenient assumption for you. Assumed we'd want to move,' Simon heard him repeat, in a tone of appalled sarcasm, to Madge. 'I think your mother would like a word with you. Yes. Here she is now.'

Christy wondered how many people were involved in this conversation. No doubt the rapacious old crone herself was hovering too, enjoying the row created by her will.

'Simon? Now I hope you're not going to let this go to your head. I mean there's no question of you and Christine living here –'

'Here name's Christy. Why not?'

'Well, it's just not your sort of house, that's all, and the wrong sort of area. So far away from that gypsy place.'

'As a matter of fact I wasn't planning to live in it. I'll probably sell it. I'll let you know when I've decided.'

A loud consultation took place in sobs and hisses.

'Hello? Simon? I think we'd – Madge says – we'll have a meeting about this, all of us, Rose too.'

'But Bernard, it's only in Victorian novels that families have meetings about wills. What is there to discuss?'

'You're turning us out of our house and you ask what there is to discuss?'

'I wish you'd stop talking as if you were the sitting tenant and I was the unscrupulous landlord. You could buy any house in London if you chose.'

'Darling?'

'Yes Madge.'

'Why don't you come to dinner on Saturday and we'll talk about it? Just the three of us and Rose. Merlin's not interested in all this, is he, and I'm sure your friend won't want to hear about our sordid affairs.'

'Yes. OK. See you then.' Simon put the phone down and collapsed, exhausted, on to a chair.

Merlin came rushing down the corridor. 'Are we going to go and live in Grandma's house?'

'No. Do you know that'll be the first time in years Madge has succeeded in getting us all together, alone, around a table. They say money drives people apart but in our family I think it's the only thing that keeps us together.'

Simon looked at Merlin apologetically, because he hadn't

225

meant to insult Madge and Bernard in front of him. If only to protect himself when Merlin became as critical of him as he was of them.

'So you're going to be rich,' Christy said thoughtfully.

Merlin was defiant. 'Well I think money's nice. We could buy a car and some new clothes and go on a proper holiday, in a hotel with a swimming pool. And eat in restaurants every day.'

'You'd better go and live with your grandparents again if you want all that,' Simon said sadly.

'No. I didn't say that. But if we've got some money why can't we enjoy it? You're like those miserable people in the newspapers who say they've won five billion pounds in the *Morning Hope* Bingo game but it's not going to change their lives. Grandma was always reading out stories like that, she thought it was awful too.'

'I've always rather admired those people.' Simon thought the money was like a green miasma drifting into the room, distorting and confusing.

Christy was very quiet, suddenly aware that a Simon with money would have different needs and expectations.

On Saturday, Rose gave him a lift up to St John's Wood. In the car she was jubilant, as if the undeclared war between the generations had at last broken out and been conclusively won by them.

'I didn't know anything about it until I phoned them on Thursday. Madge was terribly offended by something, at first I thought she was disgusted by my piece on the sewers. Then she told me – I just roared with laughter.'

'So we'll both be in disgrace.'

'Why didn't Christy come along?'

'She wasn't invited.'

'I never get a chance to talk to her. I do like her though, why don't we all go out together one day? Take Merlin to the zoo or something.'

'He hates the zoo, it was our regular treat when he was living with Madge and Bernard. But – yes – of course we'll see more of each other.'

'I suppose she doesn't like me. Thinks I'm a horrible media person. What did she say about that article on toshers?'

'Not a lot. She doesn't read the papers much.'

Christy seemed to want to keep her distance from his family, except for himself and Merlin, and Simon encouraged this as he liked to keep his friendships tightly sealed in separate compartments. Now that the barriers were breaking down he felt overstretched and fragmented.

Bernard opened the door for them, wearing his urbanity again like a buttonhole.

'So glad you could both come – just family – Rose darling, how nice and summery you look. Thought we'd sit in the garden. I say,' to Simon, 'what a surprise! She always was an unpredictable woman.' Bernard was perpetually astonished by life, which preserved much of his boyish charm.

'I suppose it *was* a surprise?' Madge asked suspiciously when they were seated on the lawn around the wrought-iron table.

'Why do you ask?' When in doubt Simon always answered questions with questions.

'Well, a most extraordinary coincidence. Such a small world. We were having lunch at the "Carcassone" the other day when we saw Ronny Saffron,' Bernard's eyes popped with amazement. 'Connie's old solicitor's partner, you know. And he did mention he'd seen you and Merlin in the office, with Connie, a few months ago. I do hope I'm not being indiscreet.'

'Let's all be indiscreet,' said Rose, watching Simon's face in the light from the illuminated toadstools Madge had put on the lawn.

'Yes, we did go along there.'

'And changed her will?' Madge asked like a machine gun.

'That's right.'

'I thought so.' She hummed casually and tunelessly, fingering the glass her little man had brought her. 'Well. Cheers.'

'I always remember,' Bernard chuckled, 'when Merlin was a little chap, can't have been more than two, we used to say "cheers" when he was in the room and he'd rush off to bring in all the deckchairs. Awfully sweet.'

'He used to be here such a lot,' Madge said coldly. 'How is he?'

'Fine.'

'Getting used to the flat? And the school? And the new – stepmother, is it?'

227

'We're not planning to get married. Yes, he seems quite happy.'

'Children have to be so adaptable nowadays. I remember when you were about five you just would not sleep in a strange bed. You needed an absolutely rigid routine, same stories every night – and you Rose, you were *devoted* to your potty. A little blue plastic one with a Rupert Bear head. You carried it around with you wherever you went and *nothing* else would do. I suppose you haven't changed really.'

'Are you referring to my article last Sunday?'

'Well darling, it *was* a bit much.'

'I knew you'd think so. The thought spurred me down all those creepy, smelly tunnels.'

'I don't know why you both take such delight in upsetting me.' Madge's voice was suddenly on the edge of tears and they all sat up anxiously. 'It's a game for you, isn't it? Well I think it's very childish and selfish.'

'It isn't a game,' Rose said softly.

'How about some avocados? Salmon and strawberries. Quite a feast, Madge was shopping all morning.' Bernard stood up and swung his arms to ease his backache, his only ailment at sixty-seven.

'Sit down, Bernard. I put the timer on, my little man will bring the trolley in a minute.' For a second she glanced up at the window from which Connie's perverse and indomitable will still surveyed them. 'Now this is what we wanted to say.' She had a catch in her voice, a self-elected Queen abdicating. 'We can't stay here now. The house belongs to you, Simon, and you don't want your aging parents in the way. It was silly I suppose, we always assumed we'd stay here –'

'In the evening of our days,' Bernard backed her up.

'Shut up, Bernard.'

'Sorry darling.'

'But now we've got to move. We'll rent a flat for a few months while we look around for something. Of course we won't be able to afford a great big house like this –'

'Why not?' Simon asked.

Rose pounced too. 'Yes, why not, Bernard? I saw your first year's profits quoted in the *Financial Hope* the other day and it looked to me as if there was plenty of money to buy a house with.'

'My dear girl, it's not as simple as that. We're overextended, had to be to get the business off the ground. Now we've got cash flow problems too, taxes, awfully high overheads you know. That figure you saw doesn't go into *my* pocket.'

'Some of it must,' said his son.

'I've noticed,' Rose said, 'that the rich never admit to being rich.'

'In fact they complain about money far more than people who haven't got any,' Simon agreed.

His mother looked at him with growing dislike. 'Well you won't be able to be so bloody sanctimonious now, will you? I hope you realize how much this house is worth?'

'Yes.' He had looked incredulously in the windows of some estate agents.

'I wonder what they'll think of that down at your gypsy camp? I suppose you'll be going to work in a sports car now instead of a third-hand bike?'

'Drawing room socialists,' Bernard muttered.

Simon flushed; his face was a sickly orange in the light from the toadstools. 'It does make my position rather complicated. But then it always has been. When are you moving?' he asked as the robot noisily trundled the food out on a trolley.

Madge slammed the dishes down on the wobbly wrought-iron table. 'You can't wait to get rid of us, can you? And I always thought you had a nicer nature than Rose.'

'We're both nice, in our way,' Simon said defensively.

'What do you want him to do, Madge?' Rose asked, genuinely puzzled. 'Renounce his legal right to the house? Give it to you rent free until you go to the great theme park in the sky?'

'Talking of which,' Bernard said pointedly, 'I remember how my dear old father looked after his parents when they got old. Bought them a house round the corner so they wouldn't be lonely, and in the end paid a fortune for his mother to go into that nursing home. He always used to say, "If they weren't here, I wouldn't be here either." He always meant this to be a family house. Still, that sort of thing's considered very sentimental nowadays.'

'None of you understand.' Madge clasped her hands in her lap and twisted her gingham napkin. 'I can't eat.'

229

'Have some salmon, darling.' Bernard tucked in cheerfully. 'Awfully good new potatoes. From Cassidy's?'

'I'm going to lie down. I don't know how you can all be so callous.' Madge walked away over the lawn, determined to suffer.

The others felt a certain amount of guilt, but it was so familiar that they were able to cope with it whilst callously enjoying their meal.

'So you *are* doing well, Bernard?' Simon asked.

'Can't complain too much. Could be a lot worse. We're expanding the one near you, as a matter of fact.'

'Really?'

'Yes, we've bought up that decrepit cemetery next to the old football ground. The bulldozers should be in there on Monday, there's a lot of rubbish to clear before they can start building. Old graves and so on. Rather morbid.'

'I used to spend a lot of time in that cemetery.' There ought to be pain or at least a wave of melancholy. But his soul had disengaged itself from that area of his past. There was only the image of Bernard's fun palaces rising on the skulls and femurs of the nineteenth-century establishment.

'Did you really?' Bernard sounded concerned. He always associated contemplation with lack of health. 'I do hope that now you've got something behind you, all this drop-out stuff is going to stop. I mean you could start your own business now. We're still looking for backers as a matter of fact, get you in on the ground floor. It would pay for Merlin's education – have you thought about where you're going to send him? Sammy was saying Westminster's got a very good new headmaster, if you don't want him to board.'

His children looked at each other, sighed and laughed.

'It's all very well laughing, Simon, but the least you can do for the poor child is to make sure he gets a proper education. You *can't* send him to one of those comprehensives, why I was reading about them the other day. They're terrorized by armed gangs – children of twelve or thirteen threatening teachers with knives and guns. And drugs everywhere.'

'Dad, we'll never agree about what a good education is.'

It was a long time since Simon had called him Dad. As they sat in the garden over their coffee, Bernard felt quite fond of them both. They were rude and ungrateful of course, but they could be worse. And while Simon shouldn't have sucked up to Connie behind their backs like that, it showed the boy had more sense than Bernard had ever given him credit for. This was a nice house and they would miss it but the latest figures had been very encouraging. Perhaps they'd be able to afford an even nicer one. Company houses were very favourably placed for tax relief, Sammy had been saying. What a pity Madge got so upset.

At the end of the evening they tiptoed through the house.

'Shall we go up and say goodnight to her?' Simon asked.

'She might be asleep – not a good idea. I think it would be more diplomatic to give her a ring in the morning. Just to show there are no hard feelings.'

'Aren't there?' Rose asked.

'Water under the bridge. These things happen. Life's too short.' Beamishly he ushered them out to the car.

Madge watched them from the bedroom window as they drove off. Later, when Bernard came up, she said, 'I feel like King Larry.'

'Who, darling?'

'You know, that Shakespeare play Tommy was so good in. The one about the old man whose children were awful to him, and thrust him out on to the Heath in a howling gale.'

'*King Lear*, darling. Shall we have a look for something on the Heath?'

'I don't know why they're so unkind to me. I've always put them first.'

'They're takers, I'm afraid, and you're one of life's givers.'

'I've tried so hard –'

'I'm afraid we've been too nice to them. A bit more discipline perhaps – do you know, he's going to send Merlin to one of those comprehensives?'

'Absolutely disgusting.'

CHAPTER 27

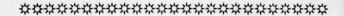

In the end they cycled up to St John's Wood in a row. Merlin, wobbling in the middle, yelled out at every traffic lights that they should have got a taxi. We look like a hearty Sunday outing, Christy thought, a family picnic with brown rice and lentils. London got richer and richer; creamy plaster squares and terraces that were more like patisserie than architecture, exquisite gardens, canopied balconies, velvety parks, butchers and grocers like smart restaurants and restaurants like palaces. They cut through the back streets to avoid the main roads, where Merlin was still nervous.

'That's a nice house,' he kept saying. 'Shall we live there?'

Past the eighteenth-century grace of Mayfair to the Nash terraces around Regent's Park, built to accommodate the courtiers of a palace that never was. In the clean morning light it all shone with the confidence and beauty of money that has had time to turn itself into something else. They stopped in the park so that Merlin could go to a playground, sat on a bench and watched while he swung and dug and climbed.

Simon was drunk on his city. 'If the Prince Regent hadn't been so unpopular he would have turned London into the most beautiful city in the world. Have you seen prints of his Regent Street? It makes ours look like slabs of suet pudding. That beautiful curve was built to connect Carlton House with a new palace Nash was going to build for him here. Piccadilly and Oxford Circus – the First and Second Regent Circuses – were lined with curved buildings. Can you imagine anything more seductive? Great sweeps of balustrades, white plaster, colonnades, beautifully proportioned rooms – but of course he didn't get away with it. As Regent and as King he was hated as a monster of extravagance and lechery. The British have always loved their sex scandals. Nash was hated too, as his architect, there was a rhyme about him:

Augustus at Rome was for building renowned,
And of marble he left what of brick he had found.
But is not our Nash too a very great master
He finds us all brick and he leaves us all plaster.

'That's the problem with architecture, you see. You can have great visions but it's almost impossible for them to materialize.'

Christy looked around. 'It seems to me he built an awful lot, anyway. It's so vain, to want to leave your indelible stamp on a city for ever and ever.'

'You will drag morality into it. Can't you see how ravishingly beautiful it would have been? Miles of elegance, sweetness and light –' and Simon, who had been in love with Nash's grand plan for London since he was fifteen, sighed.

'There's quite enough of that,' Christy said firmly. 'The whole damn city from Chelsea to Hampstead is just a rich ghetto, an exclusive club only the rich can join. And there's so much of it, that's what always shocks me. Think of each of these houses being bought and sold for a million or two.'

'I don't want to live in one, I just love looking at them. Anyone can do that.'

'Yes, but it makes you feel like a leper. And it's designed to – the keys to the private gardens, the armed guards to the big blocks of flats, the *right* food and wine, accents, clothes, furniture – they're all passwords. They don't need to put a wall around it.'

'In a way you're right. Since I was growing up here a much bigger gulf has opened up between the rich city and the poor. I think it's terrible, of course I do – but visually it's a feast.'

'I forgot you have a stake in all this now.'

'And a stake in Smiles too, don't forget.'

'Do you?' Christy unleashed the anger and misery she had been suppressing for weeks. A few days ago Lily had died of cholera, a small corpse in a tent, buried the next day in the communal pit they had dug. 'I think you're like one of those do-gooding women who used to visit prisons and slums. Everyone called them angels but really it was just their way of being rich *and* good.'

233

'I wondered when you'd turn on me. I've spent as much time at Smiles as you have over the last few weeks.'

She got up. 'You're just a bit too good at reconciling it all, Simon, and I can't take it. Such a pity there are children dying but, anyway, isn't it lucky there was enough money to preserve all these lovely houses. Sweetness and light. There's no sweetness and light for people lying in their own shit and vomit.'

'You've no right to attack me, as if I couldn't love beautiful streets without being indifferent to suffering. You're a terrible prig sometimes, Christy.'

'And you're as bland and smug as those houses you admire so much.'

As if to refute her charge, he began to panic when he saw she was about to leave. He couldn't bear to go to Freeman Castle alone with Merlin. Only with Christy would it be a door open on to the future instead of a door slammed shut on the past with him locked inside. Simon took her hands and began to plead, hardly aware of what he was saying.

'Don't go. Come with me, please come. I need you there, really, just as much as they need you at Smiles. We'll go there later if you like, with Merlin, I know we ought to. Trust me.'

They were both weeping; Simon because he was frightened that she would despise his ambiguity for all the reasons he had always despised it himself, and Christy because, for a moment, she really had been about to cycle off and leave him forever. Yet it wasn't a possibility she wanted.

Merlin, at the top of the slide, watched them and wondered why people became increasingly silly and embarrassing as they got older.

'Everybody's looking at me. Come *on*,' and he pulled them away.

It was a large brick house, pretending to be older than it was, set in its own drive and garden. Such detachment in the middle of London seemed to Christy a fantastic luxury. Merlin ran straight into the garden to see if there were any raspberries left and Simon prowled the rooms. Bernard and Madge had taken almost everything, presumably in the hope of moving to an equally big house. Christy saw in the few remaining trappings that impersonal look that houses of the rich always

234

seemed to her to have: heavy pelmets, coy bracket lights, mirrors with concealed lights, radiators in wrought-iron cages, a great deal of pink and oyster silk that suggested the house, when it was occupied, must have looked like a high-class brothel. She kept having to remind herself it was Simon's, a part of him just as her mother's house was a part of her, a perpetual landscape in her mind.

Upstairs the empty shell of his parents' bedroom and bathroom was an orgy of pink. From their window she looked down on the garden, where the flowers and leaves were acquiring a blowsy autumnal look, and on Merlin happy on his swing. She couldn't see his face but she knew he was at home here, safe, with enough space to dream in. The sooner we get him to Smiles and he sees what real life is, the better, she thought viciously. He was the image of pampered childhood. Then she remembered he'd suffered quite a lot, for someone of nine. Middle-class suffering was always psychological.

Christy followed Simon into another room, which looked strange because it was full; of furniture, books, records, pictures, even bedclothes on the bed. She lifted an embroidered cloth off the desk and found a model. When she knelt to look at it she saw a neat exercise in rectangles, cubes and diagonal lines.

'You were going to make people live in tower blocks.'

'I know.'

'A blueprint for Smiles.' She was disappointed. She had assumed that, if he had been an architect, he must have been a very good one. 'Nash wouldn't be seen dead in a place like that.'

'He was dead already, that was the problem. You can't take a spirit that's died – elegance and wit – and embody it in modern art. Our spirit is, oh, hard-nosed, angular, big, nostalgic, paranoid – even buildings that aren't fortresses have to look fortified. That underground car park I built looked exactly like a nuclear bunker, from the outside. It would take a very great architect to turn that into something appealing, and I'm afraid I wasn't one.'

As they knelt side by side she touched his hand and felt even closer to him.

Madge had left Connie's room untouched. The curtains

235

were still drawn and there was an overwhelming smell of nicotine, sickness and old age. Christy stared in amazement at the squalid jumble of unwashed clothes, dirty ashtrays, cups, glasses, old newspapers and magazines. On all the tables and on the records that had been left out there was a thick fuzz of dust. A family of cockroaches was lunching on a chocolate biscuit under a stained armchair.

'But why did they let her live like this?'

'She wouldn't let them in.'

'And after she died? Surely they could have cleaned up then?'

'I think they were too angry about her will. Thought they'd leave it to me.'

'We'll come over another day and do it. I don't want to stay long today.'

'Simon? Daddy? Christy? Where are you?'

Christy started because he just sounded like a frightened child. Finding the house creepy, as she did. 'We're up here, in Connie's room.'

Merlin stood in the doorway. 'Pooh. Fancy having to be a ghost, haunting a place like this.'

'Tangoing in eternity,' Simon said thoughtfully from the window. What a wonderful view she must have had of us all in the garden that night, he thought. 'Poor old thing,' he added, in case she was listening.

Christy and Merlin had edged out on to the landing. Simon said his farewells silently and followed them out of the house.

'What will you do with it?' Christy asked.

'I don't know.'

'So are we going to be rich?' his son asked.

'I just want to get some salt beef sandwiches and cheesecake from a place I know in the High Street.'

Christy was glad to turn her back on the house and cycle away from it. She felt her power over him increase, now that he had at last left home.

Merlin's legs were aching terribly by the time they crossed Wandsworth Bridge. He wished they'd let him stay on his swing instead of dragging him all over London, submitting him to one of their tests, which he usually felt he failed. When he used to tell Madge he was exhausted, she fed him and put him to bed, almost smothered him in a great soft eiderdown of devotion and sympathy. Now Merlin was trailing behind again; two juggernaut lorries separated him from Christy. I hope one of them runs me over and then they'll be sorry, he thought, but pedalled furiously to keep up.

'This is Smiles, Merlin.' Simon rode beside him as they turned off the main road to a hideous jumble of tin shacks, washing lines, tents and wasteland. A few dirty children played on heaps of rubble, throwing stones, and Merlin saw with horror that they weren't even wearing shoes. It was like the picture of 'A Bombay Slum' in his Ethnic Culture text book. The children rushed up to Christy and his father. One little girl wound herself so tightly around Simon that he had to get off his bike, laughing. Merlin hung back, astride his shining bike, and felt as if his father had opened a cage at the zoo and started to fondle a litter of crocodiles. He was horrified by his father's pleasure in the company of these swarming, screaming children. Tears ran down Merlin's dusty, sweating face.

'They want a go on your bike. What's the matter?' His father sounded, as usual, gentle and kind. So difficult to hate.

'I'm exhausted. Can I have a drink, please?'

'Oh dear – I should have thought of that. The water here is contaminated at the moment. There's bottled water but that's strictly rationed. You'll have to wait.'

Miserably, Merlin sat on a concrete slab and watched as three boys piled on to his bike and rode it over the ruins, yelling and leaping around on it like a horse. It would be terribly scratched. He was surprised when his father sat beside him and put an arm around him.

'When you were living with your grandparents I missed you a lot, and I became very close to these children.'

'Oh.'

'Last week one of them died of cholera, a disease you get from dirty water.'

'Is it catching?'

'Yes. But you were vaccinated against it last week, don't you remember?'

'I want to go home.'

Simon was trembling with the effort of bringing the two

237

worlds together. They didn't want to merge, and he himself had mixed feelings about bringing Merlin here. What if the child did 'catch something', wouldn't his father feel, and be, guilty? Then we'd tell my parents and they'd rush him to a good hospital, Simon thought impatiently, on Bernard's Brit-card. God, now they'll give me one again.

Merlin watched as an old black woman – all the grown-ups here were old – embraced his father, weeping.

'I'm sorry.' Simon hugged Lily's aunt, surprised at the intensity of her grief. She had always been so harsh with the child.

A man with a camera jumped out from behind a shack. 'Now tell me, Mrs Oki – how do you pronounce your name? – what were your feelings when your niece died?'

'What would your feelings be if I kicked your camera into that ditch?'

'Are you threatening me? You're Bernard Freeman's son, aren't you? Rosie's brother? I'm Stephen Rossdale from the *Evening Glory.*'

'What are you doing here?'

'We're covering the cholera story. The little angel of the slums. Now you're a social worker, aren't you? Don't you think you could have done something to save poor little Lily?'

'If you want to help these kids, run a campaign to get proper sanitation and clinics installed here. There's nothing special about this place, there are dozens of camps like Smiles around London and cholera at half of them. This city's full of fucking little angels.'

'Do you think it helps the situation to swear like that, Mr Freeman?'

'I've been working here for two-and-a-half years. There's a cholera outbreak every summer, and people often die in winter too. Why are we suddenly newsworthy?'

But Stephen Rossdale had slipped Lily's aunt a twenty pound note and was on his way to photograph the little angel's tent.

'Does it always smell like this?' Merlin asked.

'It's worse now, because it's summer and it hasn't rained for a while. That's the building where we have the playgroup. At the moment all the sick people are in there, the idea was to

238

stop the disease from spreading but it doesn't seem to have worked. There were two more cases of cholera this morning. Babies.'

'Are you going in there?'

'Yes. You can stay out here if you like.'

'Is she in there, too?'

'Christy? I expect so. We might have to stay all night.' Already he was wishing he hadn't brought his son.

'I want to come too.'

He didn't, but he was scared to stay out there alone with those wild children. Merlin paused, then bolted, fists clenched, over to his bike, Madge's Christmas present. It had been flung down in the rubble, its gleaming red body was scarred and streaked with dust. He rescued it and was wheeling it back to Simon when a voice asked if he would like a sweet. Merlin looked up at an ancient, filthy creature with fetid rags wound around its legs and a grimy hand which was offering him a packet of Polos.

'No!' Merlin shouted and stumbled towards his father, blood on his knees now, more tears streaming down his face and the laughter of the demonic children all around.

Rita and Beatrice had dropped in on Ellen that afternoon, and had stayed. Then Lily's distraught aunt had come and by seven o'clock there were a dozen people, mainly women, sitting on the caked mud outside Ellen's tent. She sat crosslegged in the flap doorway, presiding with Jack on her knee. Although the only hospitality she could offer was some thin black coffee made with UN powder, Ellen was glad they had come to her. She felt she had a role in the camp, as she had before when she helped to organize supplies and lessons in the washhouse, and planted patches of vegetables which had been dug up by dogs and children long before they could help make the camp self-sufficient, as she had dreamed. They had just agreed to sow more seeds in the autumn; Lily's aunt had contributed some of the twenty pounds, of which she was ashamed, and they all became enthusiastic and hopeful, as they looked forward to picking their own vegetables in the spring. Ted hadn't come back, and they were glad, although without his rotten supplies their diet was more limited than ever.

Since the birth of Jack Ellen had felt written off as his mother. People asked how the baby was but no longer asked what she was doing, and in fact for months she had been too exhausted to do anything. Now she felt her energy returning, as if it fed on anger, there being no other sustenance around. Since the demonstration the atmosphere in the camp had changed: Martha's arrest and Lily's death had become rallying cries, although as yet none of them knew what to rally to. They were paralyzed by their fear of ending up like Martha or Lily. But, Ellen thought, at least we're alive now. She looked beyond the faces of her friends at the vista of shacks, tents, strings of washing, heaps of garbage crowned with flies and stinking ditches with banks of dried mud where weedy purple and yellow flowers peered out like shrivelled optimists. I don't want Jack to grow up here, Ellen thought, and brushed with her lips the line where his fuzz of white hair met his sallow forehead.

It was dark outside when Christy stopped work. Inside, the candles and oil lamps gave out a light that was too soft to be helpful. The night outside the window, where it squeezed through patches of cardboard, was velvety black. Christy longed to be out in it. The sick lay everywhere in rows, on mattresses and sleeping bags and piles of clothes. Some of the mothers lay beside their children, holding them so that they couldn't float off into the ether of death. Now many of the sick were asleep but there was always somebody awake and in need of help as he or she vomited or passed grey rice water stools, as John called it. Dimelza, watching Lily in terror, had described it more vividly as soup from her bum.

John was a doctor who hadn't worked professionally since the National Health collapsed. A heavy drinker, he had drifted to Smiles out of indifference to his surroundings. Whenever he was sober he did what he could to help without proper drugs or equipment. He knew that the only way to save the most serious cases was to set up a drip with a saline solution. But there weren't any drips, so he had persuaded a chemist friend to make up the solution and when necessary, John forced it down the patients' throats. There were no antibiotics and no trained helpers. John hadn't slept for two nights.

240

Downstairs, Christy nearly fell over Merlin, who had curled up on the floor and was fast asleep. She had despaired when he first came in that afternoon, snivelling over his bike, and had been furious with Simon, who had insisted on bringing Merlin. But, for some reason she was too tired to analyze, Smiles and Merlin had to meet. Christy had handed him a mop and a jerry can of disinfectant and had promptly forgotten him. An hour later she found him doggedly mopping, rinsing, squeezing, swabbing; performing his disgusting and thankless task with his eyes down and an expression of such dignified melancholy that she could hardly believe he was the same child. Christy took off her cotton jacket and covered him with it. Her legs felt like pipe cleaners and her throat was parched. In her head were jagged flames of pain and nausea.

Simon came up to her. They whispered in case they woke the sleepers.

'Lily's aunt's arrived with Rita. They'll stay all night, so we can rest.'

'Merlin's asleep over there.'

John followed them downstairs and went out into the garden to tell the people waiting that nobody had died that night. Through the open door cool, robust air burst in, blew out some of the candles and cleared their aching heads.

Then the three of them went upstairs, sat by the window and opened one of the last bottles of sterilized water.

'There should be more when the supplies come tomorrow morning,' Christy said. 'I applied last week for water and antibiotics.'

Simon took a long drink of water. 'There was a journalist snooping around here today. If we get some publicity maybe the government will be forced to do something.'

'They did send the van around with the vaccine. That's more than last year.' John no longer expected or demanded.

'We've had publicity before but it's always bad. Dirty layabouts, living in our own filth and neglecting our children.'

Christy yawned. 'What was all that singing and chanting earlier?'

'The flagellantes,' John said.

'The what?' Simon asked.

'One of those cranky sects. I think they're from the Clapham Common camp. They wear black and stand in a circle, scourging each other and singing miserable songs. Didn't you hear the words?:

"By our blood avert the doom
Tear our century to the tomb
Repent for death is love.'"

Simon shivered. 'Have they been here before?'

'Ever since the cholera outbreak began. They're like vultures, they go all over London sniffing out death.'

John let his head drop on to his knees, then lay on his side with his forehead pressed against the cool glass and sank into the linoleum. The next time they looked at him he was asleep.

Christy and Simon sat cross legged with their arms around each other. If either of them had shifted his or her position a few inches one of them would have bumped into John or the window or one of the sick people. The room was an ocean of helpless bodies.

Simon shut his eyes and with his hands traced Christy's face, the curve of her neck and her broad shoulders, where his fingers rested. The blind loving the blind, he thought, no, she is sighted, I'm the one who fumbles in the dark. Then he opened his eyes to meet hers, which were questioning and friendly. Simon felt again his fear of Smiles, of the misery and poverty that made him feel so guilty and so insignificant. Christy has seduced me out of loneliness but I'm still crippled, I still can't make decisions about the things that really matter. Every thought and emotion comes double-sided so that sometimes it hardly comes at all. That's why love and suffering are such a relief, why Christy makes me feel more alive.

Christy thought, I need to feel this animal closeness to Simon. We're closer here than we were in that pretentious house. Wherever we go now we'll make our own space around us. If we doze in each other's arms all night we'll somehow recharge in the morning, find the energy to work and bustle and be indignant.

In the middle of the night Merlin half woke on the hard, cold floor. A broom jabbed his spine and his right elbow slid into a puddle of disinfectant. He looked around for Simon but saw only shuddering monsters, heard only the porky grunts

and groans of the sick as they lurched in and out of consciousness. Merlin got up and stumbled over them. With part of his
mind he retraced his old barefoot journey: out of my bunk,
over the carpet, open my door and then theirs, dive into their
vast bed where they lie so warm and safe and my mother's
sleeping body makes room for mine . . . Merlin climbed the
stairs and saw Simon over by the window, sitting like a
buddha with that woman who wasn't his mother. Surely they
couldn't sleep like that. But Merlin could sleep anywhere; he
launched himself across them and lay with his head in Simon's
lap.

Other new fiction from Virago

JUMPING THE CRACKS
Rebecca O'Rourke

Nearly midnight in London's derelict Hackney on a wet, windy, dark night, but not so dark that Rats (after her rats' tail hair) doesn't see the Rolls with the body slumped inside. No phone boxes work, no one else on the street: so she clutches her hideous secret and makes for home.

In the days and months that follow, Rats experiences the city with increasing menace – as though existing on the margins, a lesbian, 'unlucky in love', unemployed, a northerner, living alone at the mercy of unscrupulous landlords weren't bad enough. And her job, when she finally lands one, is more evidence of a city in decay – a seedy accommodation agency, teetering on the edge of legality. In her waking and dreaming hours, fraud, corruption and the murder glide ever nearer, as silent and threatening as the hovering Rolls, but she fights them all. Even the return of her lover, Helen, doesn't divert her from her obsessive attempts to track down the killer. Politics and crime, love and loneliness, the search for origins and understanding combine together in this impressive and gripping first novel.

Other new fiction from Virago

THE UNBORN DREAMS OF CLARA RILEY
Kathy Page

This is the haunting story of two very different women in Edwardian England who break the law, and outrage society. Clara Riley is working class, a washerwoman burdened with the memory of two children – one abandoned, the other murdered – whom she has sacrificed in the hope of retaining what little independence she has. Christina Audley Jones, her wealthy employer, is a committed suffragist: but her work for the Cause and her support for Onward House, a home for young girls, must, at all costs, be kept secret from her husband. Her utopia is a grander one than Clara's but it spurs her to similarly desperate rebellion.

When Clara becomes pregnant again, it is Mrs Audley Jones who, defying the law, organises her abortion. Neither woman, however, counts on the burden of guilt which Clara's action brings with it, and when in an unguarded moment she breaks her silence, the full weight of the law – and of society's opprobrium – comes down on them. But both women refuse to have their spirits broken and, in very different ways, confront the merciless judgement and hypocrisy of husbands and courts, and the silencing of incarceration.

Kathy Page superbly captures the social and political climate of England before the First World War.

THE CENTURY'S DAUGHTER
Pat Barker

The Century's Daughter is Pat Barker's most brilliant achievement yet – the story of a northern working-class community seen through the eyes of Liza Jarrett, born on the last stroke of midnight as the twentieth century begins. Liza never forgets her mother's humiliation in the steel magnate's house where she cleans: her childhood teaches her much about loyalty, love and fortitude. Growing up in the First World War, she married Frank – mystic, faith healer and unemployed steel worker – and, supported by neighbours and friends, brings up her children through the hardship of the Depression. The Second World War brings the greatest trial of Liza's strength, but she survives, humour intact, into the sixties and seventies, caring for her beloved granddaughter Kath, only to see 'progress' do what the Depression and war failed to do: break the community which nourished her.

This is also Stephen's story, the tale of a young community worker alienated by education and homosexuality from parents he can now hardly talk to and a job he bitterly defines as finding ways for the unemployed to pass their time. Stephen comes to Liza to offer help, but stays instead to be helped.

A remarkable mixture of naturalistic style and poetic sensibility, this outstanding novel captures flawlessly the taut, hard humour and warmth of people who have had short shrift both in literature and in life.

CRY WOLF
Aileen La Tourette

Curie has inherited one world and created another. A survivor of
the nuclear holocaust, and venerated by the inhabitants of the
new world, she protects them from the knowledge of the old,
which only she now possesses. But there is one face, Sophia's,
that shows no awe, no gratitude. Instead, her eyes say, 'We know
nothing. But you do.' In response to her challenge, Curie
recognises that she must tell at last the story of the world that
destroyed itself – the story of her own mother, Bee Fairchild, who
cried wolf at Greenham Common; the story of her sisters and
their attempt to use the ancient charm of story-telling,
Scheherazade-like, to forestall annihilation. Now Curie is the
only M-other left to face the fact that her denial of a knowledge
of evil also means denying a knowledge of good. In *Cry Wolf*, a
novel of present and future worlds, Aileen la Tourette displays
her remarkable gifts as a storyteller to explore the dangers of lying
and those of truth, and the hazards of dreaming in a world fraught
with the most concrete dangers.

Other new fiction from Virago

WHOLE OF A MORNING SKY
Grace Nichols

'There is something holy about Georgetown at dusk. The Atlantic curling the shoreline . . .' It is 1960 and the Walcotts are moving into the city from the village of Highdam. School headmaster Archie Walcott will miss the openness of pastureland; his wife, Clara, the women and their nourishing 'womantalk and roots magic'; and Gem, their daughter, her loved jamoon and mango trees. Their move into the rough and tumble Charlestown neighbourhood couldn't have come at a worse time, for the serenity of the city is exploded by political upheavals in the country's struggle for independence. Along with the sweep of events – strikes, riots, and racial clashes – daily life in their Charlestown yard and beyond gathers its own intensity. Archie's friend, Conrad, seeing and knowing all, moves with ease among the opposing groups, monocle to his eye, white mice in his pockets; through one terrible night the neighbourhood tenses as the Ramsammy's rum shop is threatened to burn; and Archie, troubled by the times, tries to keep a tight rein on his family. And young Gem, ever-watchful, responds with wonderment and curiosity to the new life around her.

In this her first adult novel, Grace Nichols richly and imaginatively evokes a world that was part of her own Guyanese childhood.

THE BAD BOX
Alison Fell

In rural Scotland of the late 1950s, Isla Cameron – hypersensi-
tive and rebellious dreamer – builds futures and explores
memories. A move from the Highlands to the Border Country
separates her from her childhood companion Ray, who remains
in her dreams as an ideal, while the reality is clumsy dates in the
back row of the local cinema.

Myth and a gritty realism interact to chart Isla's erratic
adolescence: Calvinism and competitiveness, Presley and Polaris
are as vivid to Isla as the legend she creates about the mute girl,
born of a white hind, who must bring her father back from exile
with the help of her lover, Alec. Will Alec follow her to the end
of her search? And will Ray wait as patiently for the maturing of
Isla, when her friend Wanda is both simpler and more sophisti-
cated?

Each new step to adulthood takes Isla back into the 'bad box'
of the past, which contains not only prohibitions and jealousies,
but also revenge, reconciliation and restitution.

Woven of separations and story-tellings, humour and poetry,
Alison Fell's second novel is imbued with wit and a subtle,
sensual melancholy.